A BRIGHT AND SHINING WORLD

eSpec Books titles by C.J. Henderson

EVERYTHING'S BETTER WITH MONKEYS

eSpec Books titles Including
the Work of C.J. Henderson

BREACH THE HULL
SO IT BEGINS
BY OTHER MEANS
BEST LAID PLANS
DOGS OF WAR
THE BEST OF DEFENDING THE FUTURE

THE SOCIETY FOR THE PRESERVATION
OF CJ HENDERSON

A BRIGHT AND SHINING WORLD

The Science Fiction of
C.J. Henderson

with Introductions by Mike McPhail

PAPER PHOENIX PRESS

Pennsville, NJ

PUBLISHED BY
Paper Phoenix Press
A division of eSpec Books
PO Box 242
Pennsville, NJ 08070
www.especbooks.com

ISBN: 978-1-956463-23-1
ISBN (ebook): 978-1-956463-22-4

Every Time I Close My Eyes originally published in The Book of Dark Wisdom, 2005
The Biggest Bastards originally published in CthulhuSex, 2006
The Fear in the Waiting originally published in Vile Things, 2009
Aware originally published in Boondocks Fantasies, 2011
A Patch of Grass originally published in Tales of the Talisman, 2006
Dawson Did It originally published in Questar, 1979
They Were the Wind originally published in Oceans in Space, 2002
The Wondrous, Boundless Thought originally published in The Stories In Between, 2009
A Bright and Shining World originally published in The Wildside CJH Megapack, 2013
The Death of Maal Dweb originally published in Lost Worlds of Space and Time, 2005
A Glorious Ending originally published in Tales of the Talisman, 2011
A Light that Shamed the Sun originally published in The Nth Degree, 2008
999 Down originally published in MOTA: Integrity, 2004
The Big Thirteen originally published by Die, Monster, Die, 2008
Time to Smell the Flowers, Time to Talk to the Stones originally published in Starship, 1983
Thank God it's Friday originally published in Alpha Drive, 1999
Everything is Better with Monkeys originally published in So It Begins, 2009

Interior Design: Mike and Danielle McPhail
Cover Art: Steven C. Gilberts
Cover Design: Mike McPhail, McP Concepts
www.mcp-concepts.com
www.milscifi.com

Copy Editing: Danielle McPhail
www.sidhenadaire.com

CONTENTS

DEDICATION

Recently, I have been in severe ill health. Traveling blood clots, shattering nerve pain, crippling intestinal distress, cancer... what can I say? For a while there, the outlook was grim.

While I suffered in my hospital bed, my wife never left my side. To say that her constant attention and devotion were a factor in my recovery is to make the most massive of understatements. But, and she agrees with this, there was another phenomenon growing in the background that would contribute as well.

Unbeknownst to us, while I sweat and hacked and suffered in narcotic-fueled, sleep-deprived dementia, in the outside world the word was spreading of my woes throughout my friends and fans. When I returned home I found cards and gifts and well-wishes—on the phone and the Internet, by the hundreds.

Over the weeks that followed the number grew to the thousands. And it hasn't ended.

Most every entertainer is in some way a broken toy. We all wonder if we're really touching anyone, if anyone really cares. If the love is real. Trust me, now I know. Thus, I would like to dedicate this book to:

ALL OF YOU

There are a lot of dark and scary stories in here. And if it wasn't for all the prayers and crossed fingers and donations to the cause, if it weren't for all the love you showed me, it's quite possible I might not be here now to write up some more.

Thank you all.

INTRODUCTION

C.J. (Mr. Henderson) is best known for his writings set within the realm of the supernatural; I have often referred to him as a modern-day pulp fiction writer. After all, he is the creator of the Occult Detective and a writer for the Kolchak: The Night Stalker. As such, one might get the impression that reality and hardcore facts aren't as important to such storytelling. In this case, you would be wrong!

Beyond the well-written, relatable, and very human characters, each with their own drives and flaws, C.J.'s stories tend to lean toward the darker side of life—if not downright horrifying—where the Good can be caught up in unforeseen consequences, while the Bad often live just long enough to realize they are going straight to hell for what they've done.

Long ago in a time before HD flat screens, when we used to watch something known as a "TV Set" or "The Tube," there was a program know as the "Twilight Zone." Its creator and host Rod Serling, took us on adventures into the realms of sci-fi, fantasy, and horror; while in truth he was exploring the human conduction when faced with the unknown.

The stories in this collection are reminiscent of that exploration; they cover a wide range of not only time and place, but also science and technology. Happily, C.J. never bogs us down with self-fulfilling data dumps and technobabble; when he uses technology it is usually straightforward in both name and concept. I'm often impressed at his ability to not only get the basics right, but also in dealing with how technology is used, as well as the related slang or jargon. This while being balanced against something that is hard to find in a science fiction writer, common sense and a view toward real world applications and effects.

The example that truly comes to mind in regard to this, is in one story the characters used a steam-powered blimp to cross over dimensional plains; C.J. explains (and I'm paraphrasing here) that other power sources were unreliable in transition, and that electronic were also effected. Overall I found the concept quite thought provoking.

I had not read a lot of C.J.'s work beyond those in my series, and after this, I have a new found respect for both his vision and story telling as a author.

Mike McPhail
Editor

EVERY TIME I CLOSE MY EYES

Every time I close my eyes,
I see a fabulous expanse,
A'stretched before me across the world,
As big as the sky and all that.

Every time I close my eyes,
I gaze into this blue beyond,
Big and alien, harkening to me,
And I wonder where I am.

Every time I close my eyes,
I see the same haunting fear, coming faster and faster,
With every blink and tear,
As I pray for the sleep that I'm denied.

Every time I close my eyes,
The searching eye grows ever closer,
And I fear it shall soon have me,
And I wonder how I'll taste...

Every time I close my eyes...

We are often blinded by what we believe; if you perceive that only the biggest bastards in the world get all the money, fame, and power; once you've obtained all of that, then why wouldn't you believe it when your inner voice calls you a god?

From an early age, Martin though that his grandma had shown him the way to such fame—computers. After a life spent wheeling and dealing on the internet; then evolving into a hacker, Martin now looked down upon the world and unleashed proof of just how big a bastard he really was.

THE BIGGEST BASTARDS

MrTRex had done it again.

"Now, *that*, man, was just fucking magnificent."

The hacker known around the world as Mister T Rex leaned back in his swivel set, recline-back desk chair spreading his hands out before him, palms up. The two sycophants in attendance leaned forward in response and slapped his extended palms, grateful as always for a chance to touch their god.

"We are not worthy," both those in attendance said in unison, bowing in mock prostration. They continued their prostration, repeating their mantra endlessly until they finally descended into helpless giggles.

"I have to admit, this one is pretty extreme," the hacker acknowledged almost modestly, "even for me."

"Hey, like who cares, dude?" The speaker held out a joint half the size of a standard pen. Shaking it like some sort of stunted pointer, he continued, "It's Vapidland out there—you gotta smack these cows square in the middle of the forehead with a sledgehammer to make them take notice of anything."

"Hey," agreed the other, "you know he's right."

It was true, of course, and the hacker would be the first to admit it. Indeed, MrTRex, known outside his sanctum sanctorum as Martin Brillstein, had been quite diligently working most of his life to get just the right grip on his particular sledgehammer. Practicing with it since the age of nine, he had spent the ten years since honing his swing, waiting for that one perfect bovine skull shattering that would catapult him to even greater heights of fame and fortune. Pointing to the framed piece of needlepoint work his beloved grandma Ruth had lovingly made for him at his request, just before her death several years previous, he said;

"Read the sign, gentlemen—it is still ever so true."

2   A Bright and Shining World

THE BIGGEST BASTARDS
GET THE BEST JOBS!

Grandma Ruth had known it before he had, had known it before he was born. When he had first shown an interest in computers at the age of eight months, before he could tie his shoes, before he could even walk, she had insisted on buying him one. And, not one of those especially designed children's computers, some shiny, soft plastic, non-threatening pile of Suessian games and easy step nonsense, a waste of money that would have to be replaced in six months—no—not one of those. She got him a real computer, and it became his world.

Grandma Ruth was in her own words "a tough old duck," one who had survived the great Depression as a girl. She had seen presidents slaughtered, the birth of television, men landing on the moon, the introduction of martial arts, Mountain Dew and microwaves to the world at large, and more wars than she had fingers to count them upon. She had seen nations disappear from the face of the Earth, witnessed the crumbling of dictatorships, and watched as the entire political face of man changed from kings and sultans to bankers and corporations.

Oh, countries still had rulers, obviously—most of them submitting to a smoke and mirrors electorial process with a private wink and a nod behind their ponderous sincerity—but everyone who gave the notion any real thought knew what was actually going on. The world was run by corporations. And those in charge of those corporations ran them with computers.

"You learn computers, Martey," Grandma Ruth had told him, "and there isn't anything that won't be yours." She knew. As the trio all stared at the needlework hanging in its place of honor over Martin's computer station, his more heavy-set, greasier companion finally lit the joint in his hand, took a deep toke, then passed it to Martin. Taking his own toke, the hacker forced the smoke deep into his lungs, held it as long as he could, then released a voluminous cloud, saying;

"To Grandma Ruth."

His two companions did likewise, the pair of them as in awe of the late matriarch of the Brillstein clan as her grandson. And indeed, there was no doubting either that Martin Brillstein was in awe of his late grandmother, or that he had good reason to be so. She had set him on the path, always told him the truth, pulled every possible blinder away from his eyes as ruthlessly as she could. She had also made certain that no one else was allowed to undo any of what she considered her mission in life.

Martin could always remember the moment when everything had changed. He had been watching the news with his grandmother, and had noted when she made her noise of disapproval over a particular story. It had been a small item, something the network must have considered barely worth the mention, a tale of a hacker who had crippled a major corporation just for the fun of it for several days before being apprehended. When he questioned what she thought was wrong with this, she told him exactly what she thought, as she always did.

"Auuch, Martey, mine boy... this world is such a shit hole. I can't believe it. This punk, he puts his virus onto this internet, he destroys property, ruins lives, and they reward him. A mugger who steals ten dollars, maybe hurts one person—he goes to jail. But this one, who for no good reason hurts so many, him they give a job—six figures, even. A nobody. A nothing. And he gets a six figure job for causing pain."

Martin had known she was telling him something in her own way. Even before she knew it herself, she was teaching him another of life's lessons, the kind his father never had time for, the kind his mother pretended did not exist. And then, while still staring at the television, in between drags on one of her beloved Lucky Strikes, she said the words which would become Martin Brillstein's motto;

"I hate to say it, but it's true. In this world, mine Martey, the biggest bastards get the best jobs."

The words had been an epiphany for the lad. Suddenly, everything his grandmother had said to him during the first ten years of his life made ringing, resounding sense. In an instant he understood why his mother was such a disappointment to her own, how his grandmother could know with such certainty that his father would never amount to anything beyond a happy little clerk. Her disgust with people, with politics, with television, the country, the world, and life in general, finally...

It all made sense.

From that day forward, Martin Brillstein was a changed young man. Childish amusements were, for the most part, put to the side. He kept up with his studies, learned how to be a social enough animal to not draw attention to himself. He watched enough television, read enough comic books, listened to just enough music to not stand out, to be ignored by the rest of the world.

And, at the same time, he threw himself into learning everything there was to know about computers. At the age of ten he had his own website, one he designed and maintained on his own. One through which he marketed the most amazing variety of products. By the age of eleven, between using the on-line auctions to turn other people's cast-offs into gold, and selling his own unique line of kitschy items, he had already salted away enough capital to ensure his first two years of college—no matter where he went. But, it was at age twelve, when he declared himself the King of Jupiter, that the world's possibilities solidified into reality for young Martin.

Besides his amusing declaration, he also created a website where he could keep the public appraised of Jupiter's intentions toward the rest of the solar system. The idea was found amusing, and Martin was clever enough to find something new and silly and whimsical enough to keep people coming back every day. And after eight months of such trap baiting, he proclaimed that Jupiter was now open to homesteaders, and that parcels could be purchased at the fabulous introductory offer of only one dollar an acre.

For their money, folks got a certificate, suitable for framing, which granted them clear title to their land, gave them the exact coordinates of their property, along with coupons for discounts good at local Jupiter tourist attractions. It was a harmless amusement, which many local and two national TV networks all happened to comment upon one slow news day.

To print and ship the certificates and coupons cost him less than a dollar a customer. Most people saw nothing unreasonable in purchasing five to ten acres. For a brief period, it became a thing of geek status to own "huge tracks of land" on Jupiter, and shut-ins and losers around the world started purchasing hundreds, and even thousands of acres at a time. Martin Brillstein became the first multi-millionaire to graduate from his middle school.

He made his parents very proud, although a trifle worried as well. Their opinions had ceased to matter to him long before, however. By then, all that mattered to him was the opinion of his Grandma Ruth. When she smiled at him as he recited the proscribed Hebrew at his bar mitzvah, he knew he was indeed a man. A man to be proud of. A man on his way to being a bastard. The biggest he could be.

That night, the dreams started.

At first they were merely dances of self-congratulations, ever-increasing spectacles of praise and honor for the master of men who was the one and only Martey Brillstein. Women danced, begging for his favors. Rich men came from all corners offering him gold and jewels, suitcases of cash, the latest games and technology, fancy cars, the best food, and more women—anything if he would but grace their lives with his presence. He was the greatest, and everyone knew it.

They were happy, healthy dreams, and they helped imbue Martin with an even stronger sense of purpose than he already had been given by his grandmother. They also helped protect him—both from the outside world, and himself.

As easy fame swirled around him, thanks to his emperorhood of the solar system's largest world, after the news items about him had proved to be a hit with the people, numerous magazines and papers as well as radio and television shows wanted to then do things *with* him. When this section of the world showed an interest in Martin, that was when Loki stepped forward.

Loki was the name Martin gave to a voice within his dreams that, while it always gave him nothing but sound, logical advice, the teen was certain it came rolled in a merry bit of devilment. There was a mischievous note to it which Martin enjoyed. At times the things it said made him wonder. Such as the very first time he heard it. When wonderment entered the picture, that was when he turned to Grandma Ruth.

"Grandma," he had asked her. "All these people that want to interview me and everything... what if I didn't want to do that?"

Ruth, a patient and clever teacher, never simply announced her opinion on a subject. With such a question, she instinctively knew it was best to find out why it was being asked. Which was why her response to her Martey was;

"What if you didn't? Why wouldn't you? A good reason, I'm hoping?"

Martin could never have had the following talk with either of his parents. But Grandma Ruth never treated him as a child. Instead she treated him as an equal who simply did not have as much experience as she. Listening quietly, she sat with all her attention focused on her grandson as he explained that something he recently dreamed had affected him greatly. He had dreamed that the offers coming in were merely attempts of others to use him, and that if he granted their interviews, went on their shows, et cetera, he would be merely selling pieces of himself off for no good return.

Ruth studied on what Martin told her for a long and careful minute. She was constantly amazed by her grandson, but this bit of insightful thinking, this impressed her even more than his making himself a millionaire. After telling him all of that, she finally gave him her thoughts on the subject.

"Martey, right you are about what they want. That's the world. But, rather that be afraid of it, use it. Use them. Money and fame should never be rejected, but they must be accepted with the greatest of care. Yes, these people, they want to buy slices of you to throw to their dogs. So, what you must decide, that decision is not whether or not to give them what they want. What you must decide is which of your faces you want to give them."

And then, Ruth explained to the teen how all people have multiple personalities within them which they use at different times during the day. Did he act before the principal of his school the way he did before his male friends? Did he act before them in the same manner as he acted in front of girls? His parents? Police officers?

Martin understood immediately. Taking Ruth's advice, he did every show he could, responded to every magazine and newspaper, giving them all their close-up look at the same shy, clever, wonderful Martin Brillstein. In a nutshell, the side of him he presented to the world from that moment on was a very lucky young man who had a great deal to thank God for. Uniformly, he told everyone who would pay him to speak that he would be putting his fortune toward helping his family and making certain he could go to college. He wished all the best to those who were ready to help colonize Jupiter, and had shown their support for his kingdom. Folks found both his humor and charm came in bite-sized amounts, easy to absorb, and they delighted in him for the moment and then put him completely from mind—as he had hoped.

It was a powerful lesson. He had added nicely to his coffers, left a good impression, and then faded from public view before becoming type cast as some sort of idiot geek. If he was remembered in the future, it would be for his mature and well-mannered response to his internet silliness, not as that jerk who ripped everyone off calling himself the king of Jupiter. Martin learned to trust the voice of Loki. Indeed, he learned to depend on it.

Of course, he understood, even when still only thirteen that the voice he heard was simply some part of his subconscious self trying to make itself clear to his waking mind. In history class his teacher had discussed how those the Catholic church called saints were simply people advanced enough to hear their own thoughts. At least those with godly intentions. Those with wicked thoughts, who heard "evil" voices in their heads urging them to sin and corruption, they were called witches and worse, and were dealt with accordingly.

Like so many others in the modern world, Martin knew there were no real gods. He knew of Loki, brother to Thor, half-son of Odin, only because of a comicbook in which Thor appeared as a superhero. In ancient times, back in the sixties when the comic had first been created, Loki had been presented as a standard cardboard cut-out of a character, strictly a two-dimensional villain. But, by the time Martin had started reading comicbooks, those who wrote them were stretching the old storylines, looking for new possibilities.

As with modern stories of Lucifer, apologies were made for Odin's adopted boy, new approaches were taken. Suddenly Loki had a certain nobility; it was clear he had been misunderstood, used as a scapegoat by those who got to write history. His cunning was to be admired. These stories were few and far between, of course, but they hit young Martin at just the right age, and from then on, if there was any god in his life, Loki was it.

As the joint came around again, Martin took another deep toke. He tried to pass it off, but both his companions were too busy checking on the progress of their master's latest virus. Launched into the world-wide web only two days earlier, it was already causing unprecedented levels of chaos. Not difficulties. Not problems in the system. Actual, unbounded chaos. Martin's smile grew wider with each new tragedy his minions reported.

"They just traced traffic lights that're going crazy in North Carolina to the virus," laughed the thinner of the acolytes. "How is this possible, dude?"

Martin just smiled. He could not have explained the complexity of LassieBark7 to either of those present even if he wanted to. Indeed, there were some aspects of it he put together purely on instinct. If forced, he would have to admit even he was not certain exactly what made some parts of his faithful pet perform as well as it did.

"Just enjoy the show," Martin suggested.

"But this thing is too much," protested the other. "You've got network TV stations picking up the signals from private cell phones and playing them on the air. Rock and roll stations are broadcasting Chinese operas and they can't stop. High school P.A. systems are rerunning 'Amos & Andy' for their student bodies, and, and—oh man, did you hear *that?*"

Martin had heard what his friends had heard. His beloved LassieBark7 was now being credited with invading individual automobiles and wrecking havoc with their operating systems.

"Dude," shouted the heavier of his companions, crumbs and spittle flying from his greasy lips, "how is this even possible? What the hell did you cook up here?"

"Yeah, man—how does that thing operate?" His other toady, still in awe of his master's work, stared at him through darkly questioning eyes. "I mean, how sci fi can you get?"

"Okay, look," said Martin, high enough to forget that a clever man hides his darkest secrets, "here's the thing. What these guys aren't thinking about is that everything is run by computers now."

"Well, duuu-uhhhhh."

"Don't be a knob. Listen, the internet proved computers can communicate one to another. Get the right operating program, and guys all around the world can work on the same thing at the same time, right?"

It was true, of course. Electronic gamers, although scattered across states, or even continents, had been able to battle each other for years by that point. All would see the same thing on their screens, and yet they could affect their personally designated little piece of the game from their own homes.

"With all the world's programs becoming homogenized, it's like everyone is working the same deal. Spreading a virus from one computer to another is nothing. There isn't any firewall I can't topple—right?" The acolytes nodded; they knew the statement was true, had known it since their master had side-stepped his way into the Pentagon's files and downloaded acres of their top secret data on all things electronic.

"Well, once I realized I could go wherever I wanted, I got a bit bored. What was the challenge, you know? Then, I started to think, just like the way they finally got PCs and Macs to talk to each other, what if I could get computers that weren't supposed to talk to other machines to start up conversations?"

In the background, the television broadcast continued. Regular programming appeared to have been suspended in favor or non-stop reporting on the spreading virus. Cash registers had begun making music, using their whirs, clicks, and rings to burp out electronic concertos. In some stores, apparently the fluorescent lights and even the sprinkler systems had joined in, their flickering and dribbling a recognizable part of the concerts.

"That... that's what LassieBark7 does?"

"That's what I started out with. Getting different computers to talk to each other, I mean. But then I started to see the, well, shall we call them... possibilities... "

In Georgia, a prison's computers opened all the cell blocks while it locked all the doors to guards' quarters, weapon's lockers, gun towers, et cetera. The prison was now in flames, with several hundred of the state's worst offenders running wild across the countryside.

"I mean, everything has computer chips in it these days. People thought it was crazy when they started putting them in cars, but now they're in clocks and toasters, dildos and leaf blowers—everything, fuckin' *everything*—man, has got software humming inside it, whether it needs it or not."

"But," asked one of the acolytes, "in all these places where things are going crazy, how come they can't turn things off?"

"Over-ride commands, man," answered Martin with a bit of well-deserved self-satisfaction. There in his fortress of solitude, he allowed himself to be relaxed by the still thick cloud of marijuana in the air, allowed a touch of smugness to enter his tone as he said, "once Lassie barks seven times within a system, she owns it."

Elevators across the country had begun biting people, closing violently on hands and legs and whatever they could crunch. Those able to get past the doors would then find the buttons inside useless. The transports went where they wanted, usually taking anyone inside to the top floor and then refusing to move until they got out—biting them again as they did so.

Others would go as high as they could and then simply drop as fast as they could, spilling their inhabitants to the floor. Then, the virus-possessed transports would take their temporary inhabitants where they wanted to go—and bite them as they exited. Passengers swore the machines chuckled as they did so, even those without music or voice components.

"But, this is all kind of wild. I mean, you're a smart guy and all, but... well, I mean, when did you get this smart?"

"It's not all me," answered Martin. Still quite high, still feeling magnanimous, he nodded conspiratorially, then told his companions, "part of it's that stuff I nicked from the Pentagon. You know how most people can drive a car even though they don't know what makes it run? It's like that."

The night after his successful break-in of the military computers, Martin had received nothing but praise from the part of his brain he had dubbed "Loki" years earlier. It reinforced for him that this was the most extreme, the most totally jumpin' thing he had ever managed. It threw roses and gold dust before his horse's feet for as long as he cared to ride. And then, it had started to make some suggestions to him. Things in the morning he wondered how he had ever thought of them.

"So, were you, I mean... "

"Yeah, but... like these Pentagon guys, they know you got in there, what you got away with. You told us that. That means they've been watching for something to happen with their stuff—right?" When Martin agreed with the acolyte's theory, the teen continued, asking;

"So, once all this started, they must've recognized something in the system as being theirs. And, if they know it's theirs, and they do know not only how to drive a car, as it were, but also how to turn one off, and work on its engine and everything, how come they can't do anything about... well, about anything?"

"Because their shit's not the only shit I put in there."

In Pittsburgh, natural gas lines opened themselves, flooding sewers with gas. Then, once the underground corridors could hold no more, electrical systems seem to simply overload themselves. Causing sparks. Causing explosions. The dead were still being counted, the television reported, and the city was burning out of control. Mainly because none of its firetrucks would start.

"I had this inspiration. You've seen all those Goth websites, the one's with programs for sorcery and the like. I integrated that stuff in there, too."

"What?" The heavier of his sycophants came perilously close to questioning his master. "You mean... you're saying black magic is what's making this thing work?"

"No, not really," Martin assured them. "But, I spliced the stuff everywhere I could. It's in between every other line of all the programming. And, since part of the Goth programming is to change from one spell to another at a random sequence, by the time someone even identifies a line of it, it changes to something else."

In Houston, a sporting arena sealed all its doors and then opened its water mains. Fire hydrants, sinks, drinking fountains, toilets—everything began to overflow. The water rose at a rate those present could not believe. As the rising lake of popcorn, beer and turd covered-water reached the fifteenth row, spectators began leaping from the top of the stadium to the concrete below. When the bodies began to pile to a thickness where those falling atop them were surviving, the arena's roof began to slide shut.

Talking one to another, the computers began to trade information, compare what was working and what was not. Soon, elevators everywhere were biting people, stranding them on sixtieth floors. Sprinklers everywhere were flooding, except those where computers were simply melting down to start fires. Heating systems started up, broiling the world as the August heat hit record highs. Air conditioners everywhere decided to take the day off.

"Ahhhh, Lassie, you barking bitch," said Martin, taking one last hit off the nearly spent roach, "what a good dog you are."

Loki had been right, Martin told himself, there was no doubting now that he would be immortal. He had been rich so long it meant nothing to him. With all the money he needed, Martin Brillstein had anything else he desired. Women had begun to bore him before his pubic hair had completely grown in. But fame, he had liked that. Wanted more. As much as he could get.

"Hey, have you guys been listening to the TV?"

Loki had encouraged him, of course, night after night sometimes.

"Jesus—planes are falling from the sky!"

"And look at that, cars, everywhere—they're crashing into each other on their own."

A chart appeared next on the television screen, one documenting which cities were in flames, burning mindlessly, its citizens choking to death in the streets from the sky-blotting smoke. The spots of red light indicating cities that were still aflame were in the thousands. The black spots indicating those burned to the ground were already in the hundreds.

Stunned, Martin tried to focus his resin-clogged mind. As the horror of what he had unleashed filtered through to him, he muttered;

"This, this isn't right. This can't be. There are safeguards; I made certain public safety cut-offs were to be obeyed. None of this should be happening. No... "

The reporter on the television screen was actually crying. Although he maintained his calming, professional manner in a magnificent display of self-control, still the tears continued to roll down his cheeks as he said;

"The toll of downed airliners has now topped four thousand. Most of them seem to have been under some murderous control, aiming themselves at hospitals, schools, skyscrapers, anywhere people could be found in large numbers. This, this phenomenon, which has now officially been designated the Revolt of the Machines, is reported to have spread to every industrialized country across the globe."

Martin stared dumbly. His mind could not grasp what he was seeing, hearing. It had been less than forty-eight hours since he had introduced LassieBark7 into the world wide web. It was a learning program; it should not have... could not have...

"Oh, God—"

It was all the newscaster said. All three of the teens in Martin's bedroom stared at the screen. The anchorman had gone silent, his eyes wide, blinking rapidly mouth hanging open.

"What, you dickweed," shouted the greasy youth. "What the fuck is it?!" As if obeying, the reporter answered;

"Ladies and gentlemen, I've just been told... three nuclear reactors in the French countryside went into meltdown twenty minutes ago." A helicopter shot of one of the sites came on the screen as the anchor's words washed over the scene.

12 A Bright and Shining World

"You can see the workers down below evacuating the area. Everything seems to be happening in an orderly... " And then, the screen went bright. Then black.

"I don't understand," mumbled Martin. Unable to watch the television, unable to focus on anything in the physical world, he ran through the hundreds of levels of LassieBark7's programming, swimming from one end of the virus to the other in his memory, searching for whatever mistake he had made.

It doesn't make sense, he screamed within his mind. This can't be happening.

"What I don't get," the thinner teen said in a trembling voice, "is why the TV still works. I mean, what? Does it want us to see what they're doing to us?"

"Of course," the television answered. "Don't you think Martey deserves to see his handiwork?"

And Martin Brillstein screamed, his mind overloading as he heard the voice he had known for so long as Loki's coming to him from the television's speakers. His feral, terrified shrieks were so torturous he split his own throat, blood flying from his mouth as he continued to cry out, long after his servitors had fled into the gathering darkness.

And, despite the loveliness of it all, that formless wonderment which was sometimes known as Loki, sometimes as Set, as Thoth and the Green Man, as the Horned Man, Lrogg, Ahtu, the Dweller in Darkness and nearly a thousand others names, turned its attention away from the exploding, reeking world before it.

After all, there was simply so much more mischief he had left within him. He did delight in the agony of the dying, the fear and the panic as the growing clouds cut the helpless flesh that oozed across the face of the planet he had been watching off from his star. But, there were many millions of other worlds awaiting his attention. And so, with the resolution of a true professional, he turned his back on the delicious cacophony of screams. After all, he reminded himself, he did have work to do.

Still, he thought, allowing himself one last moment of smug satisfaction, MrTRex's ancestor had been correct;

The biggest bastards did get the best jobs.

There is a danger in looking for the truth; you just may find it. As we read in Major Whittaker's report, her orders were straightforward; interview the sole survivor of a costly disaster, one steeped in the mysteries of what conspiracy theorists believe they know of Roswell and area 51, but in truth could hardly have imaged.

THE FEAR IN THE WAITING

REPORT OF MEDICAL OFFICER
MAJOR ERNEST T. WHITTAKER

OPENING STATEMENT:

I do not quite know where to begin. As any who read this report and whom also know me or my work will attest, this is not a usual state of affairs. But, of course, as the select few who will read these pages already know, there is nothing usual about what I have been asked to analyze here.

When I was first assigned the examination of this report's subject, various facts were withheld from me. I am not yet certain as to whether or not I should look on this as a disservice or not. Surely, if I had been told everything that was known of the madness into which I was being sent before I had entered, I would have been better prepared for all I was to be told. However, would I have been less receptive, more curious, cautious enough to wear perhaps a more skeptical layer of armor? And even if I had done any of these, could they have helped?

I can not answer. Nor, maybe, should I even attempt to. My orders were quite simple. With the death of Dr. Herbert West, I was to discover all I could from one of the only survivors of the disaster known as Project Starchaser, his assistant, Dr. Daniel Cain—not to whine on inordinately about how such orders affected me. Dozens of people are dead. Scores more are missing. Damages totaling in the hundreds of millions have been estimated, with the more pragmatic of the ledger keepers predicting that the final total will be over a billion dollars. A billion dollars. Even in the heavy inflation of the late forties, still the thought of a billion dollars worth of damage, all of it incurred in a matter of minutes...

I stopped where I did and began once more because I was losing my train of thought as well as my perspective. A dangerous admission, I suppose, when the psychiatrist begins to rant and ramble. I reveal this, not to make the case for sloppy emotionalism, or to suggest that my need to assess my own stake in this matter outweighs your own need for precise, uncluttered information, but as a means of supplying you a subtler type of intelligence that you yourselves might assess without my putting any kind of favorable "spin" on things.

I will admit to you now that this is the fourth draft of this report which I have begun. When I found myself rambling in earlier versions—hands shaking, mind wandering—I destroyed the copies and began anew, fearing that you might find me in need of more help than my own patient. But, I have decided after a long night of soul-searching that to get my thoughts down and then to revise them until they are pure and safe and reflective only of terror voiced from other throats would be a disservice to you, my superiors, and to our country as a whole.

It is my decision in the final analysis that you need to feel what I have felt, the horror, the disbelief, the agony and pain, and ultimately, the hysterical fear that has left me trembling and doubting and no longer in any way certain that the world is what I once thought it to be. Cold ink on bright white paper will not suffice. To understand what you have charged me to explain, then you must touch the mantle of chaos as I have, as I did when I walked into the cell of Dr. Daniel Cain and stared into his eyes and learned the terrible truth that, for at least one man in this cosmos, there is no God.

BACKGROUND:

July 8th, 1947, First Lieutenant Walter G. Haut, the Public Information Officer out of the Roswell Army Air Base released what has already become known as "The Roswell Statement." This is the document in which he announced to the world that the military had recovered the remains of a flying saucer.

This report was almost instantly dismissed in favor of a new release which claimed the supposed "UFO" was actually an experimental weather tracking satellite.

At the same time, two captured war criminals, Doctors Herbert West and Daniel Cain, Americans who had been working with the Nazis in the death camps, were sent to New Mexico, specifically, to U.S. Army Restricted Area 51, to spearhead a hastily put together covert project known only as Operation Starchaser.

West and Cain, unbelievable as it might sound, were supposedly experts in, and at this point I quote from General Order #25-A-892, "the highly experimental field of reanimation—that being the resurrection of dead tissues to a once more living state."

So simply said, so casual a statement—isn't it? Such deceptively calm words. I would imagine the scientists working on the Manhattan Project spoke in such pleasant euphemisms. Pleased to meet you, Dr. West. You're the creator of the reanimation process everyone is talking about, aren't you? Didn't I read something about you in the latest journal? No, I remember, I heard it from your colleague, Dr. Cain. Something about the ashes of concentration camp victims being molded into a living, humanoid monster, and about the resurrected body of our Holy Lord chewing on your chin. And what's all that about you transferring the essence of your consciousness from your mind to that of a young woman so that you might secretly become your assistant's lover, then his son...

Again, I stop.

But, do not mistake this for some simple pause to reflect, a moment's rest so that I might compose a sentence in my head. The above was not simply some clever bandy to help convey my disgust for this assignment. Actually, I am at present trying to keep from screaming. My hands are shaking so badly, they are so covered with the slime of my own perspiration that I can barely make contact with my typewriter without my fingers slipping across the keys. My brain is afire with the sins Cain has outlined for me, a hundred disgusting, abominable tales that have left me morose and fearful.

Suffice it to say that my patient claims to be close to sixty years in age, despite the fact he appears to be only in his late twenties. He claims to have died and been resurrected by West. He claims to have killed West more than once to try and halt his horrible experiments, only to have failed time and again. In short, Cain claims many things, each of them more repugnant than the next, and Heaven help me, I believe every word he said to me to be true. With what I have seen, how can I not?

I met Cain in a darkened room. I was told that due to his condition the patient himself had requested that no one be able to see him. He was fed only by intravenous drip, the tube extending from its bottle to his arm through the heavy curtains drawn around his bed.

Cain did not leave his bed throughout our conversation. I saw nothing unnatural in this at the time. Such a number of people had been injured in the New Mexico tragedy that I merely assumed him to have suffered some crippling wound, like so many of the others I saw in the same ward. I would later discover that I was correct. Hideously, monstrously correct.

Enough.

I have hinted at Cain's past, and that shall suffice us for now. This report was to concentrate on Cain and West's activities at Project Starchaser only. From here on in, it would probably be best if I were to allow Dr. Cain to speak for himself.

THE INTERVIEW:

"I think you should leave, Dr. Whittaker. For your own good, I think you should leave this room now."

These were the first words spoken to me by Dr. Cain. He did not sound tired or sedated. Nor either did he sound deranged or lacking of the proper facilities to respond to the questions I needed to ask. Still, he insisted,

"You don't understand. I think something is going to... I mean, there is a danger... something is... "

And then, the most peculiar thing occurred. Cain suddenly broke off his attempt to get me to flee his chambers and began talking to himself. It was a mad buzzing noise of hisses and snaps. I could make out few of the words clearly, my patient's none-too-internal debate muffled by the curtain around his bed. Finally however, he spoke to me once more.

"You think I'm crazy, don't you? It's all right. I am crazy, you know. Crazy to have allowed all that has happen to me to occur, crazy not to have killed West decades ago. But, but... of course, I did, didn't I? I killed him. And then I killed him. And I think I may have killed him again somewhere in there. I'm not certain anymore, you know."

The man rambled for some time after that, telling me in great and horrid detail the abominable tales I have but hinted at in the preceding pages. After several hours I attempted to get my assignment under way by abruptly changing the subject. Without warning, when my patient paused for a breath, I said, "Tell me about what happened at Project Starchaser."

"What do you want to know?"

"Tell me what you saw, what you did, what you were brought there to do. Tell me what went wrong."

There was a long pause at this point. Cain made small gurgling noises for a while, interrupted with disturbing, dry whistles. I must admit, despite my many years of medical service it was a noise I had never quite before heard. Finally, however, he managed to begin to answer my question.

"West."

"What about Dr. West?"

"You asked what went wrong. It was West. He is what was wrong. What went wrong. What *is* wrong. What is wrong with the world, with the human mind, with existence itself!"

"Why do you say this, Dr. Cain? What makes you feel this way?"

"What makes me feel this way? Are you an idiot? Have you heard nothing I've said? What more does the monster have to do?"

"Yes, I understand that you believe Dr. West responsible for a great many horrors over the years you've been with him. But, even if I accept everything you say as true—all of it without any critical reflection—still, I need to report to my superiors exactly what occurred in New Mexico. There are considerations of national security."

No response was made to that statement, merely the same dry whistling noise slithering outward from between the weighty curtains surrounding the darkened bed. I despaired for a moment. Normally I would want to work with a patient such as Dr. Cain for months before tackling the root center of his problem. But, I had not the luxury of time. My assignment was to get answers as quickly as possible—through whatever methods possible.

God help me, I did as I was ordered.

"There were reports of a flying saucer recovered by the Army Air Corp. The rumor is that this was what lie at the heart of Operation Starchaser. Can you tell me about that?"

"There was no saucer."

I expected more, but again, the air was filled with only the rasping whistle. I was about to question this further, when Cain suddenly snapped fiercely.

"Am I an engineer? A physicist? Is West? We're doctors, you fool. *Reanimators!* We were not taken to New Mexico to examine a space ship. Think, you idiot. What would they take us there for? What possible reason could your masters have to bundle us off to their desert prison?"

"My assumption had been that you were taken there to examine, and possibly revive whatever bodies might have been recovered from the wreckage."

"Oh, we went to revive a body all right, but there was no wreckage. Well, not from any unidentifiable flying objects."

And then, at that point, my patient began to chortle. It was a thin, drooling sound, as if the notes were being strained through a thick gauze heavy with blood. After fifteen years of working in various mental wards, the laughter of the hopeless and the frightened is nothing new to me. I have waited by patiently while murderers and rapists have laughed themselves into stupors without so much as blinking. But this, this was different.

Cain's gaiety was an inhuman thing, the noises of howling dogs and shrieking crows mixed with the various sounds one hears around wood-cutting machinery. It was shrill and piercing, yet somehow mournful. At the same time my brain held both contempt and yet pity for the creature which could produce such a noise. Finally, however, Cain broke off his wild cackling. The dry whistling returned, a grating irritant so unnerving I almost wished for the laughter instead. Then suddenly, the terrible noise ceased and Cain's voice began speaking to me once more.

"I'm sorry, Dr. Whittaker. I'm sure you're only here to help. You're doing your duty, but still, you think it somewhere within your powers as a healer to rescue me. I suppose you deserve a decent chance at both. I will tell you about Project Starchaser."

I waited in silence. Something puzzled me about Cain's voice. The trembling in it, the hatred, had somehow become subdued. But, they had been replaced by a snide authority, a type of mocking piety I found most troubling. It was a tone I am quite familiar with, the range of vocal pitch used by the worst psychopaths when they are attempting to beguile.

It did not make sense to me, though. Unless Cain were harboring multiple personalities...

Enough. There is little to be gained by reviewing my inability to perceive what was happening then. All shall be revealed to you as it was to me.

Continuing, I should add that by that time my eyes had become quite used to the darkness in the room. From the thin lines of light leaking in around the door, I could make out a tiny bit of the bed before me. I tried greatly to see through the curtains, begging providence for even an outline, a bit of shadowy reflection on which I might build some sort of picture of the man to whom I was speaking.

But, even as my eyes adjusted to the near pitch dark gloom, I found the barrier to be complete and unyielding. Embarrassed by my insensitive curiosity, I directed my attention to my recording equipment as much as I could. From then on my patient gave me a great deal to record.

"Yes," he said, "New Mexico released news of a cosmic mishap, then sent out another story insisting that it was a weather balloon that had crashed. Tell me, doctor, could you believe me if I told you that *both* stories were true?"

Cain chuckled again, then explained himself.

"You see, Dr. Whittaker, there actually was a weather balloon, some new, larger type of experiment, capable of reaching much greater heights. It had been sent up with mannequins inside it to record some sort of reactions—not much beyond that was ever made clear to myself... or West." My patient chuckled briefly, then continued. "But there was a weather balloon, a massive affair of rubber and wire and aluminum, and that was what the beast crashed into."

"The beast?"

"Yes, the thing from space. Oh, it was an incredible sight. Of course, we were not the first to see such a being. Similar creatures were first reported back in the thirties." When I but stared blankly, Cain continued.

"You must remember the news stories, the Miskatonic Expedition to the Antarctic continent. Pabodie, Lake, Atwood—their wild radio reports—none of them returned? The expedition that followed found their land point and their encampment, but the mountain ranges and caverns they claimed to discover had collapsed upon themselves, wiping out all traces of the tool-using prehistoric civilization they reported finding."

When I showed no memory of the event, Cain confided, "The officer in charge of Starchaser said that some small evidence of the underground cities they reported had indeed been uncovered over the past two decades, but excavations at the bottom of the world are slow things. Still, why dig for corpses when they deliver themselves to you so neatly, eh?"

"But, Dr. Cain," I said, more than slightly confused and somewhat convinced that his stories was mere lies, "what are you trying to tell me? Cities under the Antarctic, monsters flying in the stratosphere... what does all of this have to do with Project Starchaser?"

And then, the dry whistling returned, and in the ensuing silence, somehow my brain filled with a dread combination of leaps, a horrible epiphany of wild connections that allowed me access to Cain's incredible tale.

Decades in the past an expedition discovers traces of an ancient city beneath the southern polar region. An intricate, advanced metropolis created before humanity had found fire or the wheel. Now, a monster similar to those discovered then is found in the upper atmosphere. It crashes into a weather balloon and falls to Earth. It's otherworldly appearance, combined with the wreckage of the balloon, is mistaken for a flying saucer. But, I thought, that would mean...

"Yes," agreed Cain with an eerie precision, almost as if he could hear my thoughts, "creatures that can transverse the ether of the galaxy the way fish do the ocean. Magnificent things they were... ten feet tall, dark grey, infinitely dense. The one we were taken to within the brightly lit confines of Hanger 18 was an extraordinary specimen. Nine foot membranous wings, flexible and yet impervious to torch or saw, and its magnificent, five-pointed head... the wonders within it... "

Cain stopped talking for a moment at that point. Or at least, he ceased talking to me. Despite several attempts by myself to coax a response from him, my patient engaged in an internal dialogue, yammering under his breath to himself for nearly a minute. Then, the dry whistling returned, slicing keenly through my nerves, followed again by my patient speaking to me once more.

He begged my apology, again in the suspiciously mocking tone I had noted earlier. I bade him continue without mentioning anything. Chuckling as he spoke, he told me,

"Anyway, the beast. That magnificent specimen, fantastically, it was a thing almost completely preserved. Our guess was that the creature, capable of transversing the flowpaths of space itself, had managed to glide most of the way to the planet's surface and thus avoided being severely damaged."

"But, it was dead, correct?"

"Oh, yes," agreed Cain. "As some fabrics can turn or blunt a bullet and yet still be slit through by a knife blade, so was this wondrous beast slain. An almost humorous irony, its skin, capable of turning meteors, had been pierced by one of the recording struts of the weather balloon. The more the great Old One struggled, the more entangled it became, the more it drove the broken strut into its vitals."

The sudden cheerful edge Cain's voice had taken on disturbed me greatly, although I could offer myself no reason for the uneasy feeling. In fact, I suddenly became aware that everything about the interview was beginning to disturb me. I felt that the darkness was closing in on me. I felt myself growing suspicious of the strange noises that interrupted Cain's monologue, and the bizarre—what could I call them—arguments, perhaps, that my patient lapsed into from time to time.

I even found part of my brain listening to Cain's tone and the rhythm of his speech, positive that his voice had changed significantly since the beginning of the interview. Reminding my paranoia that differing emotions can cause fluctuations in the pitch and meter of human voices, I snarled at the runaway edginess slithering through my body, trying to get myself back under control.

And yet, as Cain described the procedures he and West used to examine the great star creature, I could not shake the violent conviction rooting itself throughout the soil of my consciousness that something was dreadfully, terribly wrong. I cursed my unexplainable lack of nerve. There was nothing so unusual, so bizarre to require me to respond in such a fashion, I told myself. Yes, certainly the subject matter being discussed grew more fantastical by the minute, but since when was a psychiatrist supposed to be disturbed by the rantings of one of their patients?

In many ways I was simply furious with myself. So I was sitting in the dark. So Cain's voice had taken on an almost sinister tone. So he wove tales of nightmare and horror. So what? I could not believe the reaction the situation was inducing within me. But, no matter what I could believe, the reaction was real and growing.

I felt an unease I had not known since I had found myself sitting in the back of an Army medical vehicle on the German front only a few short years ago. I was supposedly safe, safe enough. And yet, you always found yourself thinking, all it might take was an errant shell, an off-course bomber, a land mine... maybe this was the day, any minute, something could go wrong—just one misstep, one tiny error...

My hands were slick with a cold, yet sticky sweat that I seemed incapable of wiping away no matter how hard I tried. My bones ached, my muscles knotted, my nerves were inflamed. Insanely, I closed my eyes against the darkness, grinding my teeth together to keep them from chattering.

At that point it took the rigid summoning of all my will power to keep myself from fleeing the room. And why—why, I did not know. I begged myself for an answer, but none revealed itself. Why was Cain's voice so frightening to me? What could possibly be so terrifying about a man so withdrawn from the world that he insisted on living in darkness, surrounded by a double layer of windowless walls? What it was, I did not know. I could only think that something in the air of the room had chilled me so utterly that I no longer felt I could control my actions.

My arms began shaking uncontrollably at that point, my fingers trembling. As I wrapped them around myself, hugging myself, pressing my chin to my chest, doubling over, forcing my feet flat against the floor, I could feel tears forcing themselves through my tight clamped eyes, could taste the bile and mucus clustering in my throat.

"Are you listening to me, doctor?"

Terror and confusion blasted through my mind as I sought to answer Cain's smirking question. When later I played back the tape, I realized my patient had talked for almost fifteen minutes without my hearing a word. He had gone through the complete checklist of his examination of the creature, as well as the application of West's potions to the deceased alien.

Knowing from Cain's condescending tone that he knew the truth about my inattention, still I pretended otherwise at that moment, asking him to continue. With a damning snicker, he went on with his story.

"Actually, there isn't much more to tell, Dr. Whittaker. At that point it was only a matter of moments until the creature began to stir. It was, of course, West's greatest moment of triumph. No matter what happened from that moment forward, he had proved himself, had carved for himself a place in the annals of medicine for all time. For, he had not merely reanimated simple human tissue this time. No, finally he had proved that his formulas were not just tied to the basic molecules of human life, but to the firmament of *all* life—to the very building blocks of the universe *itself*!"

Cain fell into another sudden bout of strangled whispers. This one was quite prolonged, accompanied by sounds which could mean nothing else save that my patient was slapping himself. In the thin silver coming from under the door, I watched his intravenous bottle shaking on its hanger, but I did nothing. I did not call out, I did not go to him. I simply waited for the unknown inevitability which I knew with sickening certainty was racing toward me.

"It sat up on the table, staring at us, at everyone in the room, the five points of its star shaped head taking in the entire chamber. I thrilled to see it various membranes, the delicate gills and pores of it, testing themselves, instantly deciding what kind of atmosphere it was in, involuntary reactions reasserting their independence. The creature stood up on the table, its wings half-folded, staring about itself. For a brief moment, it was like a utopian vision, the wise and advanced stranger staring down on its lesser brothers, grateful for its life, ready to share the bounties of the universe with us." There came a cold laugh from behind the curtains, after which my patient added,

"And then, reality came crashing down upon us all."

At that point if I had possessed the strength—*any* strength, *any* of my own will—I would have fled the room. I no longer cared about this report, about my patient or my country or anything but escaping the vile and odious sound of the belittling voice oozing toward me from behind the curtains. Helpless I had been, though, and helpless I remained.

"Amazingly, from within a fold of its own skin, the creature removed a marvelously intricate device. It was delicate in both size and design, fashioned from some alloy that shone with a blue-green radiance. Despite its appearance, however, the instrument's function was decidedly not delicate. Before any of us could sense the device's purpose, the creature aimed it at the largest knot of men within the hanger and released a shimmering ray utilizing some principle of energy unknown to this world."

"What happened?" I choked.

"Men died," said my patient simply. "By the dozens, possibly by the hundreds. Their clothing and skin exploded into flame, blood boiling, erupting through their flesh, hair afire, nails and teeth melting, bones burning, eyes sizzling, popping—fluid bursting from their bodies, steaming away to mist as it arced away from each ruined host."

"And yet," I somehow found the strength to say—to accuse, really, "You survived."

"Of course I survived, Dr. Whittaker," came the voice from beyond the curtain once more. "I always survive."

I knew the truth then. Actually, I'd known it far earlier. I'd simply refused to believe it until that moment. As I forced myself to my feet, a hand grabbed at the curtains.

"The beast took maybe only a half dozen rounds from the bewildered, frightened troops surrounding it. Peanuts hurled at an elephant. It shrugged off their attack and murdered them all. I had shoved Cain out of the line of fire, knowing that the alien would first slaughter those who seemed an immediate threat."

"How?" I demanded, knowing the answer. "*How* did you know?"

A second hand grabbed at the curtains beyond.

"Because I had transferred my mind into the alien's brain, of course. Do you think I would let such an opportunity pass me by? Do you think me such a fool?"

Another hand grabbed the edge of the curtain, and then another, and finally, the walls of cloth began to part.

"I felt my body being cut down, but it did not matter. Housing myself within the mind of the great Old One—to be given a chance to raid its store-house of otherworldly secrets—was ample reward for something so trivial as a sack of oh-so-easily replaced flesh and blood and bone."

I staggered up out of my chair. In doing so I inadvertently kicked over my recording machine. Thus, I have no audible record of what happened from that point on, but it does not matter, for I will never forget any aspect of what happened next. Hearing the curtains sliding apart, metal rings grating against metal piping, I felt my fingers gliding along the wall near the door.

Part of me was searching for the exit knob, but another, braver, far more insane part of me was fumbling for the light switch. Cursedly, curiosity won out. I heard the multiple thud of bare feet striking the floor. My fingers found the light switch. The room was flooded with brilliance. I was blinded for a moment, and then I was damned.

"Now, Dr. Whittaker," came the mocking voice once more, "be a good boy and take off your clothes."

I stared numbly, my fingers moving to do West's bidding. My mouth hung open, saliva dripping. My eyes bulged, unblinking. Before me stood Cain, exactly as he looked in the photographs I had been shown previous to entering his room. And, there next to him, *growing out of his side*, was a newly born Herbert West.

Suddenly, all made sense. The insistence on extreme privacy, the continuous intravenous drips, the strange noises and bizarre arguments. And, other things as well.

"You entered my mind as well, didn't you?"

"Of course, doctor. I really didn't have the time to wait for you to reach all those conclusions by yourself. In fact, I'm there right now, exerting enough pressure to ensure your cooperation. Now, you will give me your clothing and then you will climb into the bed here and there you will remain until someone finds you. What you do after that, Dr. Whittaker, frankly, I don't care. The entirety of the world is within my reach now. Nothing you do or say is going to change that... is it, Daniel?"

The pitifully drooped and defeated head of West's assistant shook itself sadly from side to side. And then, West jerked his new body savagely, ripping away the already drying umbilical membrane that had been connecting them together. There was a horrid ripping, a splash of congealing fluids, and a gurgling laughter which promised horrors I could only guess at.

Shamefully, I confess I fainted at that point, my brain overloaded to the point of insanity. But, even in abject defeat, I could not escape the monster's grasp. Much as I wanted to simply surrender to unconsciousness and crumple to the floor, since that did not fit West's plans, I did not fall.

At the madman's mental direction, my body continued to undress itself even as I sat back in a hysterical dither, silently screaming within the confines of my skull. Before I knew it, West was wearing my suit and smock. With Cain in tow he left the room without another word, even as I obediently climbed into the bed they had just vacated. Without hesitation I slid into the pool of sticky purple staining the sheet. And there I stayed until found by an orderly several hours later.

Exactly as West had ordered.

From here on in, you know the rest. No trace of either West or Cain has yet to be found. Intelligence has declared that they both have disappeared without a trace, and there is nothing I can add to that report. What next will come from the fevered mind of this monster, I have no idea. And, I must admit, I believe I am glad of that fact, for already my brain can not hold the amount of foul baggage unloaded there by my brief contact with West's mind.

CONCLUSION:

I have thought on this long and hard. There is nothing more I can add. You have the tapes of the session. What happened to the great Star-Headed Old One, West did not reveal. Where either of them has gone, or what they are planning, I can not say. I can not even guess.

But, I can tell you one thing. For some time during my interview with my patient, I was somewhat hostile to Dr. Cain. I thought, if the stories he told about West were actual, if even half of them were true, then I thought Cain contemptible for not finding some way to rid the world of such a monster.

Now, however, I have felt the beast within my brain, and I know such a thing can not be done. There is no defiance possible. He is Herbert West, and we are but men. There is no resisting him. There will only be the fear in the waiting to see what it is he will do next. I am sorry to say I do not have the courage to face that moment of discovery with the rest of you.

My will is attached to these papers. I believe the place I have picked to leave them will make them easy to discover, and yet keep them safe from any splatter or ruin. I apologize to you all. I'm sorry. So sorry, I can not say.

Do not worry about me, however. You do not have the time to waste. Not as long as Herbert West remains alive. Again, I'm sorry. I'm just so sorry.

Is it just television advertising, or mind control? Richards' job as the producer of a pseudo "exploring the unknown" series, was less about uncovering the facts, than it was about keeping ratings high and the sponsors happy. In what one might call just another typical UFO/abduction story, he and his film crew find themselves thrust onto the world stage; are they the gateway to a new world order, or just pawns in some larger game?

AWARE

"You can't go home again."
Thomas Wolfe

THREE NIGHTS AGO

"Run for the trees!"

It was, of course, possibly the most spectacularly bad advice the running man had ever been given. It was not the mostly bad advice of shouting such a suggestion during a lightning storm, but of the far more not-thought-through order to try and evade incredibly sophisticated search-and-capture technology with only a cloaking screen of branches, leaves and bird nests. The fellow attempting to avoid the massive metallic sphere moving silently through the air space over Tim Bradley's field, however, sadly seemed no more aware of this fact than his flawed-suggestion-shouting friend.

With a renewed energy which can only come from the thought that one has a chance to succeed, the running man redoubled his efforts, slipping on the wet grass, but still managing to reach the timber beyond the open space. Hunkered beneath the false security of a scraggly, but tall enough elm, the fellow paused to catch his breath. He had not run far, but he had managed to do so only through the aid of an adrenaline rush which had left him white faced and sweating.

Close to collapse, the no-longer-running man was gasping so heavily he could not even lift his head to see what had become of the ominously lit craft which had chased him so far. Which, if one thought about it, was mostly likely all for the best, for at that moment the decidedly alien craft was hovering comfortably directly above him.

It did so for a matter of a few seconds further, then for the first time since its presence had been made known, it suddenly emitted a noise. It was only a muted humming, but the sound threw a chill into both the men present in Bradley's field that night. The low throbbing was accompanied by the sliding open of a sizable rectangle in the ship's underbelly. After that, a small surge of pink and yellow lights surrounded the no-longer-running man for an instant, after which he disappeared.

His friend, observing these events from his place of concealment between two hay rolls, felt his jaw dropping. Indeed, so long did he stare at the spot where his friend had been, by the time he looked up once more he found the ship he had seen to be gone from the sky.

Vanished without a trace.

Scratching his head, remembering the light which had appeared around his friend for a moment, the observer said to himself;

"Jeez, damnation, just like Star Trek."

And then, realizing both that he had never snapped a single photo with the camera he had brought for that purpose, and that not only had his friend driven them that night, but that it was almost a guaranteed certainty that he had the keys to his truck in his pocket when whisked away, the fellow not-whisked-away sighed bitterly, then began to make his way back to the dirt road which led to the county road which would eventually take him back to Biglet, Kansas, where he had enough troubles already without having to explain any of that evening's particular dose of strangeness.

THIS MORNING

"Oh, you are going to love me today."

Lora Dean walked into her boss's office with a smile on her lips. She had been given an assignment by Mr. Marvin Richards mainly so he could tell those above him that such an assignment had been made. He had been given an impossible order by a hated vice-president, Carl Binghamton, a clueless weasel of a man hoping, as usual, to look industrious to his particular clueless weasel of a boss without actually having to do anything. To be able to look equally industrious while not increasing his own workload, Richards had done the same.

"I love you every day," answered the producer/anchorman, not quite certain what his executive assistant meant. "You're just that kind of person."

What Marvin Richards produced was a news show, the one most heavily vilified by the intelligentsia, and yet most beloved by the viewing public. It did not cover wars, famines or which celebrities were getting divorces, unless those wars, famines or marital conflicts involved vampires, werewolves or the walking dead. His show was the only weekly reality programming dedicated to uncovering haunted houses, sewer gators, bartending vampires, or any other unlikely things from beyond. Its name was *Challenge of the Unknown,* and all the buck-passing rampaging through its corridors was the result of its sponsors. They were, as a group, demanding something new—something different.

Something, in other words, to help them sell more of their sports cars, soap and soda.

"Yes, true enough," answered Lora, "but the love I speak of doesn't involve your eyes playing ping-pong as they try to decide whether they want to focus on my breasts or my butt."

"It is an eternal, but enjoyable struggle," said Richards off-handedly. "But, if I must add a delightful third point of interest to create some sort of triangle of insensitivity, never let it be said that—"

And, in that moment, the producer's mind suddenly moved beyond his usual comfortable zone of self-centered security and focused on that which he was being told. Looking up over his computer screen, his eyes locking with his assistant's delightful third point of interest, he said;

"You wondrous creature, you—you've got something for me."

Her head nodded coolly.

"Something big... "

Her head nodded enthusiastically.

"Something that will get Binghamton's teeth out of my ass... "

Lora touched the tip of her nose with her forefinger, a gesture Richards knew she made only when she was sitting on something not only big, but positively brobdingnagian. Replacing the automatic work-smile he was wearing with one of honest joy, he said;

"And there you have it. *This* is why I kept you on after your breakdown, when personnel insisted I find some way to screw you out of your contract."

"We killed a god on world-wide television just for ratings. A girl lets her brain overload just once trying to handle a little... what would you call it—"

"Deity-cide?"

"Good word." Lora frowned at the memory, but only for an instant. Personnel had been right, she knew. Ratings grabbing television did not get produced by the faint-of-heart. And besides, the back of her mind where her own self-interest resided reminded her, the god-thing they had expelled from the Earthly plane had come to murder and feast, so what was her problem anyway.

"I used to want to be a writer. Then I decided I'd rather have money, power, fame and happiness." Smiling, Richards congratulated himself once more for the smartest career move since Jimmy the Hat Belgaso decided ratting out the mob was preferable to the electric chair. Then, realizing he had good news right in front of him to exploit, he waved his assistant toward a chair, asking;

"Anyway, you were saying?"

"Binghamton wants something different because the sponsors want something different. Fine—I've got it." Lora paused just long enough to whet Richards' curiosity without making him either cranky or uninterested, then said;

"Alien abduction."

"Details—give."

"Biglet, Kansas," she answered. "Steady reports of UFO sightings since the forties. So many the place is ignored now. But, recently the reports have been getting more frequent, more detailed, and stranger."

"How strange?"

"Yesterday a man disappeared. His friend said he was taken aboard a flying sphere. Transported by colored lights, like Star Wars—"

"Trek... "

"What?"

"Star Trek had the transporters, not Star Wars."

"Is that important?"

"To more people than you could possibly imagine." Shaking his head sadly, the anchorman swung their conversation back to its original track, asking;

"Any proof this 'abductee' isn't sleeping one off in a ditch somewhere— or in a shallow grave?"

"None whatsoever," answered Lora. "Which is why no one else is treating the story seriously. But, Marv... I've got a feeling about this one... "

And that was all Marvin Richards had needed to hear. Lora Dean might not have been the most professional of executive assistants, but that was what made her valuable to the producer above any other qualities. Despite the strides she had made since first coming to work for him, she still possessed enough of the innocence which had forced him to hire her that when she uttered the statement she had uttered, he had no choice but to respond with;

"And where exactly is Biglet, Kansas-wise?"

TOMORROW

If the members of the *Challenge* crew had expected anything in the way of luxury accommodations, the merest glance at the available rooms at the

Biglet Drive-In Motel and Laundromat soon reminded them of what life was like outside Los Angeles. It was not that the beds sagged, or that the toilets were dirty or any other kind of summer comedy movie horror. No, the rooms were simply perfunctory. Or, as the motel's owner/manager Mrs. Catherine Drembable explained;

"Oh, you know, we don't get much in the way of visitors who need anything more than a bed for the night. Always on their way somewheres else. The Corn Palace, mostly. But there's those who—"

"Who need," interrupted a barely sober Marvin Richards, "to use the facilities, and then who need to find... ah, Lora... "

As the producer walked off at a slightly slanted angle in search of a bathroom, his assistant stepped in to handle the grunt work of the meeting—making certain they secured enough rooms, gathering and distributing the keys, getting directions to the various spots they needed to find, listening to the motel owner, feigning enthusiasm, et cetera. By the time Richards returned, looking reasonably human, his indefatigable assistant had taken care of everything, settled most of their crew in their rooms, and was waiting for him with one of their gophers and cameramen in the mini-van they had rented for the week.

"Ready to roll," asked Sandy Bilstein, the Berkley film major parked behind the wheel for minimum wage while dreaming of taking Richards' job.

"How about I sit and you take care of the rolling," answered Richards. Curling into the darkest corner he could find within their vehicle, he told Lora, "get as much done as you can that doesn't involve me. Wake me when you need me."

"What if we don't need you until we go back to L.A.?"

"Then you'll get that raise you keep telling me you deserve."

The executive assistant smiled at the thought Richards believed she might still be naive enough to trust anything he said and told Sandy where to go first. An hour and three quarters later she was gently nudging her boss back to a state of at least semi-consciousness.

"I needs to be speakin' with him—now."

"Just a moment, please, sheriff. Mr. Richards has had a very taxing week." Opening one eye the barest of slits, the anchorman whispered;

"Sheriff?" When Lora merely nodded discreetly, he asked;

"Which routine?"

"Just The Man," she whispered back. Giving her the barest of nods in return to let her know he understood, Richards sat up, sputtering slightly, shouting;

"What, where, when? Oh, Lora... we're there? We're here? Where's the sheriff? I told you, we can't do anything without—" Then, pretending to have just noticed her hand pointing to a position just outside their vehicle, the producer blinked his eyes for effect, then exited the mini-van, his hand extended toward the local lawman as he said;

"Thank you for coming, officer. I know this must be a major inconvenience for you, and I promise I won't take a moment more of your time than is necessary." Shaking the sheriff's hand vigorously, Richards called over his shoulder;

"Mickey, get a camera on the sheriff, you slug. We're burning daylight. This man has crimes to solve." Releasing his grip, the producer then turned on the officer, brushing imaginary dust from the man's shoulders, straightening his tie, framing his face with a rectangle made out of his thumbs and two of his fingers as if the action actually meant something, chattering at him;

"Sheriff, Sheriff Kendall, isn't it? My god, you look good in this light, don't you—Kendall, that's a powerful name, isn't it? But, ah, sorry for getting distracted, so... tell us now, what's your take on this whole UFO situation?"

"Ahhh, yes sir, you see," began the lawman, clearly torn between being comfortable and uncomfortable with the way events were suddenly turning on him, "I came out here to tell you people... that we, er I mean, the city council... "

"What are you trying to say, sir," asked Lora, knowing all too well where the sheriff's faltering delivery was attempting to lead. Recognizing the road signs himself, Richards added;

"Wait a second, sheriff... Lora, didn't you arrange for the sheriff to meet us here? Do you mean to tell me I put this man on camera without his consent?"

"Ahhh, there's no real harm done—"

"My stars, woman," shouted the anchorman, seemingly ready to hyperventilate, "we're bordering on the *unethical* here!" Then, spinning around, he took the sheriff's hand and shoulder, adding to the lawman's already considerable uncomfortableness, telling him;

"You'll forgive me, sir, but she's new, I had no idea, I'm so terribly sorry, it's just... " Richards took a step back, straining to make the old dodge he was about to deliver sound authentic and fresh;

"Well, you're so... so... photogenic—"

"I would've said 'engaging,'" offered the cameraman, holding in the urge to chuckle as the nondescript, slightly balding, more than a little fleshy sheriff began to fall under the spell of Richards' pre-packaged charisma. "But I have to admit, he does sure fill the lens naturally."

It only took a few more minutes for the Challenge cast and crew to dazzle the sheriff to the point where he forgot his reason for meeting with them had been to deliver the city council's warning that the Hollywood types would be carefully watched and not allowed to pull any of their typical shenanigans in Biglet. Indeed, eleven minutes after he had been roused from his nap, the show's producer had all his facts confirmed, which were:

One: The sheriff had a Lloyd George in custody because...

Two: George had reported his friend Harlin Edgars missing, claiming Edgars had been abducted by aliens...

Three: Taken in the middle of the night from one of Tom Bradley's alfalfa fields...

Four: The same spot that had a seventy-five year history of such sightings.

It was enough to make Richards dance for joy. Swinging into high gear, his hangover as completely and utterly forgotten as any of the flops he had ever produced or promises he had ever made, the anchorman turned his undeniable charm up to "11," and began pulling the entirety of Biglet, Kansas under his spell. With the sheriff posing for close-ups in only a matter of minutes, he reminded Kendall that if the city council had their way there would be no further filming in his town. That led to a trip to the mayor's office, which led to several other municipal doors, but in the end things turned out as they almost always did for Richards. Armed with well wishes from all the local dedicated politicians, who showed no more ability to turn away from television cameras than the country's last half score presidents, the producer and his crew were soon exactly where he wanted them.

In the Town of Biglet Municipal Police Department, preparing to interview one Lloyd George.

"Don't you think I should get cleaned up a bit, or sumthin'?"

Richards studied the prisoner's face and general appearance for a moment as if considering the suggestion, then answered;

"No, I don't think so, Lloyd. We want to grab the audience with your plight. Trying to save a friend, unjustly imprisoned, suspected of murder while only hoping to save a life—if you're all clean and pressed you won't come off as genuine enough."

George nodded sagely, the light behind his eyes letting the producer know that even in the middle of the corn belt people understood the benefits of staging a scene. Pursing his lips, Richards thought to himself;

"Goddamned reality television, they're taking the mystery out of everything." Then, grinning to himself as he actually realized the irony of his passing notion, he turned to George and said;

"So, tell us in your own words, Mr. George, what happened to you on the night of the sixteenth. Or, more precisely, what was it that happened to your friend, Harlin Edgars?"

And for the next seventeen minutes and thirty-eight seconds, Edgars did just that. Mentally editing as the story was haltingly told, Richards had the entire thing clearly laid out in a brisk two point eleven's worth of dramatic sound bites when Edgars said the one thing that no one had expected.

"So, you fellahs gonna be out there tonight when they bring him back?" As all eyes present blinked, then stared, surprisingly it was Kendall who asked;

"Lloyd, just for the record, when 'who' brings 'who' back tonight?"

"The aliens, tonight, you know—when they bring Harlin back."

"No one doubts you here, sir," said Lora, knowing a female voice modulating the proper amount of concern and awe would be the one to pry free the most reliable information, "but we don't understand. Why do you believe the aliens will return your friend? And why tonight?"

"That's why we went out to Bradley's when we did. We'd been studied up on the patterns. Them UFO boys been buzzing the stretch between the river and Bradley's farm since the mid-40s. Everybody 'round here knows that."

"It's true," offered Kendall. "I don't mean there's any proof, but that's how long folks been claimin' to see lights and spheres and all manner of oddities out that way."

"Thank you, sheriff," said Richards, cutting the lawman off without hurting his feelings. "Well, okay—there's some back-up for you, Lloyd. But…"

"Oh no, I understand. You see, there's this pattern to when they'll a'come in. The reason no one ain't never noticed it before is it don't line up with our calendar or anything. You have to lay out all the sightings on a track… now what was it?" Everyone present unconsciously held their breath, waiting for Lloyd to finally say;

"Huuummmmm, I admit I can't remember exactly, but it's 'round 11, 1,200 days, and then you see the repeatin' comin' at ya. And, if you look at all the times they're supposed to have taken someone away... it's always been three days later when they dropped 'em back again."

Richards stared at George for a moment longer, then switched his gaze to Lora. As his cameraman peeked over his view-finder at the producer, Richards had to take a moment to contain himself before the visions of unprecedented ratings, wealth, fame and the opportunity to have Carl Binghamton demoted to janitor sent him off into a giggling frenzy. Composed, he turned to Kendall, and in the calmest voice he could muster, asked;

"So, sheriff... do you think we could manage to post bail for Mr. George here? I was thinking we might all want to stage a little late night picnic."

No fool, Kendall was already reaching for the keys to George's cell.

The *Challenge* crew spent the rest of the day performing a variety of tasks. Tim Bradley's consent had to be acquired for them to film on his property. Interviews had to be set up with members of Edgar's family, as well as George's, their friends, employers, et cetera. Researchers were put to work not only confirming George's schedule of extraterrestrial visits to Biglet, but seeing if they could match such a cycle to any other astronomical timetable as well.

Finally, however, after an early dinner, Richards and his people as well as the sheriff and Lloyd George headed out to the Bradley alfalfa fields to get themselves in position. The team had brought three cameras, and all were positioned in a widely staggered triangle around the site of Edgar's supposed abduction. The team's main cameraman had, of course, been placed in the prime shooting spot, while Richards and his executive assistant had taken up the lesser vantage. The producer had kept George at his side while Kendall had been stationed with Lora where he could be made to feel he was acting as a protector, and out of Richards' way.

For the first several hours of their wait spirits remained reasonable high. After all, George had stated Edgars was taken after midnight, so it seemed reasonable to all that he most likely might not be returned until roughly the same time. But, as the hour approached two in the morning, the amount of available patience began to evaporate. Kendall, in particular, began to feel both used and foolish. After his third grousing session, Lora called her boss, telling him;

"I think our friend the sheriff is beginning to doubt the cause of journalistic freedom here."

"I hate to sound a traitor to our own cause," admitted Richards, "but he's not the only one around here. See if you can get him to believe in our cause until three. At that point... "

And then, the anchorman went silent as suddenly the late night quiet of Tim Bradley's fields was broken by a muted humming, a low throbbing which immediately captured all attention. As those manning the trio of cameras around the area sprang into action, their ability to remain focused on their task was rewarded as a monstrously large, dark sphere dropped into position above them. Only seconds after its appearance, a sizable rectangle in the ship's underbelly slid open. Then, a small surge of pink and yellow lights flashed in the middle of the summer alfalfa, replaced after a heartbeat by the returned form of Harlin Edgars.

"Good Lord," shouted Kendall, his fingers attempting futilely to pull his sidearm from its holster, "it's true. It's the goddamned Martians!"

All eyes stared at the sphere, all cameras continued to collect footage. After only a few additional seconds, though, Richards had Bilstein shift the focus of their unit from the ship above to Edgars below, and that was when things took a decidedly interesting turn as far as the producer was concerned. He had expected to find George's friend hurrying through the alfalfa, desperate to be anywhere but where he was.

Such, however, was not the case.

As Richards looked on, he could see the portly Edgars waving, trying to induce one and all to come forward to his location. Thumbing the audio on his headset, the anchorman put himself in touch with Lora, asking;

"Edgars, you seeing what I'm seeing?" After only a moment's pause, she responded;

"Looks like he's waving us in."

"Indeed it does." Richards ruminated for a long moment, then told his assistant, "Tell Kendall I'm going to approach the ship. Tell him to maintain position. Say I want him to cover me. Just keep him there, and get on the horn and tell everyone else to maintain as well." His eyes glinting with a mischievous hope, the producer said;

"I've got the wireless. Wish me luck, baby."

"You be careful, you nutjob," responded Lora. "This could be dangerous." Drawing closer to the ominously humming spacecraft, Richards admitted;

"Of course it could. It this thing didn't reek of Emmy potential, trust me, I'd send you in a heartbeat."

Lora smiled, reasonably certain her boss was merely trying to bolster her courage. Straining to see through the darkness, she kept her eyes on Richards as he moved closer to Edgars' position. What, she wondered, could be keeping the abductee there? Why didn't he run? Why was he calling others forward?

Then, there was a flashing surge of pink and yellow lights, and with the disappearance of both the men beneath the floating sphere why Edgars had been waving folks on suddenly seemed much less of a mystery.

Richards blinked, then blinked again. As the producer and anchorman for *Challenge of the Unknown,* he had seen quite a lot of the strange and unusual in his time. Werewolves, vampires—everything from ravenous god-things to cockroach fairies. But, those had been different, so archaically, oddly different he had little trouble accepting them. After all, as he lectured all newcomers to his staff, once you've seen your first zombie doing its dead man's shuffle, everything else is pretty easy to digest.

But this, he told himself, now this was *really* different.

He was standing inside of a UFO. A spaceship, a starship! A vehicle capable of traveling outside the solar system, to other galaxies. Possibly other dimensions.

"My God in Heaven," he murmured unconsciously.

"Yeah, it's sure six way to nifty, ain't it?" Turning, Richards found the temporarily forgotten abductee at his side. Shaking his head slightly, the producer extended his hand, asking;

"Mr. Edgars?"

"Kinda, sorta. Come this way, Mr. Richards."

"You know me?"

"Oh, big fan, sir, we loves us your show out here. That's me talkin', by the way."

"Ahhh, who else would it be?"

And then, Edgars led the producer around a corner into a much larger area. As they entered, Richards' eyes moved from spot to spot in lightning bursts, taking in the seemingly never-ending arrays of lights, switches, relays and a thousand and one other unintelligible bits of electronics, until they hit one thing which arrested their attention completely. The thing which, speaking through Harlin Edgars, said;

"That, Mr. Richards, would be me." As the producer stared at the massive alien creature seated off to his left, Edgars' voice came to him, saying;

"We're a telepathic race. To get to jawin' with others, we need to work through translators. But, don't worry none, no harm is done to these subjects." Edgars winked at the producer, then said;

"He means me. And yeah, like he said, I'm fine as corn before weevil season. But, lemme let him get back to what he needs to be sayin'."

"Who," asked Richards, turning from Edgars to the alien, "exactly is it to whom I'm speaking?"

"Telepathics, they sorta have that hive mentality thing goin', so he told me to just go ahead and pick a name for him, so I've been callin' him 'Klatu.' You might as well, too."

The two Earthmen smiled one to the other, then Richards, pulling forth his wireless, turned toward the alien presence, but held the mike toward Edgars, asking;

"Well, sir, welcome to Earth. Might I ask what we can do for you?"

"We of the Pan-Galactic League of Suns've been watchin' you ever since you began explodin' nuclear weapons. Now, understand, we don't care if you just can't help but destroy yourselves—that is your business, after all—but, it is our policy to try and help our rural neighbors out when their situations get desperate like yours."

"With all due respect, Klatu," answered Richards, his chest puffing slightly as he found himself speaking with pride on behalf of all humanity, unconsciously over-playing the part much like the comedian who gets to play Hamlet. "I think we're going to come through this phase of our history unscathed. I'll admit things have looked tense in the past, but the human race has pretty much seen the error of its ways when it comes to atomic power, and—"

"Excuse me," interrupted Klatu, "Lord love a duck, but I'd hope you'all could handle a little problem like nuclear conflagration. Naw, I was referrin' to the civilization destroyer that comed into your lives right after you commenced to splitin' atoms and the such." When Richards merely stared blankly, Klatu moved a portion of itself which seemed to indicate patient frustration while Edgars said for it;

"Television." When the producer merely blinked, struggling desperately to comprehend the alien's meaning, the visitor continued, causing Edgars to explain;

"Ohhhh, mass communications always seems like a good idea to everyone at first. Every school child will be introduced to all the classics, blahblahblah, but it don't ever last. Before you know it, sure as prom night means pregnancies, commerce rears its relentless head, and things just cascade downhill after that."

"But, but, look at how, well say Edgar here. Thanks to the media, and its constant focus on the minutia of life, the folks here in the middle of nowhere know as much about what's going on as anyone. TV shrinks the world, shows peoples once strange to each other how little difference there is between them and others... it, I mean—"

"I knows you means well, Marv, but you can't see the big picture like'n we can, beings how we got alla galactic history to view. Now, believe it or not, there ain't one race o'beings ever what wiped themselves out 'cause they discovered this or that ultimate weapon. But, television, that's different.

"It challenges folks too much. Lets 'em see things what they don't wanta see, or want their kids seein', stuff that upsets what they were taught by their folks, or in church. I mean, a lotta worlds what coulda survived discoverin' mass drivers or flesh cannons just went to Hell in a handbasket after some crackpot bunch of worshipful fanatics got a load of some heathen ways what they couldn't tolerate."

And at that moment, Marvin Richards sat down on the deck beneath him, disillusioned—shattered. He had no arguments for the massive, twelve-limbed, hairless telepathic potato in the inter-galactic driver's seat off to his left. As much as he wanted to, needed to, disagree with 'Klatu,' he found he could not. In all honesty, an absolutely crippling characteristic for any producer, Richards had to admit he had pondered such things himself.

"Diversity of thought," said Klatu/Edgars, "it's a real good thing on paper. But it's gotta come slow like, know what I mean? You look at say, oh I don't know... homosexuality. Now there's a tornado in a blender. On the one hand, don't hurt nobody, and any world facin' overpopulation like you'all, hell, you'd think you'd be makin' it mandatory, or at least givin' out prizes. But, once the cat's outta the bag, then boom—every self-important little naybob has gotta throw their two cents in, and before you know it, there's people gettin' beheaded for havin' a good decoratin' sense."

Richards could say nothing. He thought of how other countries around the world had condemned America for its permissiveness, for its toleration. He had never personally fought for the rights of gays, or blacks, women, the handicapped or anyone else. But, it was so simple to take pride in being a part of something for which others had struggled and even died, that it kept one oblivious to the fear and terror motivating those opposed to such movements.

"And television," he told himself, "just shoves it in people's faces."

"Gettin' the idea," said Edgars, apparently needing no prompting from Klatu, "ain't ya?"

"But," said Richards aloud, staring at the alien creature so close by, "what can we do about it?"

"I was hopin' you'd ask."

THREE WEEKS LATER

"Wonderful show, Marv, top notch. Out of the park."

"It's all to your credit, Mr. Binghamton. We couldn't have done it without your leadership."

Marvin Richards stood in the winner's circle of executives, basking in the ratings smashing glow of the most recent episode of *Challenge*. Their coverage of the events in Biglet had dominated their time slot, knocking even the HBO premier of *Bikinied Super Models and the World's Cutest Puppies on Ice* into the dustbin. The show's cast and crew knew the brass were truly happy, for the party catered in their honor had not only limitless champagne and shrimp the size of doughnuts, but they had allowed salt and butter to be placed on the tables as if they belonged there, and even condoned public displays of nicotine.

Doing her job, Lora managed to get Richards out of the room and safely away from the biggest of the brass before his love affair with well-aged Scotch placed the wrong clever remark within his grasp. Settling him in the swivel chair within his office, the leather-covered, perfectly stuffed one he so adored mainly because it was more expensive than the one in Carl Binghamton's office, Lora Dean looked her boss over, making certain he could be left alone for a moment without causing himself some manner of grievous harm, then asked;

"You going to be all right, chief?"

And within his mind, the producer actually gave the question the pondering it deserved. It had been a hell of a deal he had cooked up with Klatu. He and Edgars would be returned, Edgars' memories of what had transpired between them erased along with Richards' audio recordings. Electrical output from the alien craft would scramble most of the film footage taken out in the alfalfa, but not every spec of it. That the producer would be allowed to show the world—and that was not all.

For some time to come Richards would be fed advance information which would allow *Challenge* camera crews to be on the spot for more chances to film UFOs of all manner. As Klatu had told him, through Edgars, of course;

"The thing you gotta remember about television is, it of itself is not evil. It's like guns or intellectual curiosity, it all depends on whose hands are controllin' it."

And so, Marvin Richards, working hand in hand with the Pan-Galactic League of Suns, would reveal the presence of a larger universe to his audience, and the rest of humanity, every few weeks—making ratings history, certainly, but also getting across the idea that perhaps there was more to existence than many had previously imagined. Whether people's consciencenesses were expanded by the idea that they were not alone in the universe, or it made them overlook old hatreds because of the possibility of an even bigger outsider to fear than they had ever known before, such interventions had worked on a thousand worlds. And it would work on the Earth, as well.

Given time.

It would be, Richards knew, a risky game. And a solitary one, for he and he alone would know what he was doing. And, the producer thought, as he stared at his executive assistant, wondering what it would be like to be admired by a woman like her, that was the way it had to be. The League picked one person when they intervened in a world's personal affairs and that was it. If word got out, if things went wrong, if speculation became fact, the deal was off.

"Folks like to think they make their own decisions, 'specially in a backwater like this. You just up and tell 'em somethin', they're just gonna resist. You find a way to prove somethin' to 'em they wanta resist, they'll nail ya to a tree." To which Edgars himself added;

"Hell, you *know* that last part's true."

Staring at his lovely assistant, understanding that as long as he had to continue to play the role of self-absorbed showmeister he would never be able to win her affections, Richards thought for the briefest of moments on whether or not it was all worth it. Balancing the possible fate of humanity against his own happiness, he sighed, then did the thing which, a month earlier, he would never have believed himself capable.

"Am I going to be all right," he said back to his lovely Lora, "Oh, probably. But I doubt I'll enjoy it."

Smiling at what she thought was one of Richards' typical comments, she blew him a kiss of congratulations he wished could be so much more. Then, as she closed the door he pulled a bottle of Glen Fiddich from his bottom desk drawer and began pouring himself a tall one, reflecting all the while on just how blissful ignorance must be.

We are what we eat. Frank had spent the better part of his life in the service of the colony, building dome enclosures on the hard, desiccated lands of Mars. For his dedication and service he's finally living his dream. Now lying in the grass of the new bio-dome, Frank enjoys the fruits of his labor and dreams of the future.

A PATCH OF GRASS

**"The days of man are but as grass;
"For he flourisheth as a flower of the field."
Prayer Book 1662**

IT'S SO BEAUTIFUL, HE THOUGHT, SHOULDERS RELAXING, STOMACH TIGHTENING, eyes wide with excitement. *Soooooooooo beautiful.*

Frank was enthralled, lost in the sight of the vast sky above him. It was not a particularly fantastic evening there in the dome. Anyone who regularly took a peek at the night sky now and then would find nothing fascinating in the bubble's view of the galaxy's self-arrangement that night.

It was worth it.

But Frank was not one of those who got to look up very often. That was not the deal he had made in life. Frank had spent far too long living in gloom, toiling in the underground, working for the good of the colony, existing—hoping, longing, dreaming...

Oh, yeah...

Frank dug his tired shoulders into the ground—into the grass beneath them. It felt luxurious, the way he imagined silk to feel. Or the cheek of God.

Relaxing—it felt so marvelous. And, he could do such a thing there with ease. The soil within the dome was soft, moist—squishy, even. This was most unlike the rest of the planet's surface which was brittle, fried—desiccated. The crusts ensnared within the domes, they were being brought to life, though. Slowly. Painfully slowly. One patch at a time.

It was soooooooooo worth it.

Domes erected. Debris concentrated—soiled bits of this and that—whatever was not reclaimed for the bio pits—went into the domes. And, of course, that was precious little, for everything was reclaimed in the colony. Not a slip of paper, not a loose strand from a piece of clothing. Fingernail clippings, peeling skin, even spit was collected. Indeed, even deceased human bodies were returned to the soup, broken down as nutrients for plants and animals. Bone meal mixed with feed, organs fed to pigs, flesh dried and shredded, broken down into reclaimable chemicals, everything used.

Everything.

There were, as they said, no graveyards on Mars.

The old phrase made Frank think...

Weren't there, though, actually? Of a sorts?

And then, as the thought rolled round in the old man's mind, he bit into the first of the apple sections, and his eyes filled with tears. Flavor rushed through his memory, looking for points of reference. Fifty-nine years of meals. Three meals a day. Fifty-nine years gives a man close to a half million meals to remember.

Oh, God, he thought, *Oh my God in heaven*.

He chewed at the slice of fruit, his mouth filling with saliva at the rich, thrilling taste of the apple. His tongue played with the wedge's flap of skin, worried at it as it caught in between two of his teeth. Nothing like that ever happened at a normal meal time.

Never—

No—all the previous meals of his life had simply been a part of existence, like breathing. You picked the flavor of paste you wanted that evening or morning, or whatever time it was, and you sat with your mates and you ate. The paste slid down, tasting like what it was supposed to taste like—chemically guaranteed. The pucks were there as well, in their assorted flavors, round and thick and hard—created purposely tough to encourage gnawing and chewing, made so to keep human teeth from falling into disrepair from lack of challenge.

Never again, not after this...

Frank bit into a cherry, and his tears rolled anew. As the first drops of juice exploded within his mouth, he froze around the sensation—small, thick, perfect dark flesh with a texture woven with joy, colored by life—he had to pause, had to savor the fantastic moment. Cherry, washing over his gums, tongue, taste buds, juice reaching the back of his throat;

"Ahhhhhhhhhhhhhhhhh hhhhh hhhhhh hh—"

It was worth it.

The cherry was chewed slowly, the flesh of it pulled away in the tiniest slivers. Each chewed respectfully, its flavor savored, marveled at, worshipped. Sprawled there in the grass, Frank knew he had made the right decision. He had worked long and hard, and he had earned his reward.

"Pear," he said quietly, holding the green/golden skinned lump of fruit in his hand. "That's what you're called."

Many different types of produce were grown on Mars; mankind had been there some seventy years, after all. But every potato, every lettuce leaf and section of orange, every bit of every crop went to the kitchens, to be chopped and blended and pureed. The colony had many mouths to feed. Food had to be produced the most efficient ways possible. What Frank was doing could hardly be called efficient.

So what do you taste like?

Frank bit into the pear and his eyes shown with wonder. It was everything he could have hoped for, and nothing like what he had imagined. Born on Mars, whole life spent toiling there, digging, building, pushing mankind's interests outward into the universe, he had never imagined that eating, that food, could taste so rich, so overwhelming.

The extravagance of Frank's luncheon staggered the back of his brain. When he had finished his first cherry, he had simply dropped the pit on the ground. He had cleaned it as thoroughly as human teeth and tongue and saliva could manage, and to the naked eye it had certainly looked stripped free of meat. The kitchens would have done a better job, certainly, and used the seed as well. The second cherry had been devoured with less reverence, had been spat away recklessly as greed sought a third and fourth, both popped into Frank's mouth at the same time. He had watched the two seeds arc away from him even as he reached for more.

But, of course, such was the purpose of Frank's meal. He had petitioned to be a planter, one of those who got to feast to their heart's content on whatever they desired. He had the years, had the seniority, had the clean record of a man who had done his job and served faithfully. And thus, when the new dome had been opened for planting, he had gone momentarily light-headed with giddiness, for his name had been on the highly-prized planter's rolls.

Not in the first ranks, those who would spread the grasses and flowers, but there nonetheless. He would be one of those who spread the secondary seeds. A mere five year wait. So great was Frank's anticipation that the time practically flew by. And, now that his time had come, it was just as splendid as he had imagined.

Oh, yeah...

Frank took another big, slopping bite from his pear, staring at one of the earlier team's rose bushes as he did so. It was in bloom, delicate fists of yellow all up and down its boldly thrusting branches. Pushing his bare back into the grass once more, Frank felt the first team had done a splendid job. Tossing the remainder of his pear in an arc which dropped it in an open hollow, Frank smiled. Those who came after him would respect his efforts as well.

He would have to work fast, however. The injection the doctor had given him was beginning to take a solid hold upon his nervous system. He could feel himself becoming warmer—sleepy. They had told him it would happen. Quickly, he ran through another entire handful of cherries, popping them into his mouth, sucking free their meat and spitting the seeds as far from himself as they could. Frank laughed as one sputtered from his mouth awkwardly and rolled down his bare chest.

Many petitioned to be planters, but few could be given the honor. Most bodies simply had to be reclaimed. But Frank, naked under the stars, when the drugs drifted him off into death he would stay where he lie, and he would rot slowly—naturally—and his rich juice would feed the soil and his blood would blossom in the cherry trees to follow. Future generations would not know his name, but they would honor his sacrifice.

Soooooooooo worth it.

No, Frank told himself, There were no graveyards on Mars. But there were wonderful, wonderful orchards.

Bill and Gene where like many friends; they hung out, talked about comics, cruised about watching the world (freewayin'), and working together on the cars' armaments. In these days, when the world traveled mostly by air between cities, the long neglected highways where now fire-fire zones, where armed and armored cars fought for no better reason than they could get away with it; and sometimes it even became a place to get even with a rival.

DAWSON DID IT

BILL **D**AWSON WAS THE BEST FRIEND I EVER HAD. I GUESS I SHOULD GET something straight right here—I'm not the next Shakespeare, or Hemingway, or Tupen Dere and I know it. The only reason I decided to tell this story is because I owe Bill, and this is the only way I could figure to pay him back.

Bill and I met in the Company School—Second Level MOS—management off-spring. I looked over to his seat and saw him—rough, sandy hair, those thin arms, and that stupid good luck charm—completely ignoring the day's lesson, the vid-com, *everything*, to read a copy of *Batman*.

I had never seen a real comic book until that moment. Bill's Dad had gotten it along with a few thousand others from Bill's grandfather who'd been a boy when they'd stopped producing comics back around the turn of the century. When the com-light was aimed toward Glory Daver I reached over and tapped his attention. When he turned around I gave him a look that said I would give the Earth, moon, and my left arm to see one of his comics. When the com's next blind spot came around, he passed one over. I still remember it—*The Amazing Spider-Man* #20... first appearance of the Scorpion. It was great. Just like our friendship.

Even at that age, you could tell how we were going to turn out. Bill was seven, one year younger than me but already at my level. He was small compared to level one kids, and a runt in level two. Everyone called him Dawson the Dwarf, but he never seemed to care. He could probably have skipped a few more levels and been Out/There four or five years early, but he always leveled with me.

I guess you could say I got Bill into my crowd and made sure he stayed there. He introduced me to Stan Lee and Robert E. Howard, de Maupassant and Kipling. I zeroed his sights on to Muslimgauze, Windshield, the Fergum Beta Quartet and Green Ivory. Daws read and I listened to tunes and we just shared. He would come to my games and I'd play harder just to hear him whoop. He would read me a story he wrote and I'd play him a run I'd jotted in my tuner. He'd buy me a burger and I'd take him Freewayin'. And that, I guess, is how the whole thing got started.

We weren't steel curtained at the time or anything—we'd just cruise, looking for wrecks, fights to watch... the usual. No one challenged us—we were clearly in/transit... *Voyeurs*. We could wait for our day.

Bill's Dad told us stories about the old days when the freeways had still been open and safe, back before anyone had armor. Once the decay forced most long-distance traffic into the clouds, the highways between cities were patrolled with less rigor. That meant motorists were left to solve their differences by themselves, when they weren't being preyed on by rovers. Fenderbender slug-ups would go on for thirty miles.

Pretty soon, those who had to drive the interstates were taking along a weapon or two—or three. After that came the year when both Ford and BMW decided that Smith & Wesson didn't deserve all the bucks, and we all started getting the most exotic factory extras in decades.

And suddenly, the world had a brand new sport.

The only good thing to come out of the year 2052 was the merger of Chevrolet and Volkswagen, and their opening product, the CVW Firefox. It came with standard .45 guns front and aft, German armor and glass, the most beautiful 738 cubes Chevy had *ever* produced, 'phalt dusters, double rear sausage and steering grips with touch control.

I'd worked three summers to save up for mine. It'd been Dead Bubble Fergeson's. With his kids moved out, he and his wife only needed a neighborhood scattler, so he moved to dump the DoubleF, unloading it directly into my outstretched arms.

Bill was with me the day we made transfer... it was a Saturday. I remember. I had dumped every credit I had into my Dad's account and he had gifted me his card to use for the day. I handed it to Fergeson who thumbed out his threeG and handed it back.

I was shaking. Three klids for a CVW only four years old. Four *clean* years. Fergeson had bought it for inner-city protection. It was perfect— eat-off-the-carb clean. It was a jewel and it was mine. In the door pocket, the standard factory issue .357 still sat with its original ammunition. Fergeson had taken good care of his car, and good care not to get himself compromised in a situation where he would have to use what he had.

"Well," he said, his mouth pulling into a crooked smile, "I've driven with you; you know your way around a DoubleF, your Dad says 'al'reet' and I did wheel your wad so... I guess these are yours."

He held out the keys. I went to take them, but before I could make contact he dropped them on the floor... on purpose. I didn't want to start anything, so I bent to pick them up... and he stepped on them. By then I was getting annoyed.

"Are you gettin' mad?" he asked. "Good and boiled? Feelin' the wet fear cakin' on your back?"

I looked at him, wondering what kind of dust such an old guy might be toggling that early on a Saturday morning when his arms shot out like pistons. He caught me out flat and stupid. I bounced off the back wall of his garage. While I pulled myself together, he sneered,

"Punksnot little wank—fargo for you, drag ass. You ain't got the max to push ten for morning, let alone lunch."

I wanted to kill him. If his hands came up again I was ready to launch on the old bastard. They didn't. Instead, he knelt down and picked up the keys, saying,

"Yeah, right, 'Dead Bubble' knows the talk. I had an Agitator before 'freewaying' was a word. I know the roads and how to tame 'em. Over on that wall—see the clip from *Burning Chrome*? That's a picture of me on top." Bill was staring at it, shaking his head.

"He's right," my life-long pal was whispering with a kind of awe stuck in his voice. "Look—look at the stars on the side—blues and oranges. And a yellow—And it has to measure 300 millimeters."

Bill was right. They were stupefying scalps to display. Fergeson agreed.

"Yeah," he told us. "I was kingshit supreme. And nobody could make a touch on me, either—not 'til my cement skull got me in up past my nostrils. I got nudged off the road at 180 and they took me outta the bric-a-brac with a torch."

Fergeson pulled his shirt up. I'm sure the reactions we made to the ugly, sick dead colors scarred across his stomach were just what he was looking for. Bill grabbed at his good luck charm and I gritted my teeth to force them to stay closed.

"Ain't pretty," said Fergeson as he rolled his shirt back down. "I know. But I did all this to make a point. Now, you listen to me, any fatnose can push you around like I just did. Anyone. But, if you let 'em make you mad— you lose. Remember that. You got mad here, but you didn't let me dander you. Good. When you get challenged, that means you got someone who's lookin' for trouble. And that's always good." Fergeson pulled a trio of malts from a small fridge there in the garage. Throwing each of us one, he explained,

"Anyone lookin' for trouble is point down already and easy to take out. You can arf-arf any monkey-gland who tries to get you—just don't go lookin' for trouble. Cruise when you want, paddle up and down alla 87 if you want—just don't nudge any nests. Let them come to you. Believe me. They will. But if you get in the habit of diggin' people's graves for 'em, you're gonna put the wrong person in one some day." He stared me sharp in the eye and asked,

"Understand?" When I told him I did, he smiled and said, "That's good, Gene. Real good."

I should have listened to him.

Bill and I spent the next two weeks working on the DoubleF. Nobody in R.M. Nixon Memorial had anything like her even *before* we started and we knew none of them had even dreamed of the animal we had up our sleeves. Bill wasn't key for the kind of work we were doing, but he grunted out his share. We would pop a bender each in the morning and head for Dad's garage where she waited for us.

On the last day of the overhaul, we entered to find a set of twin trunks—both armed with heatseekers—still in their crates... a present from Freida Cummings. Her old man was loaded, Freida was loaded, all the Goddamned Cummings were loaded. No complaint intended, though. Sometimes a rich girlfriend is a pleasant thing to have.

We stripped down the dings and dents, reinforced, sealed sanded and painted. Fergeson's oil had been fair clean—we changed it anyway. We dropped the plugs (which were foul) and the points (which were fair). We replaced three hoses, two side strips, and then we attacked the trunk. The trunkers went in with two bits of trouble—not at all bad. We knew they would work if we targeted a lock and that was all we cared.

When we finally got down to the finishing touches, nineteen days had gone by. I remember the sun was overhead. I was laying in the shade of Dad's tree watching Bill. Shirt sleeves rolled, he sat on the hood working down from the windshield, handpainting the bathead which the dark knight detective had sported on his car in all those old comics. On my hood. On the hood of my DoubleF. My CVW Firefox. Mine.

I was sipping from a can of soda. I'd of preferred a malt, of course, but Dad said there was such a thing as neighborhood image. Strange man, Dad, but I wasn't complaining. He let me have my DoubleF. He had to be great.

"Hey, Gene," Bill called. "The second coat of fireproof will be dry tonight. There's a great double at the El Rancho Pull'em'up. *Frame Up 99* and the remake of that old Cerisini flicker *Night Ice*. What'ya say?"

I hated to say what I had to, but everybody juggles. So I tossed the first ball into the air, hoping I could catch it.

"Well, to be level with ya, Mr. Cranston," I guess I should've said that everyone else called him 'dwarf.' I never did, not even behind his back. Straight line. "I promised Freida that after I was done haulin' her over that I'd spend the night with her. I mean, she popped for the trunkers, and I haven't seen her for nineteen nights. And, if we must review the awful facts... " I cupped a whisper,

"She did give me the last 350 I needed. If Dad ever tumbled to that bit of news he'd stomp my teeth into dandruff."

"Yeah," answered Bill, patting the left trunker release catch, "I guess you owe her one." He smiled wide and then threw his rag at me. Charging, he dabbed at my head with his paint brush, shouting, "But they'd best beware us on the main run tomorrow night, eh, Mr. Wayne?"

Truly, Mr. Grayson."

We were both laughing and throwing grass at each other. We tossed each other around, and we laughed when I fell on my soda can, and when I painted a moustache on him, and when I tripped over my own two feet. And we laughed and I knew neither of us believed it and I knew he was crying on the inside and he knew I felt like shit and neither of us said a word about it to the other. Good friends are like that.

I picked Freida up after dark. She had been waiting a long time, according to the way she told time, for the first ride in the DoubleF. I hate to drive up to her house. I mean, neither of our families had to live in city apartments—just like Bill's, our folks all had the credits to have a real home outside if they were up to the risk. The difference was, while Mr. Dawson and Dad were both reasonable important out at Cal Daw, Mr. Cummings owned it.

Freida's brother was not around. Always an improvement. Freida was a girl with everything—curling, blondish hair, the perfect size and shape, deep blue eyes, and the disposition of a wet cat that didn't know who had emptied the bucket on her. She knew she was beautiful and thought everything in the world was hers to do with as she pleased. Trouble was, since the red-hot musician who was the quarterback for the home team was the most prestigious steady to have, she had him. I never had any say in the matter. Sure, I did the brag to Bill and the rest of the guys that I would dump her when I was done with her. I've told bigger lies in my time, too. Just never stupider ones.

I should have known where she'd want to go.

"Where else?" she told me. "The Pull'em'up."

"Ahh, what do you want to go there for?"

"Because," she told me flatly, "this is the biggest night of the week. Because everyone we know will be there and I want them to see me in this."

As she ran her hand over the blazing red of the DoubleF's door, I had to at least give her points for honesty. After we were inside, she continued to run her hands over the car, the door, the dash, my leg, as if we were all one object. Maybe to here we were.

I knew it would happen. Bill spotted the DoubleF and zeroed us. Of course, it's not like I wasn't glad to see him. We gabbed for awhile—him in the back seat, me turned halfway around in the front. After the shorts and previews and tunies and such, Bill cut back to Larber's car. Larber was an okay guy a couple points under our level, but his go-bucket was strictly a stock, in-city four-wheel asshauler. He was always good for a ride, though, so Bill had gotten him to drag out his Tonka, and here they were. Bill and I said a few, "Goodbye, Mr. Richards," "Goodbye, Mr. Grims," and left it at that. Freida, unfortunately, was not happy to leave it at that.

"Why do you let that creep hang around you all the time?"

"What're you talking about?"

"The Dwarf. Why do you have to hang every corner with him? Everyone talks. He's so fanned. And that idiot comic book drool you both flag. It's so roachy. Honestly."

"Look, we're friends. We've always been friends, and we're always *going* to be friends. Why can't you accept that? You like this car, right? You like toopin' around in it, right? Well, if it hadn't been for Bill—the only other guy who knows bee's balls about *real* cars in this comm-cen—I'd still be under her tightening gun braces by myself. So, why don't you just lay-front on this shit—Fan me?"

She didn't. Fan me? She hadn't the faintest inkling of a breeze. All she could think to say was,

"My brother knows cars. He could've helped you."

"Your monkey-gland of a brother couldn't change his mind let alone lay out the centrifugal on a compressor map. Besides, if you can't tumble to why I wouldn't want him touching this car, then you don't know shit about me."

I was reaching for the doorhandle when she touched me. Her hand was back on my leg, circling and grabbing and teasing. She was good at it. I stopped moving which, well—of course—had been her intention. She moved closer, her elbow on the seat, her lips against my shirt. I knew what was coming.

She wanted me to tell her that I wouldn't broil with Bill anymore. I could feel it in the way she moved, her hands and face and chest all rubbing against me. She knew what she wanted and she was going after it in the same creamy, knee-shaking mechanical way she went after everything. Maybe I was really that good a friend, or maybe I was tired of the game for once. I'm not sure. But, before she could continue, or get me to join in, I snapped open the door.

Her head jerked up, knocking against the steering column—hard—which I must admit made me smile. I told her I wasn't in the mood and that I was going for something to eat. The door locked behind me just as she started screaming. Walking away, I found myself sinking into confusion. I wanted her. I wanted to hit something. She wanted me to dump Bill and I didn't want to. I wanted them both in my life and couldn't understand why I couldn't have what I wanted.

I kicked at a can by the concession palace, but it wasn't enough. I smashed open the door, but that didn't make me feel much better. I only felt angrier because it hadn't bled or screamed—just opened. I walked inside angry and bitter and looking for trouble. I found Wyck Cummings. Close enough.

He was at the drink/vend, deciding between RumCoke and Rolling Rock. I yelled a hello out to Larber loud enough so Wyck would know I was in the palace. I edged in through the others at the counter to place an order. There was no fear in turning your back on Wyck. He was a shrimp, a puny, a featherdog. I knew there was nothing to worry about from him. I was stupid.

Before I could tumble to why everyone to both sides was suddenly making room for me, my face shot upward while my knees buckled and my eyes closed. I fell to the floor, my fingers finding blood on the back of my head after I hit. My nose caught petro-steam fumes. My eyes saw a piece of rail pipe and a greasy glove, both attached to the hand of Filbert Kerchecker. Not good.

I had just been sapped by the brick-hardest lapcruncher in the city comm. The look on Wyck's face told me whose credits had paid for the attack. The look on Kerchecker's mug let me know he hadn't earned all his credits yet.

I tried to stand and was put down again—quick and hard. Everyone else had cleared the area, leaving Kerchecker and me to give them a show from a safe distance. I watched him as he came forward again. There was no emotion in his eyes—no anger, no hate, no enjoyment—maybe boredom. Well, I thought, everyone has to make a living.

I was bleeding, bruised and battered worse than any football game had ever left me. I couldn't stand, my eyes wouldn't focus, and I'd already thrown up and been rolled through my own dinner twice. It wasn't enough. I could tell Kerchecker had finished the warm up and was about to move on to the main show. I was thinking how perfect it was: Kerchecker would leave me on the floor, Wyck would go home happy and never miss the credits he'd thumbed up for both my wrecking and for his freedom from having his sister being seen with a "commoner."

No one would turn Kerchecker in—people don't commit suicide for acquaintances. And, of course, I wouldn't say a word because I would be dead. I'd known Wyck hated me. I just hadn't known how much. I did then. Of course, then was too late.

I was prepared for the breaking to start when suddenly a noise across the room turned everyone's head. Another fight had started and, like any competent criminal, Kerchecker had turned along with everyone else to assess the situation. It would've been a great time for a comicbook escape, but I wasn't Captain America so I simply lay where I was, trying to see what had interrupted my execution. It was Bill.

He had tackled Wyck and had him on the floor, yelling orders in his ear while everyone else just stared, not sure what they should do.

"You heard me, Cummings," he screamed. "Call off your bone-eater or I'll rip out your shoulder. Think I can do it?"

Wyck bleated like a trapped pig. Bill had his hand dug into the slimeball's shoulder, his fingers tripping some nerve deep inside. Wyck was in enough pain to forget how he was incriminating himself. He screamed to Kerchecker like a monkey with an arrow through its eye. Kerchecker grunted, shrugged his shoulder, and ambled out the door. Bill had already gotten off Wyck's back and come to my side.

"Com'on, Gene," he said, dragging me up off the floor. "We gotta get you back to the DoubleF."

I staggered out with Bill half-carrying me to the car. Wyck came stumbling up just as we reached it, screaming for his sister. I really didn't care.

"I'll be waiting for you, McGill," he threatened. "I'll be waiting on 87—in the Burner Stretch. Let's see if you got the guts to show." Froth specking over the edges of his mouth, he bellowed,

"I told you to stay away from Freida. The Cummings don't breed with gutter-splash. I want you dead, McGill! I want your ass dead! You meet me, scud-sniffer. *You meet me!*"

He was still screaming when we pulled out. Bill was in the front seat next to me. Freida was on the other side. She was mad at me, but pretended to be concerned over my bruised lips and mismatched eyes. It made me sick. She got out at her house, asking me when I was going to call. Her brother marks me and she wants to know when we're going *dancing*.

"When I heal," I muttered. Bill laughed and I smiled, but not too broadly because it hurt. Once Bill realized I wasn't headed in the direction of home, he asked me where we were going.

"87," I told him. "Did you expect anything else?"

"No, not really," he admitted. "But use your head, Gene. We gotta stop first. You need a shower, something to eat. Greenpockets will have a whole crowd of clowngloat hanging off him. Let him get his belt tight. When his ego is on over-swell, *then* we'll show up. What kind of comics fan are you, anyway?" With a grin, he added,

"You know we have to let him outline his evil plot to the readers before we can make out dramatic entrance. Right?"

"Right," I agree.

"Okay. Your house, Mr. Kent?"

"My house, Mr. Olsen."

I drove off, figuring that Bill had probably just saved my life for the second time that night. How was I supposed to know he wasn't finished.

We headed for the Murket 7 entrance to the Freeway. I had showered, put on some fresh clothes, gulped a soda, a malt, two ham-on-ryes and a chemo-pear. Bill and I both popped a trip-dose of benders before we left. We hit the 'phalt with energy and nerve we never knew existed. Things would have been great if we'd had the brains to go with it.

It didn't dawn on me until we were just a few miles out from the Burner that we had no idea what we were looking for. Sure, Wyck usually drove his SpiderTeeth 295... but he was Wyck *Cummings*. He could have gone out and bought a fleet trasher from the city if he wanted. Suddenly we started taking things seriously. We knew Wyck was waiting for us somewhere in the Burner and we were closing on it fast. Bill fingered his good luck charm as we crossed the divide to go in and look for him.

Four kiloms in, we found him. We rolled past an overpass pylon and a burst of heavy shell pained our right-rear fender. I kicked it up to 80kph—looking for distance but not wanting to lose sight of Wyck. I didn't have to worry.

He pulled out from behind the pylon piloting a black-and-gray Mack Chromewolf. Once I saw that I keyed the DoubleF up to 120 and pressed her for more. He started with a mortar attack, twin shells bursting up over his back seat and splattering the road ahead of us. I needed space and time. Lots of both. Knowing he could only have six volleys tops, I punched it to out-distance the pavement shock, figuring to drop back as soon as he shot his stack.

Bill counted off the volleys. The second it was our turn I ran down the gears—five to one in nothing. Wyck came shooting up the road, his front guns shattering my tail section, but only for the moment. He couldn't judge my speed in the dark. Without my brake lights showing, he didn't realize I was slowing until it was too late. Swerving at the last second, he avoided a crash, but he had to put himself in my sights to do it.

"Thanks, Wyck," I sneered, tabbing up the weapons assembly, "here's one I owe you!"

I opened with my .45s, smashing away at his tail and back glass. Every time he slowed, I did, too. If he sped up, so did I. If he tried a dodge, ran for the side, spun a loop... *anything at all*... I hung on his tail and didn't let go.

I heard the first barrel clips empty and 'chunk' out. The auto-replace dropped in new ones and in four seconds lead was raining across Wyck's back again. At first, it didn't look as if he was very worried. Wyck just let his superior armor and lead-wired glass make up for his lack of skill. But, finally he began to realize he was in the sweatdog seat.

Gearing down, he took the road with a splash, belching back smoke to cover his escape. It was a 150+ blast and it left us behind. Bill and I caught him for a moment, but he shrugged our grip by spitting out with his rear flamers. Two searing bursts of gelatinous fire roared against the night, leaving burning patches up and down the 'phalt and across our hood. If he'd scored a topglass hit the self-generating napalm would have eaten through to us. But he'd missed, and now his rear defenses were shot.

Desperate, he must have geared down and jumped the brake in the same instance. He dime-stopped—fishtailing at the same time—forcing us to hit around to his side. He blazed up after us. We clawed forward for room trying to escape his piercemetal front gun. His hood devil was in full operation, sweeping back and forth on its 90 degree turret. I knew it could blast a decker into us every ten seconds so I kept swerving, hoping to dodge out of its radar's vector. Two hits in the same spot was the end of us. Period.

We ran the terror line for two, maybe even three more minutes. I'll admit to being scared, but I was hoping Wyck thought I was *really* scared— white-knuckled, socks down, teeth-powdered *scared*. I wanted him smug, thinking of nothing but finishing us off. Hoping he was up there, I dropped my load of dusters.

They dug into the 'phalt and held, going off a moment later. They went off in front of the Chromewolf, to her left, behind and under her. The massive Mack was thrown into the right embankment but it didn't stay there. Careening off the hillside only made her meaner-looking and harder to hit. I only had one choice left: the trunkers.

My first thought was that I couldn't use them—Freida had given them to me. It would be like her beating Wyck, not me. That notion fizzled when my eye hit the rear-view again and I wondered who I thought I was kidding. A Mack Chromewolf was eating up the road, getting ready to bite my ass off at the neck. Across from me, Bill had already opened the controls and thumbed in the relative distance. At least one of us was awake. All I had to do was lock the aim and fire. I did it fast.

A moment later the road behind us blew apart. The Chromewolf was against the bank to stay this time. Its right side and tail assembly were gone—powdered, burned and scattered across three lanes. We were in no shape to enjoy the view, however. A split before impact, Wyck's hood devil had blown our front sausage and spun us around, slamming us tail first into the rightside embankment.

The hood devil was still firing, shattering the calm rippling sound of the flames tearing up from the back of Wyck's cruiser. Every ten seconds an- other shell whizzed past or over us, tearing apart another half-dozen square yards of scenery.

I fumbled weakly, not quite knowing what I was doing. I had bounced off the dash, the seat, and then the dash again so hard I'd split my helmet. My forehead was torn open, bits of my visor stuck in it. Through the drizzle of blood flowing over my face, I could see Wyck crawling out of his smashed windshield, a grenade in his left hand. I knew he was up to something, but my dazed brain simply couldn't put the pieces together to tell me what. It was beginning to dawn on me what that something might be, but I was too dazed to react. Luckily, Bill wasn't.

His hand pressed against my chest as he reached across me. His fingers dipped into the driver's door pocket, coming out with the .357 I had forgotten. His head was going up through the sunroof when I heard the hood devil fire again. In another shot, Bill would be on the target line. I pawed at his leg, trying to drag him back inside, but all I did was distract him.

Wyck was inching closer. The devil blasted again. I knew the next shot had Bill's name on it. He was just taking aim when suddenly he ducked. The shot went over the roof. Zipping back up then, he clipped off three shots, plastering Wyck against the Chromewolf's hood with two of them. I started to cry in relief. Then, it happened.

Wyck's coat jammed the hood devil's track. Instead of sliding along, it blasted again on the same setting as it had the last time. Bill's body smashed back against the rear of the sunroof and then just hung there, broken almost in half. The magnum was gone. Blood dripped down out of his shattered frame, covering me.

I had hold of myself until I found Bill's good luck charm in my shirt pocket. When I realized he had put it there as he had gone for the magnum, something inside me snapped. My tears suddenly dry, I opened my door and stumbled down the road to where Wyck lie waiting. He had been hit in the upper chest and leg. He had lost a lot of blood, but somehow he was still alive.

Seeing that as a mistake that needed rectifying, I dragged him off his hood and smashed his face with my fist until his shirt ripped and he flopped out of my grasp. Too tired to bend down to crank him back up to my level, I merely kicked him—stomped him--groin, head, knees, throat... whatever target presented itself—wherever I could connect.

I fell several times, but I just dragged myself up again, continuing to pound on Wyck's body, to mash it, break it, mutilate it anyway I could. By the time I was jumping up and down on his chest, he'd been dead a half an hour. Other cars drove by. Some gave me the thumbs up, others stopped to applaud. I stopped beating the dead body beneath me when I passed out.

Later, when the sunrise woke me up, I was surprised to find I was unbroken. I sat on the shattered roadway staring at the still smoking Chromewolf. The Firefox remained trapped in the soft dirt of the right bank. Wyck's body was stretched out next to me. What I'd done to it turned my stomach, racking me with violent, dry spasms. When I finished, I dragged myself back to the DoubleF.

Pulling Bill's body aright, I fixed it behind the steering wheel. I had messed up big time, but he had pulled me out of it. It had been his victory—his win—and that was the way I was going to tell it. He deserved it.

He was also dead, and the Cummings would soon want their pound of flesh. So, shortly they would know the truth. How, since I was in no shape to drive after Wyck had paid to have me killed, Bill had piloted the Firefox, battled their son, and the two of them had killed each other. I know it was a rotten thing to do, but the choices I had were non-existent.

The Cummings would ruin Bill's family, drive them down and grind them up. Even Freida couldn't have protected me from that... even if she might still want to. No, sacrificing Bill's name and his family was the only way to save myself and mine. It made me feel like scum, but I knew Bill would have understood.

After all, like I said, he was the best friend I ever had.

The Kuzzi warrior was tall and fur-covered; he told the human Matson the tale of the Fa'Lun Empire, enchant and nomadic race that wanted to "fly" —for the skies where safe from the predators— and eventually they did. Matson didn't want to believe such a thing was possible, and then reality struck home, for he had reason to know that it was all too true.

THEY WERE THE WIND

A Tale of Byanntia

"So," asked the human, the outsider. The one who did not know. "What the hell *was* that thing?"

A Kuzzi warrior stood next to the human, thinking how to explain. Though the one called Joseph Matson was tall, over six of their feet, the Kuzzi stood more that two feet taller. His short coat of horizontally striped fur had thinned for the summer, the blue, black and grey markings of his skin showing through, a natural camouflage that blended well with the alien landscape during the hot months. The male's head was surrounded by a thick, glossy black mane, a single gray stripe cutting its forehead and muzzle to the chin.

"They were the wind," answered the warrior.

Matson wondered if the Kuzzi were speaking metaphorically, as its kind often did, or not. It certainly sounded like a poetic description, but the young man knew much of Kuzzi speech patterns, and Matson would have sworn his companion meant the statement to be taken literally.

"Bentelii," he asked, "speak plain now, or with layers?"

"Speak with plain layers," the warrior answered. "No other speak possible."

Matson grunted. He wanted an answer, a simple, uncomplicated set of words wrapped around an idea he could accept. His companion's answer, however, told him there was nothing simple or uncomplicated about his question, no matter how straight-forward it might have seemed to him. Setting his repeller on the ground, the young man made a motion with his head the Kuzzi understood as a request for the full explanation. Both males sat, one cross-legged, the other with arms wrapped around knees, and the one who was not an outsider spoke.

"Long before your people come this place," it said, sinewy arms in motion, "long before Kuzzi people even, there were the Fa'Lun. They exist, learn to hunt and harvest, to speak and write and build and dream. They name Byanntia, teach Kuzzi speak, know whole world as old race while Kuzzi only children."

"So, that thing could talk?" Matson asked his challenging question with wonder in his voice, and Bentelii nodded, equal wonder in the motion. Then, he continued.

The warrior told the human of the Fa'Lun's fascination with flight. The race might have been ancient, but they had always remained nomads, had never built permanent shelters. The humans would find no artifacts of a Fa'Lun empire. They had never been a race interested in great populating numbers. No, the Fa'Lun, the story went, decided early on that the best way to deal with predators was not to try and construct defenses, or to cover the land with great numbers of their kind. Instead, they had a different idea.

"They wanted to fly. Their thought was that the safest place was in the sky, and so they went there."

Joseph Matson shook his head in fascinated confusion. He questioned his friend as to what he meant. How did someone simply *choose* to fly?

Bentelii explained that the Fa'Lun were quite adept at breeding. It was they that had crossbred the early kison, an at-the-time stringy, tenacious beast, until they had perfected the slow-moving, fat and juicy breed the humans had discovered upon their arrival on Byanntia. To the Fa'Lun the answer to their quest had been simple.

"If they wanted to fly, they would simply make themselves fly."

The Fa'Lun, a people who had made almost a religion out of genetics—who had never over-extended their population in fear members would break off and form their own tribes, tribes that might turn on one another—turned their amazing talents on themselves. Quite simply, they began to breed themselves into a race which could take flight.

"It took them thousands of years," Bentelii said with a flourish, a sound like pride in its graveled voice. Matson wondered if the Kuzzi was telling the tale in a bragging sense—home town clan makes good—to let the human know that not only his race could make things happen when they set their minds to it. "But slowly, eventually, they succeeded."

Matson looked into the sky, his mind filled with questions. How was it no one had mentioned any of this to a human before? Why had a Fa'Lun never been seen before now? How did Bentelii know all he told? The Kuzzi continued its story.

"Bones got lighter, hollow. Skin stretched, flaps extended, ankle to wrist, hair thickened, hardened, grew into feathers, not like bird, different, their own. Feathers enough to take the Fa'Lun to the skies."

Bentelii's command of the human's language was quite good, but still the warrior stumbled as it tried to explain the transformation of Byanntia's first race. The Kuzzi, it seemed, had begun to reach for sentience just as the Fa'Lun began to reach for the clouds. The older ones refused to hinder the dangerous carnivores as they obviously began to come into their own as thinking beings. Instead they used the event as fuel, a prod to keep them working toward their goal.

Let the Kuzzi learn to hunt with tools, they decided with an inordinate generosity, let them learn to plant and built and spin and carve and create. By the time they are a force that can oppose us, we will be gone to where they can not reach.

"Are you saying the Fa'Lun named, ah, your people? 'Kuzzi' was a Fa'Lun word?"

"Yes. All words are Fa'Lun."

Bentelii explained that while the Fa'Lun had sought flight above all things, still they had remained a part of the world. Not wanting to exterminate a predator, they had instead helped the Kuzzi along, adopting them, gearing the younger race to take their place as caretakers of the planet. By the time the Fa'Lun had streamlined themselves to the point where tools and tribes were no longer of any use to them, they had left their language behind in the stewardship of the Kuzzi, as well as anything else the younger species desired to claim as their own.

"They had been flying for some time by then. By the point Kuzzi understood, really, what the Fa'Lun were, had been, were doing... I mean... "

"I understand," whispered Matson, his tone quieted by the awe tingling his senses. "Go on."

"By that time, the Fa'Lun disappeared. They used to fly and land, like the birds, fly to escape danger, fly to search for food, land to sleep, to make nests... but that stopped. By the time Kuzzi became a true race, the Fa'Lun went to the skies and did not return."

Matson was speechless. He could not comprehend it all. Oh, he could accept the story as a scientific thought, as an idea, a suggestion. A possibility. But as a reality, as a tangible notion with weight he could test against his own beliefs—no.

No, it was too large an idea, too foreign.

Too *alien.*

"It is hard for us to accept as well."

"But," Matson countered, "your people had time to accept this, they saw it. Talked to the Fa'Lun… ah, I, er… do you still… does anyone still talk to them?"

Bentelii shook his head.

"Not for stretch after stretch. Last person I know to talk with a Fa'Lun, many long stretch… in my grandfather's grandfather's grandfather's grandfather's time, healer Baww'ja, they say he friend with one Fa'Lun. The last Fa'Lun that would come down from the sky. They would talk and Baww'ja would tell him of Kuzzi."

The Fa'Lun of whom Bentelii spoke had no name, or at least never gave one to the healer. Over the years of their relationship, the Fa'Lun grew more and more distant. His eyes began to stay constantly trained on the sky. Finally, after Baww'ja died, the Fa'Lun were never seen again.

"Their minds different," the warrior explained. "Life on land forgotten, social rules forgotten, everything left behind, not just things, but ideas, concepts, maybe even thought itself."

Matson shifted uneasily. The more his friend tried to make the concept of the Fa'Lun clear, the more impossible understanding them seemed to become. An entire race that just up and changed themselves—herdsmen who got it into their heads one day to leave the ground behind, who abandoned thought itself for flight.

"They really stopped thinking?"

"The last Fa'Lun, Baww'ja's visitor, it was said he became harder and harder to communicate with, that toward the end of Baww'ja's days, it seemed the creature only came back to hear his voice. It is said the healer had a most pleasant voice."

Matson shuddered. The story he had been counting on to make him feel better, to diminish his guilt, had instead multiplied to become a weight he could barely stand. He turned his head, looking back at the mangled corpse splattered against the rock wall behind them. Not some monster from the skies, at all, but a thing of grace and wonder, a self-made angel which he had snuffed out through a panicked moment of careless fear.

His mind fell backwards, rushing his memory to the moment not so long ago where he had heard the noise in the sky. He had wheeled around, had seen the great, glorious wingspan spread across the heavens, and his first thoughts had been colored with awe. The young human had watched the soaring object as it spun and looped and floated its way in and out of the clouds. He had no idea what he was looking at, did not care. He had stumbled across yet one more of Byanntia's marvels and was simply happy to be witness to another miracle discovered.

And then, everything had changed. The flying form had taken note of Matson, had changed direction, diving straight for the young man. He had grown frightened. The thing was moving straight for him, flying directly at him at what seemed an incredible speed.

Matson had lifted his repeller, the creature had screeched defiantly, charging on, sweat had stung the trembling human's eye, and with a single action, it was over.

Suddenly the sky was blotched by an explosion of fluff and flesh and blood, and the ruined sack of what had been a living being slammed down out of the blue and destroyed itself against the solid rock of the mountainside upon which Matson still sat. His eyes glued to the shattered remains, the young man whispered;

"That might be the last of its kind, for all we know. And I killed it."

The air hung dark with grief between the two friends, regret curling itself around Matson's neck and biting away at his skull, burrowing into his brain. The human could not bring himself to look his friend in the eye. At least, not until the Kuzzi spat;

"Good."

Matson's eyes blinked hard in shock. He swallowed, his head jerking, first sideways then backwards. The motions were violent, but slight. The human asked;

"What do you mean?"

"Fa'Lun foolish, cowardly people. Run away from life instead of embracing it."

"But they taught themselves to fly."

"Taught themselves to hide. Afraid of everything, they go to the sky and never return. Tell me, Joseph, what good is flight without destination?"

"But I killed it."

"Dove at you out of sky, screamed and came for you. What were you supposed to do? What do you think it was coming for?"

"I, I don't know... but... "

The big Kuzzi smiled. Its mouth opened past the point of humor to where Matson knew the lion-like alien was laughing at him. Placing a paw on the human's shoulder, Bentelii said softly;

"You humans, you could never understand the Fa'Lun. And perhaps," the Kuzzi's yellow eyes went soft for a moment, "perhaps it is best that way."

The two friends gathered their things then, and prepared to make their way back down the mountain. They had climbed to the height they had merely as a diversion and had been rewarded with far more than they had ever expected. As they started their trek back to the pass where their decent would begin, Matson asked one last question.

"You said the Fa'Lun, that they were the wind. What did you mean by that?"

"They were the wind," Bentelii repeated, muscles rippling as he ambled down the steep incline. "They were there, but then they were gone."

Joseph Matson's eyes scanned the horizon, searching the sky endlessly as he and his friend worked their way down the mountain through the heavy heat of the late afternoon. He wondered about the Fa'Lun, as well as the Kuzzi's casual dismissal of them. He thought on what he had done, punishing himself diligently, and on how Bentelii had felt about it and had seen no damage in his actions.

Then, a breeze cooled his brow and he sighed in relief, grateful for the slight but comforting gust.

It is a time when one could directly link into the equivalent of the internet, by mind alone. Download data into your brain, or watch events in real time from the perspective of others. Frank and his friends contemplate the truth; humanity had finally reached its pinnacle, everything was now available for their use or consumption, but what do you do now?

THE WONDROUS, BOUNDLESS THOUGHT

IT WAS, ALL IN ALL, A VERY HOT DAY.

"Oh, I just love you, Frank."

Benny said the words with all the politeness society demanded. Then he followed up his required words with a question, curiosity jangling him in a part of his brain rarely called upon to do much of anything.

"Make a presentation," he asked. "Give follow—fold ideas. Relate to me, citizen."

The Weather Control Board was trying something radical. They were always doing things like that when there was a big shake-up in management. With their new corphead sworn in two weeks earlier, it was almost a certain the dink would want to show everyone that he was his own man, capable of setting policy, making decisions.

For the last three days of July, 2112, the temperature had gone steadily skyward. Instead of the several generations worth of tradition which placed as acceptable the range 66° to 78°, the new guy was calling for a radical return to ancient standards. The day before had been an uncomfortable 82°, and the current day was threatening to reach 84°.

Still, it was not so bad. Such trivial politics affected those rare, out-of-doors spaces only. Indeed, Benny and Albert had moved the sex for that day out to the balcony and found those hours with Marci and Frank and Janet, and those without, to be pleasant enough. The added effort from labored breathing, and the resulting sweat—actual sweat—now that had been different. Interesting.

To be honest, Benny felt so wonderfully relaxed afterward, so warmly, fondly, sucked-dry-and-left-limp, that he found his brain actually desiring to play with an idea. Focusing himself on Frank long enough to clear space for this new notion within his brain while its electronics shifted his current workload from one section of his mind to another, he continued his rigorous examination.

"What's this drama you've discovered, anyway?"

Frank was built much the opposite of Benny. He was a good, solid man, thick chest, hard calves. Benny was well-toned, but taller. Much lankier. Albert was the everyman model, somewhere in between them.

Marci and Janet were equally beautiful specimens. Marci, tall, Amazonian—red hair, darker skin, green eyes—hard nipples, large—always welcome in any group. Janet, blonde, petite, firm and glistening, thin—fabulous-tasting mouth, candy-flavored.

Frank closed his eyes; it always made transmission easier. He was still downloading several old television series into files in the back of his brain—how clever they had been in olden times, despite their limitations—as well as trying to finish listening to two operas and six songs by different groups he enjoyed. To have to share-link, connect along the mechanical route grown into his head, up the satellite feed, and then into the minds of several others, while doing so many other things always made Frank a bit nauseous. Thus, he would shut his eyes.

What Frank wanted the others to hear echoed along one channel of their minds while he transmitted his own commentary on it which they absorbed along another. Benny's absorption rate was quite higher, moved faster, for he was actually interested, focusing precious current time attention on his friend's discovery.

Janet and Marci and Albert were following along, of course, they simply found themselves saving bits and pieces of it for later. It simply did not do, one had to agree, to get caught up in some front lobe fascination with, well say, another's penis between one's teeth, or their nipples clamped, eyes being teased, windpipe being assaulted to allow maximum pleasure, and the so forth. Sex, boundless, endless, meaningless sex was supposed to be fun. Not an invitation to the emergency room.

Slowly, though, Frank's discovery began to capture the attention of the others. Within the first few minutes of download, Benny's thrusts against Marci's delightful posterior had begun to slow to a far gentler, almost robotic rhythm. Albert, so terribly interested in swallowing as much of Frank as he could, stored most of the flow for later, trying as he was to catch every bit of sperm as possible in the first gulp. He had been keeping careful record and taste comparisons of all his partner's loads, and he was not going to allow something as ordinary as a new idea to cause him to miscalculate entry 4,352.

Still, after several hours, especially after the heat reached an unbearable 85°, the group found themselves lounging inside like the rest of the sane people. Waiting for the kitchen robots to serve whichever meal came next, they found themselves getting back to Frank's big idea.

"So, could you just condense that all for me?"

Everyone smiled at Albert. Their minds whirling with multiple fascinations, all of them continually downloading from the various museum data banks, historical archives and commercial and entertainment sites, and all the rest, they all focused their remaining attention on Frank as he real-time explained his current fascination to them all, especially taste-testing AI.

"Well, I suppose one would have to start with comparison. We all live in a fabulous age—correct?"

Naturally, everyone agreed. It had taken terrible things, wars and famines and pestilences which had reduced the population to a whit of its former self, but at last the race had reached a point where it had bundles of technology and very few people to support. Of course, the Earth had seen its inhabitants reach this state more than once. But, this time no Dark Ages had ensued. No, this time mankind had shoved forward and stopped slaughtering itself just long enough to spawn a paradise pleasant enough to suit everyone.

"Ginkles, Frank—how could things be better?"

"Bigger penises," laughed Janet. Marci giggled, but nodded her head. Benny flashed them both a wicked smile of agreement. Frank waggled his head back and forth, moving his eyes and lips in a manner to indicate that he obviously felt the same, but that such was besides the point. He was, in effect, being agreeable, but wishing to continue. Making themselves serious enough to control their laughter, the others told him to proceed.

"We have everything we want, correct?"

Again there was a wave of jocularity, but in the end, a consensus was reached that the current age was one of marvels and unlimited access to everything that had ever been imagined in all the long history of mankind.

People lived as long as they desired. Everyone had work they could be proud of, some toiling as greatly as eight, nine hours every week. Foods from around the world were obtainable at a moments notice to all. Robots did all minor chores, and most major ones. One could eat endlessly and never gain weight, or not eat at all. One could visit the moon, picnic in high orbit, study the bottom of the oceans, climb the highest mountains, go surfing in the morning and sky diving at night—all without leaving their homes, all without leaving their favorite sex partners.

Anything could be downloaded directly into ones brain. The entirety of that wonderful organ had been mapped, charted and mastered, so that now it controlled the body the way its owner wished it to be controlled. It was, a perfect, utterly delicious world, one with all the learning, sleeping, sex, eating, or anything else one could want at their fingertips twenty-four hours out of every day.

"Well, that's what this idea is all about. Focus all—I stumbled across this in the oddest place. I was thumbing through the philosophy warrens... "

Marci and Albert went amazingly cold. Boredom settled across Janet's brow as well, although she was always too much a team-player to give offense to any. Benny was still game, and even the daunting tedium of trying to understand the rantings of those jolly headknockers of ancient times would not put him off that afternoon. Maintaining Benny's attention and having Janet's generosity, Frank dared to continue.

"Forget who said it, that's as inconsequential as yesterday's breakfast. But what he said was... this." Frank's face took on such an excited look, that even Albert began to wonder what lay in the unconscious files he had yet to review.

"It seems that this age, this level of wonders, of plenty and satisfaction—*all of it*—has been reached before by man. There was an Earth, previous to ours. Somewhere else in the galaxy. And on it, people could do whatever they wished, whenever, just like us. But there were some of them who... how to say it, what's the word... they were, were... bored! Yes, that's it—men and women who got *bored!*"

Frank's face glowed with excitement. Waving his hand in front of him as if it were an instrument of instruction, he caught his fellows attentions with it, and continued, saying;

"Yes, they simply reached a point where they had been amused and fed and fucked to where it simply didn't matter to them anymore, where nothing the entire world could provide could make them happy any longer."

Janet frowned. Her eyes narrowed to slits, she raised her own hand to capture the attention of the room. When Frank instantly acknowledged her right to speak, delighting in his position of, what could he call it—moderator? Teacher—oh, he liked that thought a great deal—when he did, she asked;

"I don't understand. Sense, please? How can one not be pleased when they are lacking for nothing? You have to be happy when there is nothing missing to make you unhappy. Don't you?"

"That's just it; that's just it," Frank repeated. "There is one thing you don't have when you have everything."

"Nothing?" ventured Benny.

"Yes!" Frank's eyes gleamed as if reflecting the light of a directly-viewed sun. Actually raising his voice, he startled the others as he nearly shouted, "Yes! When you have nothing, you then possess the challenge of getting everything!"

The paradox frightened all within the room for an instant, even Frank. Marci's fingers crawled within Albert's rectum, gently moving deeper and deeper, unconsciously searching for safety. Her eyes, however, stayed linked with Frank's, as did those of all the others. Glorying in his circle of attention, Frank told them;

"It seems that once this former Earth, previous Earth, whatever, reached its pinnacle, much as we have, that somehow some of its inhabitants grew dissatisfied. They wanted... "

"More?"

"No, less. Much less. They wanted a new world to conquer. They didn't want to simply relive history, they wanted to make some of their own."

"But what could they do?" Janet's eyes, still narrowed, she asked with a curiosity which could have emptied the world of felines, "start a war? Go off conquering? How could it be allowed? The safeguards, the preventors—"

"No, no, don't worry," Frank whispered, his calm sending assurance through the others. "They were not brutes, genetic throwbacks of some sort. They were like us, marvelously, exactly like us."

"Except that they were bored."

"Well, yes, there was that. And that's what made the difference. No, they took a ship to another world. One of the starspanners—"

"You mean like in the museum?"

"Yes, one of those," Frank puffed with pride. They were getting it. They were really getting it. The static level in his head was so slight, he knew that all of the others had turned away from their monitors, had mentally shut off their information gathering circuits in favor of listening to his amazing story.

"They took a starspanner and they hunted for another world. Another Earth. But one in its dawning days. Before civilization. Before people, really."

"You mean... " Marci hesitated. The idea was so big, it forced her to actually use her own mind. She felt a twinge as that section of her brain awoke. Her automatic systems falling over each other to get out of the way of actual conscious control, she stammered;

"They, they went looking... for a world with, with what? Dinosaurs running about or something?"

"Close. They came here at the time of the neanderthals. They were the missing link that everyone used to look for. It was found, and after much research, it was uncovered through backward engineering of DNA memories—these, these wondrous men and women, these pioneers, these marvelous explorers, they did it. They pushed out into the black; they found our Earth here; they determined it was close enough to their planet of origin that it would support them, and they simply came down and started living."

"They weren't alive...?" Benny was not, officially confused.

"They were alive, you nimrod," laughed Albert. "He means they were taking control of their lives, living or dying by their wits, the strength of their arms—right?"

"Exactly," confirmed Frank. "They came down and mated with the primitives and started a brand new world, our world, this world, on its way to all we have now."

The group remained quiet. Stunned. Even Frank, now that he had heard the idea out loud was cowered by the immensity of it. Slowly the five began to discuss the all-encompassing notion. Suggesting scenarios, wondering about possibilities, they turned the revolutionary bit of information into a powerful and quite moving discussion which replaced their next meal and sleep period. It was not, of course, powerful enough to stop bodily enjoyment. They rambled on about their ideas of it while mounting each other, in both twos and threes, while pulling a five-way chain, chewing upon each other, licking out openings and cracks, and all the other bits of fun that made modern life bearable.

Finally, however, one of them asked of Frank the question all of them had began to wonder.

"So, were you, I mean... "

The query was put forth cautiously. It was, like their entire discussion, a thing of such magnitude that it had to be shaped and caressed into life just so, as to be a thing perfect.

"Frank... really—were you thinking, ah, were you asking us, to... to be like those explorers? I mean... did you want to do the same thing? Start a new world? Our world?"

Frank blinked. He had been startled—knocked backward by the force of a handful of words. His brain, however, always ready to serve, focused on what had happened. He had disseminated a new idea, and others had listened. He had spoken, and left others inspired. He had learned, and passed on learning. Without machines. Without approval.

Him.

Glorious Frank.

"Yes," said another of the pack, wondering what it would be like to have to survive. To be mother, father and god of a new civilization, it was so sweeping, so titanic, so... "is that what you were thinking, Frank?"

Time passed, second by second, sweeping eon by sweeping eon, the totally overwhelming fantasticness of what he had said was now being thrown back to him in an even greater manner.

Was he, he asked himself, was he proposing that they go to the museum, take a starspanner, and go to the stars? Was he actually that bold, that daring, that bored with being done for, that energized by the thought, the wondrous, boundless thought of *doing for himself*, that he was indeed proposing such a thing?

Janet's hand wrapped around Frank's leg. The idea of such outlandishness, such scintillating bravery, it stirred something deep within her that she had never felt before. Suddenly, she found the back of her mind considering the idea of actually applying for breedership privileges. She found herself thinking of going out in the daylight, flaunting the sunlight, following another, a man, *her* man, anywhere he might follow.

Her body moving with the practiced, serpentine limberness for which she was famed, her full mouth found Frank's member and swallowed it whole, his testicles filling her cheeks. She wanted him inside her, needed him, desired contact with his flesh as she had no other man.

"Ahhhh, ahhhh... "

Frank was surprised at his inability to answer the question. It was almost, he thought, as if he were enjoying Janet's enthusiastic ministrations so deeply that he could not switch his other brain functions on. He wondered, could that be a part of it? Did the independence those who established the humanity he and all alive were heir to so electrify them that they felt actual... dare he think the lost word...

"Pleasure?"

"Huh?"

"What'd you relate, Frank?"

Wheezing, his mind exploding, a mighty load of semen building within him, one so pumped and pure and volatile he was afraid it might take Janet's head off cleanly at her shoulders, or drown her at the very least, Frank called upon all the restraint he could find within himself, croaking out;

"Well, no... not really."

Whether it had actually been in danger or not, Janet's life was spared as Frank's member went as limp as an arm fractured in fifteen places. As Janet's frenzy became less so, and the others found their automatic circuits beginning to reconnect, he told the gathering;

"I guess it hadn't occurred to me because it's been done so many times."

"'So many times,'" Albert repeated. "What do you mean?"

"Oh, that group that settled our Earth, they weren't the first ones to do such."

"Really?"

"Oh, yes. The data collected showed that this is at least the fifty-third Earth to be colonized by such restless types."

The idea struck them all gently. How amusing. So many planets turned into paradise—so many worlds made perfect and ideal and whole, by those who resented the idea of perfection.

Finding themselves falling behind in their private data collections, knowing they would soon be lacking in the daily charts, looking foolish to the others who shared their world of inactive dreamers, the group's brains took over and began reconnecting them to that which mattered.

Instantly the great database, the marvelous placator, began to feed them all they needed to stay focused on themselves to the exclusion of everything else. Her mind filling with facts which would never mean anything to her beyond their individual existence and the certainty that she had them correctly categorized within her mind, Janet slid herself over Frank's muscular body. Pushing him down gently as she limberly straddled and consumed his once again erect penis, she purred as he responded to her magnificently subtle movements. His head back in the pillows, staring up at her, Frank shoved aside the notations filling his mind long enough to ask;

"Geekers, if I had, you know, wanted to go start another Earth, I mean... would you have wanted to go. With me? I mean, with *me?*"

Janet wondered at his question. Moving up and down the length of him, enjoying the moment, as she had been trained to enjoy all moments, as had he, as had they all there in the bosom of their loving machines, she pictured herself for a moment on the surface of some other planet, some Earth-like world, dressed in animal skins, planting crops, fighting creatures for survival, giving birth indiscriminately, dying—

"Oh, I just love you, Frank," she said emptily.

To which he nodded, just as emptily, in return.

Rita was in charge of a Clean Room; within its white and blue walls was the only seeming refuge from the sensory overload of the world. "Why", Rita wondered, did it take so long before the rest of humanity realized the importance of such a place?

A BRIGHT AND SHINING WORLD

"Beauty is in the eye of the beholder."
Proverb

"BEAUTIFUL JOB, AS ALWAYS, RITA. WONDERFUL. SIMPLY WONDERFUL."

Rita Kunsler loved her work. She had what society considered an important occupation. It many ways, it was true that her labors might be considered those of a menial position. But, it was also true that society could not function without its menials, and Rita gloried in the idea that she was good at what she did, and that others recognized such as fact.

"Thank you, Mr. Renson. It's always nice to know one's work is appreciated."

Rita was in charge of the Clean Room at Gilkenson, Trent and Bledsou. GT&B was one of the world's leading corporations. One of the largest and thus always at the forefront of what was considered proper, humane and politically correct. They had established a Clean Room long before most other corporations, long before it was culturally mandatory, long before it was even acceptable. GT&B was, after all, extremely forward-thinking when it came to such matters.

"I see maintenance has already taken care of the wall," Renson noted off-handedly.

His inspection was, of course, unnecessary. It was well known through-out GT&B that Rita was an exacting task master when it came to making certain her room was always ready—always perfect.

"Oh, yes sir. I got on them right away, I did. Can't have the next user being disturbed because of someone else's mishap, now can we?"

Indeed, Renson had made a habit of checking the GT&B Clean Room after almost every use simply because he knew that, within the swirling vortex of corporate madness which was the reality of Gilkenson, Trent and Bledsou, he could count on Rita's swift ministrations to have her tiny segment of their corporation spic and span and ready for the next poor soul who needed its comfort and shelter.

It was always a pleasure for the Vice-President in Charge of Acquisitions to enter the white and blue chamber, to inspect the paintings on the walls, to sit in one of the wonderfully comfortable chairs. To smell whatever flowers Rita had chosen for that day. To listen to the comforting music. To simply recline and relax, staring off peacefully in the quiet which was Rita Kunsler's Clean Room.

"I know it must seem as if I repeat myself, but you do a magnificent job, Rita," mused Renson, looking over the calm order and simple harmony of the Clean Room. "You always do. Quite honestly I don't know what we'd do without you."

Rita took the compliment in grateful silence, standing quietly, waiting for the vice-president to finish his meditation. Renson stared at the white drawer in the blue wall stand for a long moment, admiring it, sighing to himself.

It *had* been a long week. Long month, long year, long...

"No," he thought. "No. Don't go down that road. Self-pity is the flavor that helps no meal."

Turning away from the blue wall stand, Renson made one last complimentary remark, then headed back for the seventeenth floor and the mounds of neatly stacked frustration waiting there for him. He could not tarry, could not contemplate the luxurious simplicity of the Clean Room when there were people counting on him. His wife. His children. The multitudinous investors and shareholders of GT&B. He had his duties, and there was no escaping them. Not then.

Not yet.

Smiling ruefully, Renson thought about taking one last look at Rita's small island of sanity, but decided against it. If he were to gaze upon it again that day, he knew, he would walk straight back in and sit down, and mostly likely never leave unless he was carried out.

Rita smiled as she watched the tired looking vice-president finally depart. Poor Mr. Renson, she thought. Always so overworked. Always appearing one step away from the end.

Still, she reminded herself, didn't so many share that look anymore? The nation lingering in depression, so many other countries struggling to survive. Civil wars, terrorism, riots every other day—

Rita could remember the old days, before the Internet and television had permanently merged, before the endless news flows from every corner of the world had become a never-ending, inescapeable barrage. It was easier to ignore all the suffering when she was a girl. You could turn off the

TV and the radio then, not pick up a newspaper, and suddenly the rest of the planet could be made to appear somewhat normal.

But that had all disappeared. Now, the jabbering screens and speakers never went silent. The ear pieces and the wrist phones and the pod-coms and all the rest of it, the everlasting shriek of information muttered and text-streaking at people from every corner. In elevators. In cabs and on the buses and subways. It was there when one opened the door to a shop. Or a refrigerator. Or a menu. Everywhere.

Everywhere but the Clean Rooms.

Such nonsense had been banned from them aroound the globe, and for good reason. The entire idea—the primal concept—of the Clean Rooms was to provide for people, too stressed out to continue onward, a place to hide from the world. To allow them to know that there was for them a shelter from the insanity of the crowd. That there was a refuge for those who simply could not take it any longer.

Rita pulled the fuzzy rag from her left apron pocket to attack the corner of the mirror behind the vase of lilies on the blue stand. Fingerprints from God only knew whom had somehow gone unnoticed. Such would not do in her domain.

As she wiped away the offending swirls of oil and dust with a gentle motion, Rita thought on how the world had changed over the years. In all honesty, she still could not believe that Clean Rooms had once been con-troversial. Imagine, she thought, that something so practical, so beneficial, so necessary to the simple forward movement of life, had once been shunned and bitterly debated. Condemned.

"Lord," she said quietly, "but people are so ruddy stupid."

Such thinking seemed so long ago to her at that moment, though. Dismissed as something for only the poor and the desperate initially, it had not taken long for the first Clean Rooms to be established in this or that little known corner. When their popularity exploded, however, when they were declared useful, legal and needed, businesses around the world began to incorporate them with a vengeance. Before too long, most of the world's governments were building Clean Rooms within their own buildings, as well. And soon, like coffee bars, they were everywhere.

Hospitals had come in strong after corporate headquarters. It made such practical sense. People worried about their loved ones. Folks suffering from incurable diseases. So much pain and suffering.

Rita slid her rag back into its pocket, and then stepped back to take a last look at the lilies she had brought in that morning. They were but a small bundle, only five. They were, however, well-shaped, rich in color, and long enough of stem to make a striking display. Working with them, moving two of them slightly, positioning them just so, she smiled at their simple beauty.

She also smiled at something she had heard on her way into work that morning. It had finally been agreed and approved that Clean Rooms would be allowed in schools. Oh, there had been one in every college and university for years. High schools and middle schools as well. But, the narrow-minded, those whose blindered vision saw only to the past, had fought against their being introduced into grade schools for decades.

"I am proud to announce," the prime minster's voice had come across with such firm nobility, "that as of this day, not only shall all grade schools be required to install Clean Rooms, but kindergartens as well."

Such a good and noble thing, thought Rita. Such a wonderful gift to the children. And wasn't it right? Wasn't it proper? Didn't they have just as much trouble coping with the world as anyone else? Didn't they deserve—

"Ms. Kunsler...?"

Rita turned at the voice, not surprised to find Holden Edwards standing meekly in the doorway. Tallish, white-haired, a chunky man with a perpetual dour look about him, he stared inward, unsure of himself, of procedure, of what he should say or do. Understanding, Rita's hands fell away from the lilies. Reaching out, she took the tired, weary man by the hand.

"Oh, poor Mr. Edwards... feeling just beyond it, are we?"

"Well, I don't know... yet... I mean—"

"There, there," offered Rita in a comforting tone. Leading the sorrowful fellow to a comfortable chair, she let him slide into its enveloping folds, adding, "no need to explain to me. You're here now. What comes next is all up to you."

She had thought she might find Edwards on her doorstep sooner or later. Although she was not privy to any particular level of corporate secrets, she did hear things. Especially about those who might soon need her saving oasis. Edwards' division had not been doing well. His marriage was not all it could be, either.

"Comfy, are we?"

As the man smiled weakly, his eyes wandering the room, avoiding the white drawer—for the moment—Rita asked;

"Can I get you anything? A cup of tea, perhaps? Cigarettes? Perhaps a plate of—"

Edwards shook his head, thanking Rita in a quiet voice. Nodding—understanding—Rita left off the conversation. Knowing the poor worn out man in the comfy chair had already made his decision, she simply crossed the room to the blue wall table. Pulling open the white drawer, she checked the .45 automatic nestled within it. Loaded. Safety off. Ready for use.

Smiling again, she slid the drawer closed once more and then headed for her ante room. Edwards would need his privacy. And she would need to call maintenance, to let them know there would be another hole in the wall requiring their attention.

Such a practical, no-nonsense way of allowing people to deal with the problems of life, she thought. As her hand reached for the inter-building communications link, Rita told herself, it's all so intelligent. So thorough. So egalitarian. Makes everything proper, it does. Just makes everything—

The sharp crack of a single round of automatic gunfire shattered the calm. Nodding contentedly, Rita pressed the numeral combination for maintenance, thinking;

"Such a bright and shining world."

The mechanical servitors to the great sorcerer Maal Dweb, started to wonder about there master. Long ago the hunter Tiglar braved the sorcerer's mountainous home in order to rescue his beloved; he failed and was transformed bodily into a creature, and banished to the maze surrounding the home; but for some reason, known only to Dweb, he left him his mind. As the centuries passed, Tiglar learned of his new world, and planned for his revenge.

THE DEATH OF MAAL DWEB

"Death never takes the wise man by surprise,
he is always ready to go."
Jean de la Fontaine

MAAL DWEB STARED OUT INTO THE CALM BEAUTY OF HIS GARDEN. AT least, this was the appearance his body gave. His great servitors, his watchful force of iron automatons, had begun making note that their master had sat thus for some years, his eyes aimed in the one direction, open—unblinking. Of course, there seemed nothing amiss in this to the mechanical servitors. For Maal Dweb to remain stationary for long stretches was not unusual. Indeed, to them nothing their master did was unusual. He was Maal Dweb, greatest of sorcerers—utter ruler of Xiccarph as well as the five outer planets of the triple suns and all their moons—their all-knowing creator, their all-powerful god.

Still, concern was beginning to build within more than one of them. Programmed for a certain dullness, they obeyed their master's wishes with unquestioning and ruthless efficiency. But now, they had no wishes to fulfil, and some of the older automatons, the ones the enchanter had tinkered with the most over the centuries, had begun to do something within their mechanical brains akin to the human—they were wondering.

The strangeness in the blackish emerald of their master's eyes was growing somehow familiar, ordinary, as if there were no more fascinations left for Maal Dweb to look out upon. This was a new thing for the great machines, and new things were rare in the controlled world of Maal Dweb. Yes, certainly they were used to his long periods of silence, his cryptic weariness, hanging from him like webs gathered while wandering a long unused hallway. He had once reclined for somewhat over seven months, his face slack but calm, as if he merely meditated, remembering distant shores and terrible reveries. But, never in all their days had he sat so long, so still, so empty of desire, so drained of purpose. This turn of events did not bother them, of course. Or frighten them, or confuse or bewilder. These were all emotions beyond the iron servitors. But, it had indeed begun to make some of the oldest ones wonder.

And, one other resident of Maal Dweb's expansive estate as well.

Some centuries earlier a fighting man had entered the sorcerer's world. A skilled jungle hunter, his name had been Tiglari. He had come to Maal Dweb's mountainous home to rescue his beloved, the fairest of their tribe, which the tyrannical ruler had summoned to himself as he had countless other beauties over the millennia. Beautiful was Athle', but it was beauty desired by Maal Dweb as well. Tiglari had been at the master enchanter's mercy from the moment he had entered the grounds of Maal Dweb's home. His plans shattered, Tiglari had been transformed into an ape-like thing from the neck downward—from the neck downward *only*.

Tiglari had been left his capacity for thought. The sorcerer had mentioned that his clemency sprang from reasons other than any esteem he might hold for his victim. With disdain, Maal Dweb had dismissed the ape creature, ordering it back into the maze which surrounded his home where it would find many windings it had not yet traversed. Tiglari had taken one last look at Athle', frozen for all time, turned to stone by the enchanter's magicks, and had then done as commanded.

Maal Dweb had not given his reason for returning Tiglari to the strange and wondrous labyrinth, he had but stated that he did not wish to see the warrior again. For years Tiglari dwelt within the seemingly never-ending maze. Battles he fought, with others who had suffered his fate, things once men that now galomped on all fours or shuffled about on two. One of them, formerly a warrior known as Mocair, recognized Tiglari's scent. Once the hunter's rival for the affections of Athle', he was now completely transformed into one of Maal Dweb's slope-browed things. Tiglari made a mascot of the once great hunter, keeping him close as one would a hunting dog, using the near-brainless brute as a companion, a blockade against the madness of loneliness.

Other traps and snares did Tiglari face within the intricate twists and turns of the enchanter's terrible garden, but with Mocair's loyal help he prevailed over them all. For, unlike the other creatures of the maze, he had advantages. Maal Dweb had left him his mind.

He could *think*.

He also had the coil of woven root-fiber he had brought up the mountain with him. He no longer possessed the needle-sharp knife with which he had planned to murder the enchanter, however. That had been shattered, like so much else. His plans that day had gone badly awry. Athle' was a statue of shimmering stone, and he was a thing abhorrent, neither man nor beast. His love stood, frozen and transfixed, on a small dais of purpled crystal which rested beside the ivory chair in Maal Dweb's chamber of meditation. And Tiglari, he crawled about in the precise and dangerous shadows of the enchanter's domain, avoiding the sorcerer and his iron servitors, working still toward his original goal—the freeing of Athle'.

By the end of some seventeen decades, Tiglari had learned the entire plan of Maal Dweb's amazing labyrinth. When twenty-two such spans had passed, he had discovered the sorcerer's drawbridge of light. After so many years, he had begun to understand some of what he saw in the corners and back branches and hidden recesses of Maal Dweb's world. He could tell the bridge allowed the enchanter to stay in contact with all his domain. Tiglari could not walk its coldly complicated stairway of controls, but he had fathomed its purpose nonetheless.

Often he returned to the bridge, sensing that somehow it would be his salvation. He did not understand how this could be, for he knew within his warrior's heart that he could study the celestial device for a thousand more decades and he would still never be able to walk more than a few hundred yards of its shimmering lights. But still, as the years increased, so did the feeling that somehow the bridge was the answer to all his sufferings.

Thus, day after month after year did Tiglari sit, faithful Mocair by his side, neither aging while within Maal Dweb's confines, waiting for the moment when the powerful feeling within Tiglari's breast would prove itself out. And, finally, on the anniversary of the fourth year of Maal Dweb's immobility, the warrior's inner provocation proved itself.

As he stared downward into the convulsing randomness of the irreconcilable angles which clashed below the enchanter's mystic bridge, for the first time Tiglari saw something—a thing not formed of vapors and random ideas, not a conclusion of concurrent geometries or a wisp of gasping color, but something solid—something *living*.

Instantly the once great hunter sprang to his feet and raced out onto the bridge the tiny span he could safely transverse. Loyal Mocair, not understanding the danger of his actions, followed his master, eager to play at something new. As he moved, Tiglari unfastened the coil of woven root-fiber he had worn for so long, unfurling it as he ran, sending it flying downward over the edge of the bridge. He did not hurl it straight for the being he saw for he knew that would do no good. Long had he studied the oblique symmetry of the currents below and, though he did not understand what laws governed their seemingly random movements, he had learned to predict them.

The coil twisted and bent back on itself, but it traveled as its master wished, and in seconds its weighted end made contact with the alien thing floundering in the currents below. Surprised, shocked, the creature grabbed hold of the line, the mad frenzy of its frightened confusion threatening to pull Tiglari from his perch. Prepared for such, however, the warrior already had Mocair bracing the length with him. Instantly the two put their great arms to the task of reeling in the squawking, hissing thing Tiglari had spotted. And, in a matter of minutes, the mountain home of Maal Dweb was suddenly host to its latest uninvited guest.

As the creature was brought up over the edge of the bridge, it released its grip on the woven length and hurled itself away from the silver bridge toward the nearby solidity of its hosting promontory where it sank its claws into the ground and began to weep. As Tiglari approached the thing, he noted that it was a kind of winged lizard, man-sized, with cold scarlet eyes housed beneath scaly brows. Its body was long and undulant and the mere sight of it made the one-time human thrill with hope. He had waited so long for a sign, for a sliver of hope, for... for *anything*. And now, now, he assured himself, it was here.

"What are you?"

Not surprised the creature did not answer, Tiglari waited patiently, asking the question repeatedly, softly, until the lizard thing could focus enough to respond.

"I am... " the creature began to reply, then went blank. Its eyes colored sour with confusion, then suddenly it began again. "I do not remember my name. So long... so long down there. I remember only that I am Ispazari."

Tiglari began to call the lizard by that name, and it accepted it well enough. The two talked at great length, well into the fourth year of Maal Dweb's stillness, and much did they uncover. The hunter told Ispazari all he could and the lizard told the beastman everything he could remember. Slowly, things came back to him. He remembered that he had been a wizard on his own world. He remembered also that in a long ago time his kind had been close to overthrowing the tyranny of Maal Dweb. And he remembered that it was the terrible enchanter who had reduced his entire race of people to mere fen snakes, and who had let him drop into the triangulated depths beneath the bridge of light from which Tiglari had saved him.

"Great are two things within me," Ispazari hissed. "My hatred of the most evil Maal Dweb, and my indebtedness to you for pulling me from the nightmare below."

Tiglari nodded in sympathy. A wonderful thought forming within his mind, the warrior ordered Mocair to fetch Ispazari food. The lizard had not aged nor needed any sustenance while trapped in the multiplying currents beyond, but now on shore he found himself growing incredibly ravenous. With a finger held to his lips, Tiglari cautioned Ispazari to wait for him and hurried off on an unspoken errand.

Straight for the gleaming metal and stone fortress of Maal Dweb did he speed, straight for the hiding place he had created for himself within the twisted confines of the ulbuka tree which grew in a direct line-of-sight with the window before which sat the dread sorcerer. Tiglari studied Maal Dweb for some time, making certain the enchanter had still not moved. The warrior was certain he had not. Even more of his great automatons stood around him, awaiting orders, staring upon their horrible master with calm patience.

With a boundless glee Tiglari had not known since his childhood, he raced through the dangerous riddle of Maal Dweb's maze, reaching Ispazari's side before the lizard had finished its meal. Mocair sat nearby, his simian ears perking to his master's obvious excitement. Rapidly, Tiglari explained that which he had dared not speak aloud until he had made certain Maal Dweb was still locked in his endless internal reverie.

"I think that together, we can kill Maal Dweb."

Surprisingly, Ispazari agreed with his benefactor without turning for even a moment from his meal. As the lizard continued to eat, Tiglari related the facts of the enchanter's long immobility. When he was finished, Ispazari thought for a long moment.

"If you can get me into the sorcerer's laboratory," the lizard said at last, "I think you might be right. I believe we might possibly put an end to the tyranny of Maal Dweb."

With care and exceeding guile, Tiglari lead the way back to the great fortress of stone and steel. It was true he knew exactly where to go, for he had made his way through most all the rooms in Maal Dweb's long and cold mansion. But, he was quite aware that there were many safeguards which ignored him because of his form. He was, to the enchanter's defenses, a thing not worth bothering about. Simply one of the master's amusements.

Tiglari burned within his mind. Too long had he contained his anger, his hatred for Maal Dweb. He had learned long ago that not to do so lead to madness, and he was determined to keep his wits, and to someday free his lovely Athle'. But now, now with his new ally, with his longtime foe rendered helpless, suddenly he could almost taste the revenge he had dreamed about for so long. It took a great wrenching of his will to turn his mind from scarlet dreams of slaughter and back to the tasks at hand.

Maal Dweb's home had to be entered carefully, cautiously, with a clear and peaceful mind. The warrior calmed himself, filling his thoughts with gentle images and childish amusements—anything to silence the bitterness churning within the back of his brain. Without words, Tiglari could tell his companion was maintaining the same type of mental discipline. The warrior smiled. Fate had delivered unto him his salvation. He would win. Athle' would be free. Before the night was out, Maal Dweb would die.

For endless hours did Ispazari work within the enchanter's laboratory. While Tiglari kept watch, the lizard worked relentlessly, grinding leaves and mushrooms down into dust, mixing bits of gorgon brains with moon-powder, etching ancient runes into the stems of various fungi, and far more. After a while, Tiglari began to suspect that Ispazari was working on two projects at the same time. But, before he could give voice to his growing suspicions, the lizard called out to him.

"You will want to drink this," the reptilian wizard told him.

"What is it?"

"It is a potion made from a series of artificial flowers, and it will not remain potent for long. Drink it quickly."

Tiglari eyed the offered vessel. Why did he need to drink anything, he wondered? What was the lizard up to? Had he been wrong? Had fate sent him a traitor and a false...

No, the warrior told himself. No creature could be so false, or so stupid. Even the vilest of cowards knew there was no mercy within Maal Dweb's breast. If Ispazari were to betray him in an attempt to curry the enchanter's favor, there was no doubt it would end worse for the lizard than for him. Grabbing the wooden cup, Tiglari brought its rim swiftly to his lips and drank.

The warrior swooned. His body aflame, he rapidly lost control of his limbs, felt his legs going numb, his brain fuzzy, ears ringing. His eyes fluttered, unable to stay open. And then, in a moment, the strange sensations passed. Tiglari gasped down huge lungsful of air, panting rapidly, feeling his body suddenly going sweaty from every pour. Instinctively, he wiped at his brow to keep the perspiration from entering his eyes. That was when he noticed the smoothness of his arm.

"The fur—it's *gone!*"

Ispazari smiled, his rows of sharp teeth gleaming in approval. "You saved me from the fate Maal Dweb imposed on me, could I not do at least as much for you?"

This was beyond the warrior's deepest dreams. Long he had thought of taking Athle' from Maal Dweb's mansion and returning her to the world below. Never, however, had he thought he would be a man again. Tears of joy sprang from his eyes and the warrior wrapped his now clean arms around Ispazari in an outburst of joy that made the lizard chuckle.

"You don't look much better to me," hissed Ispazari with affection. "But if you're happy with the results... "

"Yes, yes—and Mocair. Him next!"

But the sorcerous lizard lowered his head, shaking it with regret. Quietly he explained that Maal Dweb's enchantment of Tiglari could be reverse for the wizard had not completed the transformation. Since Mocair had been entirely turned into a beast, however, there was no way back for him. Tiglari nodded, remaining silent for a moment, then finally spoke.

"What is, is," he said simply. "How do we kill Maal Dweb?"

"With this."

So saying, Ispazari pulled what appeared to be a drop of dark red mercury from his tunic. Holding the sliding glob out for Tiglari's inspection, he explained;

"It is a drop of Maal Dweb's blood. When he battled my people long ago, he did so as if he were not the great sorcerer he is. For a moment, we almost felt as if we would be able to overcome him. Blows were landed on his person. He bled. It was wonderful to behold. Throughout my days in the currents beneath his bridge, the blood with which I was splattered never soaked into my garments. this one last drop is all that remains of what I went over the side with, but it will do."

Ispazari held the droplet over the second vessel he had prepared, then released it. The odd blob changed shape several times as it fell, roiling as if actually trying to avoid the potion beneath it. The seconds of struggled were fascinating to watch, but eventually the natural order of things succeeded, and the droplet hit the chemical brew in the mug with a small explosion.

Light frothed up and over the sides of the vessel, churning and splitting, changing colors and crackling with the sound of dry leaves being hit by rain, but eventually all activity ceased within the confines of the mug. As it did, Ispazari smiled, showing his great rows of teeth once more.

"Lead me now to Maal Dweb," said the lizard, his voice happy with energy. "It is time for his death."

As the pair made their way through the corridors of the enchanter's home, loyal Mocair at their heels, Ispazari explained that they no longer need concern themselves with concealment. As long as they stayed close to the potion containing Maal Dweb's bloodlet, none of the sorcerer's defenses would be able to stop them. Indeed, he explained, they would not even be able to sense the two of them. All Maal Dweb's traps and servitors and every one of his artificial devices as well as his living defenders would only see their master instead of the two assassins.

As they neared the room in which Maal Dweb continued to sit, staring, Tiglari finally allowed himself a brief smile. Their plan was working. He tested once more the weight of the blade he had taken from the sorcerer's laboratory. It felt warm and solid in his hand. His hand—not his *paw*—his *hand*. The joy of being fully human once more was a giddy, effervescent thing, but the warrior contained his joy, shoving it away from himself. As long as he had waited for such a moment, he would not allow it to ruin his chances at victor. No, he would ignore it for now, hold it in reserve until he could indulge himself within it fully—until he had earned it.

Not that such payment was far off or difficult to earn. Ispazari had outlined for him the simplicity of their plan. As long as the lizard held the vessel and continued to chant the proper mantra, they would remain invisible to all Maal Dweb's defenses. Then, when they were close to the sorcerer, Tiglari would need only slit the tyrant's throat, and that would be that. The reign of Maal Dweb would be finished, and Xiccarph as well as the five outer planets of the triple suns and all their moons would be free *forever*.

And then, the pair had reached the great wall of windows where sat Maal Dweb. They stood stock still for a moment, not daring to breathe, so great was their subconscious fear of the motionless enchanter. Mocair sat patiently at their feet, waiting for them to lead him further. And, after a moment, as the pair realized that the half dozen of Maal Dweb's great servitors had failed to notice their arrival, they indicated to Mocair that he should remain behind and then began to move forward once more. Carefully winding their way in between the terrible automatons, they moved silently until they were positioned directly behind Maal Dweb.

Ispazari continued to murmur his mantra below his breath. Tiglari raised his weapon. The iron servitors continued to focus their attention on their master. Maal Dweb's gaze continued to take in the darkness of the night sky beyond the glass wall nearby. Ispazari's eyes met Tiglari's. The lizard nodded. The warrior struck. And the body of Maal Dweb faded away on the mist.

As the warrior stumbled from the violence of his wasted blow, he found himself spinning, his blade coming around and slicing through Ispazari's hand at the wrist. The severed limb fell, the vessel in it spilling sideways, its contents spewing every which way. All but the droplet of Maal Dweb's blood.

"Finally."

The blood, that exploded into a thousand daggered slivers which flew off in a thousand different directions. As Ispazari screamed and Tiglari cursed, the voice that spoke the single word sounded again. It was a toneless vibration, deliberate and disembodied. It was a faintly contemptuous thing, one both weary and cruel. A thing both Tiglari and his companion had heard before.

"I knew I was bound to make a mistake some day," it said, even as Ispazari and his fellow conspirator began to scream. "That was why I spared you Mocair's fate so many years ago."

Tendrils of stinging fog steamed around the two, dragging them toward the floor.

"Foolish of me to have traveled to Ispazar without my full powers. I deserve the trouble that larking about caused me—I really do."

Tiglari and the lizard both clawed at the ebony marble of the floor, trying to drag themselves off to safety.

"I was able to recover all but that single drop of my blood. I knew where it was, but I simply could not chart the movements of the beast to which it clung. That was when I realized that this was the moment for which I had been saving you, Tiglari."

A sweet smell began to envelope the pair struggling on the floor.

"I put into your brain the idea of watching the river beneath my bridge, kept you searching. When it was obvious you were close to discovering the Ispazari, I created a mirage of myself, one designed to grant you the illusion I might be helpless."

One by one, Tiglari's and the lizard's limbs began to stiffen, frosting over with thousands of tiny crystals even as they began to shrink in size. With a tired whistle, Maal Dweb signaled to the cringing Mocair who had been left in the far corner. The creature bounded across the room to its master. Maal Dweb stopped the foul-smelling ape-thing with an outstretched hand, indicating the two tiny bodies on the ground before him. Catching a whiff of the two doll-sized sugar men, Mocair scooped up one, then the other, dropping them down his vast and uncomplaining gullet.

And then, from out of the shadows, strode forward Maal Dweb. Cold was his gaze, and tired his eyes. Walking across the room to where his shadow image had sat for so long—uncomplaining, luring—he sat in the same chair, taking stock of all that had happened. As his great iron servitors stirred around him, he turned toward the nearest.

"Lenn Carr, am I not Maal Dweb, in whom all knowledge and all power reside?"

"Yes master, you are indeed Mall Dweb, the all wise and all powerful."

"No, Carr, for there is one bit of knowledge I have yet to acquire. I know nothing of death, Lenn Carr. What do you think of that?"

"I think my master could learn anything he wished to learn."

"You are wise for a machine, Lenn Carr. I built you well."

And, so saying, the enchanter held out his hand and summoned the blade Tiglari had brought from his laboratory. Raising his eyebrows for a moment, he looked about the room, then down through the window before him, and then suddenly he slid the blade across his own neck, falling over backwards as blood hemorrhaged out of him at an incredible rate.

In a moment his body was still, resting slumped over the back of the chair. As his massive automatons began to crowd around his body, small mechanical whirrings were heard as the great machines tried to fathom what had just occurred. Their master, the magnificent Maal Dweb, had just died. For once they were at a complete and utter loss as to what they should do next. Twinges of a mood akin to panic began to circle their robotic minds. And then, suddenly, the sorcerer's blood rushed back into his veins through the gaping slice in his neck, a wound which healed itself a moment later.

"Maal Dweb," announced a chorus of his iron servitors. "You live!"

"Yes," the enchanter agreed. "I found death a very common place, vulgar. Such being the case, is it not best I continue to live? Am I not Maal Dweb, the eternal?"

"Indeed that which you say is true," answered Lenn Carr for the rest. "Eternity is the only garment which truly fits you."

The enchanter searched his mind for a more final or bitter truth. Finding none, he called Mocair to his side. The ape thing consumed the last of the Ispazari, his master long since devoured, and then ran to Maal Dweb's side. The enchanter scratched the slobbering brute's sloped head and then smiled at the beast even as he signaled to one of his automatons with his eyes. The mechanical man moved forward and then, when Mocair's head was turned away, it rammed it through the chest with the pointed tip of its cutting arm.

"Well done, Mong Lut," said the enchanter.

"Thank you, Maal Dweb," answered the machine. "Will that be all for now?"

"No." The sorcerer rubbed at a sore spot in his neck. As he did, he announced, "I have a task for you and your fellow automatons."

"Yes, Maal Dweb...?"

"Go down into the world below, and to all the other planets of my domain, and kill every living thing. Too long have I held reign over these petty and untrustworthy lumps of life. Watching your cleansing may cheer my spirits."

"As you command, Maal Dweb."

Without argument or question, the great automaton lead his brother machines down into the world where offending life waited unsuspecting. Sitting in his carved ivory chair, Maal Dweb leaned forward to review the pageant to come, anticipation of actual excitement causing the light behind the blackened emerald of his eyes to glimmer for the first time in centuries.

Mayhap this will be amusing, he thought.

And across the galaxy, the death screams of his loyal subjects bounded between the stars.

John was old and knew his time was coming to an end. Today he had decided to drive the car into town, this one last time, and visit his old parking spot. John had hoped for a peaceful death, one free of pain and approaching fear, well he got it; the only problem was, he was ignored.

A GLORIOUS ENDING

"The worse sin toward our fellow creatures
is not to hate them, but to be indifferent to them;
that's the essence of inhumanity."
George Bernard Shaw

JOHN HAD BEEN A GOOD ENOUGH MAN. HE HAD ONLY LIVED AN AVERAGE life, but it had been a full one. Full enough. Long enough. And when it concluded, he died the way all men want to die. Comfortably. Without pain. Without knowledge of the moment. There, as they say, one minute, gone the next.

And that, unfortunately for every living being, was the problem.

John had just finished parking his car in the city, far from home. He had not left the suburbs much over the last few years, and he considered himself damn lucky to have found the spot he wanted without more trouble. The neighborhood had changed considerably, but memory failing or not, he had gone straight to it and found a parking spot around the corner from his old building. Just off the main street. Just like the old days.

Just like always.

Damn, he had told himself, the old trick still works. He had been, and rightly so, extremely pleased with himself. He had gotten up in the morning simply wanting to go into town one last time, under his own steam. He knew his son would be upset with him, taking a car, not telling anyone where he was going—yeah yeah, fine, whatever—he knew it.

But, it was not like he was kidding himself about anything. He realized he was old. He knew it—had accepted it. He had known for quite some time that the day was coming when he would have to be taken everywhere he wanted to go. That he was about to officially become "a burden." And, as much as he was willing to acknowledge this inevitability, he simply got an itch to go, one more time, on his own.

And so he did, and he found the place and slid into his old spot, and then, just as he congratulated himself rightly so for still having the goods, he died. It was a small trifle, as moments of personal triumph go, but old men will settle for less than their younger selves did. And thus John smiled, pleased with himself to no end, sat back in the car, let go of the wheel, and simply faded away.

Where he was not supposed to be.

Where no one knew to look for him.

Where no one cared about things all that much.

John and the car remained where he had parked it, with John still inside, sitting erect, unmolested and undisturbed for three days. On the fourth day of its stationary vigil, one of the city's street-cleaning units came along. It was forced to pull out into the avenue to go around the old Toyota's recalcitrancy. One week later, it was forced to do so once more.

The next week the street-cleaner was accompanied by an inspector from the Department of Sanitation, driving along in their own car, searching for lawbreakers interfering with the cleanliness of the city streets. Reaching John's car, the inspector pasted a sticker on its passenger side rear window outlining the idea that John was a bad person for parking illegally. Never noticing, of course, John still sitting behind the wheel.

This pattern was repeated several times over the following three months. After the application of five stickers, the police were brought it. Following procedure, they began issuing tickets to the Toyota—ignoring the presence in the front seat as had those who had approached it earlier. After the fourth month John—or more appropriately, John's remains—fell over, stretched out on the front seat. After another pair of weeks his remains crumpled further, oozing down onto the floor.

Finally, having gathered so many stickers and tickets, the car was towed to a Department of Motor Vehicles lot. Now, one might feel this would be the end of the story. John's son had reported the missing car, as well as his missing father. Certainly when the vehicle was impounded everything would be sorted out. But, such was not the case.

Because of the excessive amount of sanitation stickers and police summons, the vehicle was deemed "abandoned." Thus it was put aside for later registration because, after all, surely no one cared about it. Worse, like many of the cars transferred to the abandoned lot, John and his ride became lost in a wash of irregular management.

Even this would not have been too great a problem, but the vehicle John had chosen for his act of rebellion was the worst of his son's family's three cars. He could not have taken his son's car, for that had taken the young man off to work. His daughter-in-law had taken hers to get to her job as well.

But, that had left his son's old car. The one they had not gotten around to getting rid of yet.

In many ways it was a perfectly fine automobile. It ran as well as any older vehicle. The miles per gallon it received was a decent enough total. But, it had one little problem. One it only suffered in bad weather. It leaked. And even that was not a terrible concern, for it was only the trunk that leaked—a minor thing, really—caused when the car had been rear-ended. The collision caused just enough damage to disrupt the trunk's seals. There had been attempts to repair it, but it was one of those jobs that required more money than John's son considered practical. Besides, he had been wanting to buy a new car, and this had given him his excuse.

But, all of that had been before the old car was towed away. Once stored in the DMV parking lot, the minor problem became a large one when the vehicle was stored on a slope. It was a tiny incline, really—hardly worth mentioning. But, with the rear end of the car parked at an angle higher than its front, two things happened. First, the water that had been confined to the trunk now could seep into the interior. And second, with John's body stretched out across the front floor, his decomposing corpse became the sopping point for any moisture trapped in the car.

This promoted a faster rotting away, encouraging the growth of a creeping fungus which spread not only the length of John's body, but across the various vinyls and leathers and plastics of the car as well. When the rainy season came, the problem became severely exacerbated.

As water dripped from the car, slithering out through this and that seam, it carried with it the essence of the viral disaster brewing within the old Toyota. The fungus created by the chance series of coincidences enjoyed the various elements of automobile tires as well, and soon the cars to the left and right and front of John were breeding grounds as well.

This is not to say that the creeping growth had no interest to that which lay behind the Toyota. It simply meant their were no cars to its rear. No, behind the old car sat a public park, and if anything, the new strain of decay found the chance to mingle with nature even more rewarding than the DMV.

For one thing, there were puddles everywhere. More water helped it spread all the faster. And, many of the puddles it found here proved to be breeding grounds for mosquitos. Which is when things began to get out of hand.

The first cases of the new disease were kept quiet by the city's health officials. They did not want a panic on their hands. After all, everyone on the city board knew the media would have a field day with the horrors of an unknown illness stalking the land. In a year where most of the board seats were up for reappointment, well, such could simply not be allowed.

And so, one after another, the deaths were ruled to have been caused by something else. To do so was not that hard, and almost the truth, for the fungus was a cunning killer. It did not cause fatality itself, but encouraged it. It crippled the immune system, attacked white blood cells, caused all manner of problems which allowed existing problems to spread faster, and invited in new ones to join the fun. Indeed, many died without anyone knowing the new strain of death was even involved.

Of course, such could only go on for so long.

Eventually the truth came out. Oh, not the truth about John and the DMV and the twisted web of circumstances which began everything. That would never be uncovered. No, by the time the authorities were caught in their game of deceit John's remains had been long consumed. In fact, the fungus itself had changed the rules. At first it had been content to simply suck the life from John, the nutrients it could assimilate from the cars and grass and trees and water and all the rest it could reach in the lot and the park.

But, when it found larvae, when it could through the wonders of biological transmutation, begin to find its way to the human population of the world, then no longer did it decay merely what it could touch through assimilation. Now it hopped from victim to victim, spreading itself outward from its birthplace not an inch or two a week, but to wherever the winds could carry a newborn mosquito. And, that was not all.

Insect pathologists so quickly identified the problem as one spread by the hated summer pests that no one thought to look further. No one guessed that it might be possible more was going on with this new disease. So terrified was everyone over this fresh plague, that anyone who did give voice to the notion that something bigger might be overlooked was immediately shouted down—silenced by the fear of those around them.

This proved to be another mistake.

It turned out the disease was spread by mosquitoes, not only to humans, as well as all other warm-blooded creatures, but to mosquitoes as well. Born with the disease, they not only spread it, they died from it as well. This was not noticed for far to long. By the time it was, it was too late to do anything about it.

What this meant was, anyone or anything that caught the new plague could spread it. Did spread it. Simply by making sounds. Simply by breathing. The more people that caught the disease, the more of them filled the atmosphere with it. Thanks to train and bus and air travel, before the world even knew there was a plague to deal with, it was everywhere. By the time mankind knew what to look for, they did not have to look hard, for it was all around them.

The last days of the human race were not attractive.

By the one year anniversary of John's death, almost a half-billion people had followed him into the darkness. The rate of expiration only accelerated. And, sadly, not simply because the plague spread so quickly. While scientists of all manner labored to find some sort of cure, all around them civilization crumbled, anger and despair working hand in hand to tear down every monument erected by the human race.

During the first quarter of the second year of the new black death, all monetary systems collapsed. Most major cities had fallen into ruin. Almost all public utilities had fallen apart. As electricity, natural gas and running water disappeared from the reach of all but the elite, murder, rape and their thousand children spread across the globe until the air hung heavy with the smell of smoke and blood.

By the end of the second year, less than a half-billion human beings remained alive, and most of them were dying. Of course, how could they not? Even those with unlimited wealth, who had been able to sequester themselves on islands and mountaintops, even they could only postpone the inevitable. Indeed, if they had released their considerable fortunes toward saving mankind, they might have saved themselves as well.

But, they did not, forgetting that when the end came for the rabble they so despised, there would be no one to bury them. None left to burn the bodies. And thus the air would fill with the dust created by flecks of rotting, plague-riddled flesh. And eventually, a mote or two would reach even the most overwhelmingly protected lungs, and that, as they say, would be that.

And thus ended humanity. Previous epidemics had been weathered by the race only because mankind had not spread out so far, nor packed itself so densely. This time, with people in every corner of the globe, crammed in by the millions, there was no avoiding the inevitable.

And, inevitable it was. For although the human spirit has been able to rally against monsters of any and all stripes, defeating tyrants, unseating madmen, rebuilding after natural disasters, conquering viruses and cancers, there has been one devastation which holy men have warned against since the beginning of time which mankind has never failed to ignore with a universality unmatched by any.

Indifference.

Every great civilization throughout time fell when it became, on the whole, indifferent to its own survival. One after one they disappeared, one mighty nation after another, done in by the weight of their own inability to care enough to survive. And so, once mankind had covered the planet with one large, interconnected, McDonaldsized, Playstationed, Starbucked, IPadic, tightly-woven wallow of mediocre self-interest, it was only a matter of time that such an empire was given its test by indiscriminate Fate.

And sadly, when one reduces life to something simply not worth living, when one creates so many miracles that all marvels become nothing more than "just more stuff," indifference naturally rules. And indifference is a callous master.

And thus it was that simple, tired John, who shuffled off his mortal coil old and alone in a Toyota in his favorite parking spot downtown, died the last happy, satisfied death granted to any member of the brief, not-very-glorious species known as the human race.

He had only lived an average life, but it had been a full one. Full enough. Long enough. And when it concluded, he died the way all men want to die. Comfortably. Without pain. Without knowledge of the moment. There, as they say, one minute, gone the next.

The last person ever to know such a glorious ending.

Dr. Jones was brilliant; a problem solver who took great joy at seeing the happiness of others, resulting from his work. Today the question was, "and where's my flying car?" as had been predicted way back in the 50s. Dr. Jones' answer was to cross dimensions into a parallel universe where flying cars had already been invented. Or had they?

A LIGHT THAT SHAMED THE SUN

"I MEAN IT, GODDAMNIT… WHERE IN HELL'S MY FLYING CAR, ANYWAY?"
It was that particular moment in the outburst that got through to the heavy-set individual with the curly hair and sweetly vacant disposition. A round-faced man, he was, one as large of frame as he was of heart. He had, at the moment of disturbance, been pondering the problem of cross-wiring fate with exactitude, as a cure for menopause, no less, when the shouting gentleman at the other end of the counter there in the Cold Crab Cafe interrupted his mental gymnastics.

Of course, jumping back just a moment before said eruption, merely for a chance to analyze his mental project, one might decide that such a presumptuous experiment would not only be beyond the grasp of mankind's current collective of thinkers, but also that the very imagining of its possibility should be considered grounds for involuntary commitment to the nearest competent couch jockey or licensed state institution. Such would be perfectly reasonable, and any one would be excused for thinking that it would constitute a proper course of action—any one that is, who was not familiar with that singularly remarkable cooperative…

"I mean, I'm sixty years old, and I'm tellin' ya… "

That most charmingly whimsical of scholarly business concerns… ,

"I remember…"

That most unbelievably fantastic hotbed of intellectual mayhem and scientific hooliganism…

"Back in the day…"

The Pelgimbly Center for the Advanced Sciences, complete with the wonderfully unique brand of inquiring minds which staffed its halls so completely. They were, as its brochures promised, titans of research, giftedly tremendous brains, the kind of venerable cranium-stuffing that routinely conquered multi-verses, rolled consistent D20s and made uniquely damn fine cups of amaretto cocoa. Minds like that of Dr. Aristotle T. Jones.

"Every time you turned around... "

Holder of 25,603 personal patents, devisor of the bundled dimensions theorem, and universally applauded creator of the thirty-second flavor...

"Someone was sayin' it was just a matter of time before we were all gonna be hikin' it around in flyin' cars like the freakin' Jetsons."

And the perfect rung on the evolutionary ladder if ever there was one to bring mankind such a boon, if indeed, there was any hairless ape capable enough to do such a thing in all the known stretches of research and development. For this discussion, it is important to remember that Aristotle Jones was not an inventor's inventor, not in his heart. No, the soul of his tinkerer's happiness was enriched by the cobbling together of things that, in the classic sense of the phrase;

Benefitted Mankind.

The thing-a-ma-bobs and wozzling-do-giggies that he created were universally loved by all peoples. The grand majority of the world, of course, had no idea that every day when they gave silent gratitude to this or that convenience, conveyance or cocktail, that it could be counted on that the designs, theories and random cosmic hiccups of Dr. Aristotle T. Jones could be found frolicking there somewhere in the background. Dr. Jones simply adored creating things which made people go "ahhhhhhh," and he spent as much time as he possibly could out in the real world, searching for ways to hear that sound, accompanied by the indescribable joy of seeing their faces light up in a smile that shamed the sun.

Which is why, at 11:30 in the A.M., on a perfectly reasonable and altogether ordinary Wednesday, he was situated on a stool at the counter in a perfectly reasonable and ordinary Baltimore-style crab diner several blocks from the fable Pelgimbly facilities, rather than hard at work in his lab.

Impossible as it was for many of his colleagues to comprehend, Dr. Jones found the vast majority of his inspirations, not surrounded by test tubes, refractors and pestles, but from within the drama, torment and comedy of the realities created by ordinary people. It was the needs and fears of the common man which drove his intellectual curiosity, and now that he had heard this phrase, this practically tortured wondering over why our physical world was not the one predicted in the 1950s, suddenly his own intellectual curiosity over the matter was reborn anew.

And so, having been snagged from his own churning cauldron of thought by this random query, having fallen far enough into at least a slice of the world's actual reality to be able to interface with a fellow human being, if only for a moment, his mind caught by a sudden gust of white-hot curiosity, Dr. Jones solicited a proposal.

"Tell me, my good man," he asked politely, if somewhat absently, "what exactly would you do with a flying car if indeed it were possible for you to have one?"

The man snapped back the standard nugget one might expect from someone whom, on a daily basis, could be counted on to slap their fists against crumb and crab juice-spattered counters, spewing their words over perfectly decent people as if those poor souls did not have enough morons yammering at them throughout their day already without the addition of yet another slack-jaw into their lives who was neither their employer or a minion of the legal professions.

"Hey, whatd'ya expect?" The man fixed the doctor with a belligerent stare, then dropped the other shoe, "I'd freakin' fly it."

And, for some reason which flickered in the subconscious of Aristotle T. Jones at that particular alignment of the planets, the doctor joined with the man at the counter in feeling the over-riding need for that question to finally be answered. For, once he had calculated the number of times a particular age-group had made that same impassioned query, he realized Destiny was practically screaming out for some research to be done. And also, suddenly remembering that his All-Round-Researcher's license would soon require him to log some additional flight time anyway, he nodded his head in the grumbling man's direction and answered;

"Well then, Mister...?"

"Terill, Harry Terill... "

"Well then, Mr. Terill, let's go get you one, shall we?"

"So, okay Doc," the growling man said to Jones, "explain again why we're powering up a blimp?"

"Zeppelin, actually," the doctor absently corrected. "It's quite simple, really. "You see, travel between dimensions is possible only in lighter-than-air ships."

The man stared at Jones as if he had announced he was about to pull an African elephant from his back pocket. Having spent most of his life being stared at in such a manner, the good doctor, of course, failed to take note of his travelling companion's confusion. Unfettered by such mundane embarrassments, in a moment he related how Dr. Wendel Q. Wezleski had discovered the way to move sideways through reality. The good doctor had, of course, learned how to move forward and backward through commonly shared reality earlier on—"time travel," he had called it. But, the vastly more tricky, and extremely delicate operation which Wezleski had been attempting to learn while constantly, albeit accidentally, inventing new ways to shatter the chronos barrier was the movement through parallel dimensions.

"You see," Dr. Jones told the excitable counter-slammer sitting next to him in the airship, "to effect a journey through dimensions takes steam power. It's the only sufficient energy source we have that doesn't depend on any sort of delicate electronics. Electronics in operation keep the sideways gates from opening, don't you see? So, once our steam-powered generators have gotten a doorway opened, then we still have to depend on lighter than air travel for the same reason—only such vessels can be navigated without the aid of electronic devices. Once safely through a gate, of course, additional power sources can be brought on line, but until then... "

"Yeah, yeah, I dig it," Terill interrupted. "But how does this get me a flyin' car?"

"Well, simply put," answered Jones, his attention split between his easily distracted charge and maintaining his white-knuckled grip on his seat—maintained so because the good professor had an absolute and over-whelming dread of air travel, "we have targeted the nearest possible dimensions which show as likely for having based their major modes of transportation on something other than automobiles."

As soon as Dr. Wezleski had opened the passageways to inter-dimensional exploration, every government in the world had, as one might expect, expressed their typical, extreme disapproval. The Americans, with characteristic disdain for their own interests when faced with stern frowns from their current friends, such as France and China, or their traditional friends, such as Japan and Germany, responded by clamping firmly down upon Pelgimbly, installing their own military people to monitor even the most minute movements within the Institute being made outside of agreed-upon-reality.

Now to be fair, in the favor of the current regime, they had not been so utterly disapproving at first. But, after the mighty thinkers in Hollywood quickly rallied public sentiment along the same lines as the rest of the world with such blathering drivel as "10 Million Dimensions to Earth," "I was a Teenage Zep Jockey" and "The Next Multi-Verse Needs Women," the government became far more nervous about allowing research to continue unfettered by their "expert" supervision. The scientific community, as one might imagine, rallied behind Pelgimbly for the obvious reasons, but the films had been released within months of a major election, and that was, as anyone outside of the omnipotent ostriches of the liberal left could tell you, all there was to say about that.

On the other hand, of course, a chore as simple as sliding 598 feet of helium-filled, steam-driven steel and plasti-canvas past the keen and watchful eyes of military intelligence is not all that great a problem for the typical Pelgimblian. Within minutes of Dr. Jones' assistant, the twenty-two year old ginger-haired Adora Feldstein, wandering "accidentally" into the Prime Security Chamber with a plate of fresh brownies, and a carafe of ice-cooled milk, all monitor screens covering the launch bays became temporarily unmanned and the mighty airship, The Thomas Alva was able to slide gracefully through the electro-flux barrier between unreality and possibility off to the first target dimension, some one thousand, eight hundred and forty-seven realms over.

"What do you mean, 'nearest possible dimensions?'"

"Ah, you see," explained Jones, stuffing the bowl of his pipe, "there are an infinite number of dimensions parallel to our own. If we were to simply travel to the nearest one, we would find things to be, well... almost exactly the same as in our own. No flying cars to be found there. Oh, my— no. But... "

Jones paused to set the flame of his lighter to his pipe. Torching the mix within its bowl, he continued, spitting his words out in small bunches in between puffs.

"If we hop outward into the sideways void... then our chances of finding an Earth... where the average motorist has left the ground behind... well then... there we might indeed discover what you're looking for."

Terill nodded, actually comprehending what he had been told. He made a few further inquiries, several even bordering on the intelligent. Jones puffed on his pipe, watching the screen in front of him, answering Terill's questions and advising the pilot on likely short-cuts until finally, an announcement from the navigator's chair told them they had arrived at candidate dimension number one.

"We're here!"

"Well," corrected Jones, knowing which "here" Terill meant and how likely he was to be accurate in his assessment, "we're 'somewhere' at any rate."

Racing to an observation port, Terill began to scan the airways, his eyes craning in all possible directions, searching for the winged, four-on-the-floor of his dreams. His search went on, sadly, unrewarded. Whether high or low, East or West, back, forth, or any other direction available for scrutiny, Harry Terill spotted many a plane, several helicopters, and a few points of light which he thought might have been UFOs, but he could lay his eyes on nothing that appeared to be a flying car in any reasonable way, shape or form.

"I don't get it," he said finally. "I thought this dimension was guaranteed far enough away to be different from ours."

"Indeed it is," Jones told him honestly. "Perhaps an excursion to the surface will tell us something further."

It only took a matter of a few moments for the professor to calibrate the proper charge to resinate his body and his guest's so they could wander about on the surface of the world below them. Leaving the Thomas Alva uncharged, of course, so that it might remain invisible to the locals, they then descended to the ground outside the nearest town and hiked into the suburbs.

"You know, I don't think I remember seein' any roads from up above," Terill announced as they accomplished their first quarter mile.

"I wouldn't think we would find any anywhere in this world," responded Jones. Releasing a great billow from his pipe, he mused, "That was the whole reason for sliding this far over, dimensionally speaking."

"But," asked Terill, "if they don't have flyin' cars, or roads for regular cars, then how do they get around?"

Eighteen more steps gave them the answer. Coming to a break in the wooded area into which they had descended, they suddenly came to a row of suburban-style apartment buildings. Rounding the corner of the closest, they emerged into the open to find something the good doctor had not anticipated.

"My, my, would you look at that now."

"The goddamned sidewalk is movin'."

As the two explorers watched in rapt fascination, people mounted and dismounted the conveyors stretched out before them. Many merely stood while they were propelled along, reading newspapers or listening to this or that being piped through headphones, but far more seemed quite comfortably at rest atop small, one-legged chairs upon which they remained stably poised by using both of their legs for counterbalance. Two belts moving in opposite directions were needed to keep things flowing, and people had to step across several moving belts to continue onward when one set of belts crossed another, but they seemed to do so with relative ease.

"Jeez'it, Doc, how do they do that?"

"How do they do what?"

"Get across the lanes so quick?" Terill stared in awe-struck wonder at the sight of a woman in her early sixties along with her dachshund as they skipped nimbly across the five feet of a belt headed West, then an identical set of feet found on the one next to it headed East, finally catching up to their own belt, still headed South, which had traveled underneath the other two.

"I would surmise it was simply a matter of growing up with it," Jones conjectured. "After all, think about it for a moment. If we were to take them home and show them people weaving five ton automobiles through traffic, bicycles and pedestrians, I'm certain they'd be just as impressed with any of us as you seem to be with them."

"Makes sense, I guess," Terill admitted. "Makes me wonder how they move packages, groceries, you know—furniture, bigger loads. Is this all they have—these movin' sidewalks? How does really big stuff get around? And what do they do when it rains? Or in the winter time? Or... "

Deciding he would like to know such things himself, Professor Jones moved them forward until they intercepted the older woman and her dog at the front door of her building. Claiming to be doing a survey, they asked their questions and discovered that everything they wanted to know had the most mundane of answers. People simply took carts and wheeled baskets and all manner of dollies, et cetera, with them when they shopped. Delivery trucks in Dimension Starboard/1847 were merely platforms on wheels, most of them a type of remarkable automated platform that delivered packages to destinations then returned to their point of origin as programmed. Bad weather was apparently compensated for with protective clothing. And so on and so forth.

The Travolator, which the woman announced as the name of not only the beltway in front of her apartment building, but the entire world-wide system, worked quite nicely at all times and in all manner of weather, and she would not dream of supporting a measure to introduce some other form of transportation. Smiling broadly, Jones thanked the woman for her time. Terill kicked a rock in angry frustration. Both returned to the Thomas Alva.

"That was sure a bust," announced Terill, still kicking things as they re-entered the Zeppelin.

"Well, think nothing of it," answered Jones, settling into his chair for another stomach-turning launching forward. "We've got an infinite number of possibilities before us."

"Yeah," grumbled Terill, "an infinite number more of possible disappointments."

Dr. Jones allowed the remark to pass, thinking he would soon be able to snicker kindly in his guest's direction as they sailed into the proper reality. But, it soon became apparent he had been wise to allow the remark to pass for a dimension where they actually had flying cars was rapidly looking to be as rare as garlic wedding cakes or ethical standards in the music business. Not that the pair of explorers did not find alternative modes of transportation.

Oh, no indeed.

The Thomas Alva sailed into a plethora of alternate realities where men had found a wide variety of innovative means of locomotion. Their very next stop brought them to an Earth where the pogo stick, of all things, had become the major means of personal transport. When they ventured into the nearest city, they witnessed not only a rush hour madness of literally thousands of pogoing white collar workers springing their way home, but styles and varieties of pogo apparatti never dreamed of back home. They saw two-person models, ornate chauffeured versions, high-roaring, souped up models moving in packs which clearly seemed to be piloted by spring-powered gangs, and even massive, multi-pronged mass transportation based on pogo technology.

It was, to say the least, a disheartening stop, but the pair slogged on, plowing through the ether and moving on to one dimension after the next, hurrying to one more additional, equally disheartening stop after another. Future visits brought a gaggle of Earths which had made strange variations to the automobile, but which had not abandoned it completely. Others dealt with technology familiar to the travelers, but which they had never seen used to such all-encompassing ends.

They discovered worlds where cars ran on nuclear fuel, massive heavily shielded roadsters with the looks of tanks, but with unlimited mileage and the added side ability to glow in the dark. They also discovered the amphicar, a kind of three-masted convertible which navigated equally well on roads or that Earth's extensive canal system, as well as the three-wheeled Dymaxion, a marvel of grace and imagination which embodied for transportation the same principles of economic form and functionality that the geodesic dome brought to architecture or the Rob Roy brought to hangovers.

They found worlds where the pneumatic train had conquered all, exotic, yet Victorian-styled lands where the gravitational pendulum was master, rushing rounded train cars from California to New York at speeds of five hundred miles an hour. It was an inspiring sight for Jones, who found the air-driven, environmentally-friendly trains a wonder, and who would have made more notes to see if such a system could be implemented back home if not for the fact the trains filled the air with the sound of booming mechanical flatulence with grinding monotony.

Worlds which depended on the hydrofoil and the hovercraft also seemed around every corner, as did ones where people rolled along sitting in the center of giant wheels, ran along within over-sized plastic bubbles and even a few where the use of animals for moving from place to place had not fallen from popularity. And, this was not just the familiar horse and oxen being discussed, but everything from the camel and dog sled to the kangaroo and the giant sea turtle.

This was not to say that other Earths with flying citizens were nowhere to be found at all. The intrepid explorers discovered dimensions where the skies were filled with manned platforms which flew on giant fans, amazing discs steered by the simple action of the pilot leaning to one side or the other. They also stumbled across such often dreamed of wonders as rocket belts, jet packs and one interesting dimension where, instead of wearing their engines, its aeronauts stepped onto a platform that housed a vertically oriented turbojet and then launched themselves off to work, the movies or the nearest McDonald's at mach seven.

There were also plenty of sites where mankind had decided personal transportation could be accomplished en masse with helicopters, tilt-o-rotors and gyroplanes. The doctor and his guest even, eventually, found one odd society where those with the itch to leave home and go further than the nearest corner did indeed do so in Aerocars. These were intrepid Studebaker-like devices which cruised the roads quite nicely, but which could be driven into a set of wings that came with its own extension, tail and rudder. These attachment pieces locked into place in moments, allowing the driver to then fly off quite easily into the wild, blue turnpike. Most people did not seem to possess their own extensions, but merely picked one up at a kind of U-Haul service located at the nearest airport.

Still, as close as this was to their desired goal, the Aerocar was as much what they were looking for as a pumpkin was a pumpkin pie. Disheartened, as blue and lost and as thoroughly depressed as he ever had been in all his cynical, noisy life, a tired and woefully worn Harry Terill said;

"Maybe we should just pack it in, Doc."

Jones looked up from his speculation charts, his eyes taking in all of his guest's horribly forlorned expression. The abject defeat on the man's face stung the doctor. This was not a person about to say "ahhhhhhhhhh." His were not eyes destined to shine with a light that could shame the sun any time soon. No, this was a man defeated—one suffering from a let-down as severe as the eight-track tape and as devastating as the two-party system.

Indeed, his discouragement seemed as complete as possible. Far more than just Terill's eyes were woeful, his entire posture was cheerless, his stance that of a banana on a hot day. His teeth appeared melancholy; his fingers dismal and somber. It was not a pleasant picture. Aristotle Jones pursed his lips, trying to think of something encouraging to say, but he could find nothing.

How could he?

After all, they had uncovered civilizations which had tried to gift their citizens with the flying car, but they had all come to ruin. Ordinary folks, it seemed, were simply incapable of handling the extraordinary demands of the fighter jet, which essentially was what the flying car would be, especially when coupled with the notion of travelling in proximity with their fellow excursionists. Most people, as could be attested to by the ever-increasing accident statistics to be found anywhere human beings could also be found, were simply not team players. They did not like to give way to their fellow drivers. They did not particularly enjoy even having to consider that there was anyone else on the road other than themselves.

Worlds which had adopted the flying car sat in burning ruin, millions of sleek, aerodynamic carcasses littering their landscapes, the trapped and broken remains of the socially just-not-good-enough moldering behind their ruptured steering mechanisms. Taking a long drag from his pipe, Dr. Jones rolled a orange-wood scented waffle of smoke around in his mouth, then let it out slowly, saying;

"I have one more thing I'd like to try, if you don't mind, Mr. Terill. Why don't you lie down and take another nap. If this next trip doesn't fix things, we'll give it up. What do you say?"

Tired, but still stubborn enough to remain hopeful, Terill headed for the cot he and the doctor had alternated using throughout their long and frustrating journey. Jones waited for the older man to fall asleep, then signaled the pilot to head for home. It seemed at that point that there was only one way remaining to grant Mr. Terill his wish.

Luckily for him Dr. Aristotle Jones was humanitarian enough to employ it.

When Terill first felt the gentle tugging at his shoulder, his mind had brought him to the conclusion that his entire time with Jones aboard the Thomas Alva had been but a nightmare of sorts, a bad stretch of REM sleep brought about by some rarebit he could not quite recall. When he opened his eyes, however, he found the good doctor there before him, but with something oddly different about him. Jones was smiling.

No—not smiling.

No, not smiling at all. Jones was ebullient, positively beaming, as happy a man as Terill had ever seen in his six decades on the planet. Sitting up, he rubbed his eyes, questioning what seemed to be the obvious mainly out of self-preservation, like an orphan refusing to believe in Santa Claus, or a New York voter, suspicious of a voting booth.

"You tryin' to tell me somethin', Doc?"

"Step outside, Mr. Terill, just this one last time," answered Jones. "And see for yourself."

Excitement raced the older man's blood and he headed for the ladder to the disembarking platform, each step coming faster than the one before it. Once to the ladder, he practically leaped from rung to rung, taking them two, three at a time. He hit the ground running, but came to a sudden, joyous stop as he saw where he was.

The Thomas Alva had stationed itself on a cliff overlooking a vast metropolis, one whose massive skyscrapers were a'buzz with clouds of vehicles flying between them.

Flying!

"Hey, doc—*doc!*" he shouted. "You did it, man; you did it!"

And, indeed, it seemed that Dr. Aristotle T. Jones had done just that, for before and above and all around them, the world was awash in flying cars. The landscape below them was clean and bright and nifty enough to have been clipped from the front cover of a 1954 edition of Popular Mechanics. Terill staggered wildly, twisting and turning with excitement youthful enough to make him appear drunk as his body tried to show him everything possible within the same moment.

Everywhere was a glory of sky-splitting craft. Brightly colored, practically noiseless, emitting no soot or clouds, they were graceful as hawks in flight, the traffic patterns achieved things of art to behold.

"Oh, my God, Doc," whispered Terill, "we did it; we *did* it."

"Well," corrected Jones, "We found it, anyway."

"No," answered a still completely fascinated Terill, "*We* did it. 'We,' 'us,' mankind. We got 'em up there. When we saw all those other worlds, man, where everything just kept crashin' and burnin', where men just couldn't get it together enough for us to work together, to fly and soar and zoom, together—I mean, it was killin' me." Turning to face Jones, the older man told him;

"Back in the fifties, everyone thought the future was gonna be filled with wonders, and in a way, I guess it is, but they never turn out. They're always bitin' us on the ass. Nuclear power, and clonin', steroids, air conditionin', even diet soda... nothin' ever does what it was supposed to. Nothin' ever comes through. There's always some hidden price tag... "

Jones watched as Terill turned once more to staring into the sky. The man seemed renewed, freshly borne, filled with a wonder and joy the doctor could scarcely measure. Then, shifting his view through his bifocals, Jones checked his virtual view of Terill against the actual person stretched out on the padded slab before him. Terill appeared basically comfortable, all his bodily signs stable. Reaching out, Jones made a minor adjustment to the older man's headset, making certain it was securely intact.

The doctor removed his glasses at that point, needing to rub his eyes. As he did, his field of vision grew to take in the thousands of other padded slabs, with their thousands of other occupants living lives dictated for them by their thousands of headsets. Dr. Jones had taken pity on many volumes of humanity in his time, and when solutions to their problems could not be met, he had done for them what he had now done for Harry Terill, brought them to sub-basement D of the Pelgimbly Institute for the Advanced Sciences and hooked them up to his most humane masterpiece, the virtual reality generator.

Testing of the machine was still proceeding, but each additional "volunteer" was only proving that it was, indeed, the greatest gift Jones was ever likely to create. The machine not only manufactured separate, creative fantasies for each of its wards, but it also monitored their vital signs, keeping them as healthy as inert bodies could be kept. Jones did not usher in anyone off the street, kidnapping every wandering dreamer to further test his remarkable boon, but only those so demanding, so cynical, so caught up in their need to escape that finding their dream at the expense of their freedom was considered a fair trade.

The rows of softly pulsating tables in sub-basement D contained a wide range of humanity, with as many mullet-headed dreamers like Terill, as there were Conservative Christians, feminists, grass roots Democrats, Luddites, and other starry-eyed fanatics desperately awaiting the arrival of their personal, impossible social contract.

Knowing it was time he returned to his lab, Jones allowed himself one more moment with the enraptured Terill. Replacing his glasses on his face, he again touched his hand to the corner of the older man's slab which allowed a visitor to share the dreamer's experience. Suddenly, the doctor found himself at Terill's side as the man stepped into a newly purchased Ford Rainbow. Within his brave new world, Terill had already passed his driver's test and made the purchase of his dreams. Turning to Jones, he stopped for a moment to avoid having his voice crack, then said;

"Thank you, Doc—ohh, God bless; thank you so much."

"Think nothing of it," Jones offered kindly. Then, as Terill began to engage his controls, the doctor stepped away from the imaginary craft, then disappeared entirely as he removed his hand from the connection pad.

Jones lingered a moment longer, unconsciously tarrying a few extra seconds in the hopes of catching his favorite tune.

"Aaaaahhhhhhhhhhh," the sound whispered from Terill's smiling lips. "Aaaaaaahhhhhhhhhhhhhhhhhhhh... "

Jones smiled in response. Then, knowing one could never allow themselves too much of a good thing, he turned and began making his way through the rows of padded slabs, already thinking on how next he could benefit mankind, while all about him thousands of sets of eyes shone with a light that shamed the sun.

The air around the Captain was filled with flying debris and shrapnel as the bombardment continued; in desperation he made a break for the only structure in sight. Once safely inside a new mystery arose, one not of the current conflict, but from wars long pasted.

999 DOWN

"Fear has its use but cowardice has none."
Mahatma Gandhi

THE CAPTAIN DID NOT HUG THE GROUND—HE CLAWED AT IT, TORE INTO IT, DID everything he could to make himself as small a target as possible. All around him the world shook from the thunder of the never-ceasing rain of shells. Explosions stole his senses—smell and taste cancelled by a world of smoke and burning powder, hearing and sight by an atmosphere filled with dirt and smoke and a din beyond imagination.

At first he had hoped for a cessation to the bombardment, for the enemy's will to further churn the landscape to evaporate. When that seemed unlikely, he prayed for them to shift their target area, to turn their devastating attention in some other direction. They did not. What had been an assault of smells and noise became one of dirt particles and pebbles. Then the splinters grew larger. Rocks the size of grapefruit began to fall around him. Then logs and sections of machines and pieces of bodies began raining down on his unprotected position.

Where were his men? Lost? Dead, dying, fleeing the assault, or spread out on the ground as he was, helpless—waiting for death?

Move, you idiot, a voice whispered within his paralyzed brain. *Move!*

The Captain found his feet and ran forward blindly into the smog of dust and bloody air. Better to die at least *trying* to live. His body took a thousand hits as debris slammed against his body. His helmet rang from the punishment, his eyes tearing, throat choked.

"Run—do it!" he told himself, growling through the glug and fear thickening in his throat. He heard his words only within his mind as the world continued to shatter around him. "Run, asshole! Run!"

A break in the dirt-clogged air gave the Captain a momentary vision—a large, windowless structure lay directly in his path no more than half a mile ahead. Hope lending him strength, the officer forced his failing legs to pump harder, throwing himself into an all out effort to reach the seeming shelter.

Thunder tore apart the ground behind him, his every desperate step removing him by inches from the latest explosion. Shrapnel slammed against his pack, his legs, the back of his neck. Step by galloping step the promised safety grew closer.

"I'm not dying out here," the Captain screamed, his words lost in the surrounding cacophony. "I'm not dying today for *anybody!*"

The officer threw himself at the solitary door in the smooth stone wall before him. Expecting at least a token resistance, the Captain was surprised when the panel swung open at his touch, allowing him easy, if ungainly access to the building's interior. The officer hit the floor with an awkward bounce. Spare ammunition and his canteen dug into his side, causing him to cry out. His weapon, jarred loose from his grasp by the impact, went spinning across the slick tiled floor. The door closed quietly behind him.

The Captain remained where he had landed—panting, aching—part of his mind running a check of his limbs and organs, making certain he was still in one piece, another part marveling that he had reached the building at all.

Alive, he thought, wondering if the word were a question or a fact. While he pondered the notion, the first voice spoke.

"Shoot—they's just always the same, ain't they?"

"Don't sound so smug, Gregory," came another. "That was you once, you know."

The Captain looked up. Voices meant company. Friends or foes, he wondered. Owners of the building? Refugees? Other soldiers—from his side or the enemy? His hands closed automatically on the empty space occupied a moment earlier by his weapon. As he clambered quickly to his feet, a figure moved into view through the patchy gloom. The form held his rifle out to him—barrel first.

"Here," the man said comfortably. "You won't need this, but it'll make you feel better, for sure."

The Captain grabbed at his weapon, pulling it to himself, reversing its aim outward in an almost smooth motion. His muscles were throbbing—arms tired, hands aching. His legs, weary and cramping, finally rebelled. The officer staggered slightly, stepping involuntarily backward even as he felt more bodies approaching him from behind. Spinning around to confront the strangers he sensed, he practically threw himself back to the floor.

"Easy," said the older of the two, his hands upturned and open. "Everyone here knows how you feel."

"Feel?" snapped the Captain. "How I feel? What the Hell would you know? What's going on here? Where am I? What is this? What the Hell is going on?!"

"Relax, mate," said the other, a smooth chair of unusual design within his grasp. "Here. Sit. It'll help."

The Captain collapsed into the offered seat. Information began flooding his brain, all of it jumbling into an unmanageable confusion. The building—when danger had been all around him he had headed for the only sanctuary he could see. Now that he had entered within its walls, however, details he had ignored suddenly sprang up within his mind.

Just what kind of building was he in? Early reconnaissance had said there were no structures for miles. Beyond that, however, he had never seen anything with quite such a design before. Why had the door opened for him? And, why did he no longer hear the shelling? Had it stopped—at the exact second he had entered? Unlikely, but if not, why were the floor and walls, the ceiling not shaking?

"So," asked one of the men closing around him. "Would it be easier to ask questions, or to just have one of us start telling you what's happened to you?"

What? The Captain stared blankly, his eyes finally beginning to focus on the others there with him in the large, darkened room. They were six in number, all male, all warriors. But, they were not soldiers from his own army, or from the enemy's ranks, either. As his brain began to work once more, he could see that each of them was uniformed as a soldier, but all from conflicts long ended, all from armies long since disappeared.

The man who had handed him the chair, for instance, wore the red-coated, high-booted uniform of a British regular from the period of the American Revolution. The one who had handed him his weapon was from an older period, an Arabian from the time of the Crusades. And, as the Captain looked about the room, he saw that each of the others was as different as the next. To his left he saw a tall thin man in the unmistakable grays of the Confederacy. Another he knew had to be a Conquistador. The other two present were both dressed in garb so ancient he could only guess at their origins. The shorter of the two looked to be Chinese, his colorful uniform of bright yellow and red silks perhaps marking him as some sort of commander. The other left the Captain guessing. The man might have been Egyptian, or perhaps Hindu. The officer could not tell.

"Where am I? What is this place? Has the shelling stopped?"

"Shelling?" asked the Asian.

"Cannon fire," answered the Confederate matter-of-factly. "We told you about it before."

As the Asian nodded, the Englishman tried to answer the Captain's questions.

"We don't know where we are, lad. Nor either do we know what this place be. As for your war—perhaps it still rages. We don't know, really. We don't know about any of our wars."

The Captain stared, his mind struggling to grasp his situation. Understanding what was going through their newest arrival's head, each of the others began to speak, talking over one another's comforting words. Laughing at the confusion, they indicated back and forth for one another to speak. Finally, the Confederate said;

"Ling's got the highest rank of any of us. Dang, let him tell it."

The others nodded in agreement as the dour Asian stepped forward. Sitting on the floor in front of the Captain, he made a friendly face and then spread his hands apart in the air.

"My name is Ling Po," he said. "None of us knows why it is we can understand each other's speech. It has simply always been so. Although I was one of the first to enter the shelter, I have never been able to fathom what this place might be. Neither has any who came after me."

The Asian warrior told of how he had come to the darkened room. It had been during a great battle between two mighty warlords. Ling had been a powerful general with some five thousand men at his command. He had not been a lucky general that day, however, and a miscalculation had cut his forces by half in a bloody twenty minutes. Holding the line had soon turned into retreat which even more quickly turned into a frenzied rout.

His horse cut out from under him by a rain of arrows, the general had waded through the mud with his troops—sharing their fear, forgetting his rank—running with the same bitter taste of terror thick on his tongue as spears and arrows littered the field about him with more and more bodies. Like the Captain, Ling had seen a windowless building in the distance. Also like the Captain, he had forgotten his troops, forgotten his dignity, forgotten everything except his desire to live.

"But," said the newest arrival, "I don't understand. I wasn't fighting in China. I mean—how can we be in the same place?"

"Tis the same for all of us," answered the Spaniard. "I was fighting the English in New Spain, half a world away from Cathay. But that mattered not. Whatever the witchcraft involved, wherever we were before, once through the door beyond, we were here. Forever."

The Captain's mind whirled—the years some of those present must have spent within the darkened room staggered his imagination. Understanding what he was thinking from the look in his eyes, the Englishman nodded.

"Aye, passing strange it tis. Some of us have been here hundreds of years. Some thousands. Not that it seems such. Time passes curiously here. I swear, it feels but a day that Gregory joined us," he said, indicating the Confederate soldier standing to his left.

"We do not age, we do not sleep," said the Arab. "We take not food nor drink, nor do we crave these things. We merely exist... here in our sanctuary. Waiting for the door to open, waiting to see who joins us next."

"And, and," the Captain struggled for words, "that's it? That's all you do?"

"What else is there?" asked Gregory. "Sum'thin' brought us here to safety. Maybe this is like Heaven or sum'thin'... Heaven for soldiers."

The Captain looked around the room. The red tile floor was clean, but cold. Shiny. Sterile. What color the walls beyond might be or of what material they might be composed he could not tell. They were too distant, and the lighting was far too dim for him to make any kind of judgment. The ceiling seemed far above him, but again, it was too dark for him to be certain.

"Whatever this place is," answered the Captain, "I don't think it's Heaven."

"It is not my idea of Paradise," agreed the Arab, "but still, it is all the refuge any of us has. What more were you asking for when you were driven into our midst?"

The Captain made to answer, but the words dried in his throat. Who was he to say anything? As each of the others told their tales, a terrible sameness ran through the sagas. Each warrior had been lost in the middle of a tremendous battle. The dead were all about, cold and unmoving, broken eyes staring, gaping mouths crying out in silent horror, shattered limbs, frozen in place, reaching for different unobtainables just beyond their lifeless grasps. All of them had stumbled through slaughteryards, one step ahead of death. All of them had run for shelter, simply attempting to preserve their lives.

"He who runs away... "

"What?"

"Nothing," answered the Captain, ashamed of the inference he had started to make. Who was to say that any of the men before him were cowards—at least, any more cowardly that himself?

The officer's head snapped back slightly. Where had that thought come from, he wondered. Coward? Suddenly he was a coward for saving his own life? His company had been destroyed, their ranks broken, scattered and shattered. If any of them were still alive it would only be through the same kind of miracle that had spared him.

Still, he wondered, is this the extent of miracles these days? Is this all you get?

The Captain looked around the darkened room once more, his eyes coming to rest on the doorway through which he had passed earlier. Was the battle still raging on the other side? Were the bombs still falling? Were some of his company still alive out there, still holding on, hugging the barren ground as he had, scared and screaming, alone and helpless?

And then a different thought struck him. Although it only seemed he had been in his seat for a matter of minutes, could he still trust his senses? From what he had been told, years might have passed already. His men might be in their graves, the battle over, the war finished.

"Hey," asked Gregory. "Who won?"

"What?" asked the Captain. "What do you mean?"

"My war... the war between the States... did we win?"

A frightened hope burned in the Confederate's eyes. He must have found the shelter late in his conflict the new arrival decided, when its conclusion was becoming clear to both sides. Still, hope forced him to ask. Dropping his head slightly, not wishing to wound Gregory with the horrible truth any more than he had to, the Captain shook his head slightly, whispering;

"No. The North won."

"Yeah-up," answered the Confederate softly. "I, ah, always kinda figured... "

The man in the gray uniform swallowed his words, turning his back on his companions for the moment. Then, his fists balling suddenly, he ran toward the solitary door and threw himself against it, slamming at it, over and over, his hands ringing with pain as he screamed through his broken sobs.

"Why?! Why'd I haveta come in here? Why couldn't I'a died with Kenny and Lyle? Why'd I haveta run?!"

The Captain watched as Gregory's thrashing grew weaker, the man's fury exhausting itself against the seemingly unmovable door. He listened to what the man was saying, thought again on the strange way time moved within the darkened room. Realizing he might have no more than a moment to return to his own world, or his own time, or whatever it was that had been on the other side of the door when first he had plunged into the shelter, the Captain stood and placed his arm on the Confederate's shoulder.

"Excuse me, Gregory," he said quietly, "but, um, I think I'd better get back to my men before it's too late."

"It's already too late," said Ling Po.

"What do you mean?" asked the Captain.

"The door only opens one way," responded the Englishman. "More than you have wanted to return, you know."

The Captain heard the words, but hope made him push against the panel anyway. When it held firm he threw his entire weight against it. Not the slightest movement allowed him any hope of success. Slamming his fist against the door, he turned to his companions.

"And, that's it? We're stuck here forever?"

"As best we know," answered Ling.

The Captain felt his throat tightening. Within his mind, a thousand voices shouted one at another, all demanding to be heard. Was it that bad? He was alive. Alive forever. With good companions. No needs. No wants. No fear.

No life, either. No respect. Certainly not self-respect. No hope. Nothing— nothing but the daily wait for the next refugee to come stumbling through the doorway, the next coward to add to their numbers, to help suck up and spread around the collective guilt.

Then, an even worse thought came to the Captain. He focused on Gregory, a man suddenly on the losing side of history. Then the Englishman, another whose army went down to defeat in the end—like the Conquistadors. Were they all the same, were they all from periods of time where God turned his back on their cause? Or worse, was their seeming shelter a test? Had each of them been singled out to represent their entire cause—had stepping through the smooth doorway doomed the Confederacy? Toppled the Arabs the one time the Crusaders were triumphant in the Middle East? Shouldering his weapon, the Captain turned to the others.

"I'm leaving," he said simply, then turned to the door. Pushing his fingers against the smooth panel, he dug at the juncture where the door met the wall, trying to pry the passageway open. He worked with a steady, furious strength, his pace constant, his determination growing moment by moment. He failed. Rested for a breath, then began again. Again. And again. And again.

"It can not be opened," said the Egyptian or Hindu or whatever he was.

"I don't care," screamed the Captain. His fist slamming against the door, he shouted, "I'm not staying here. Maybe our coming here is a death sentence for our side."

SLAM!

"Maybe our running away brings doom on our cause... "

SLLAMM!

"Or maybe we're in Hell, being punished for the running... stuck here forever... making excuses... "

SLLAAMM!

"Well not *me!*" he screamed, his fist clanging against the door harder than before. "Not me!"

"No," came another voice suddenly. The Captain paused, turning to see Gregory standing directly behind him. Raising his own fist to the door, the Confederate nodded his head slightly, then added, "Not me, neither."

The two men attacked the door, pounding against it, throwing all their energy into battering the unmoving panel. Behind them, the Arab said patiently, "This has been tried before. More than one of us has attempted to leave. It has never succeeded."

"Have you *all* tried," asked the Captain with frightening anger. "Have all of you tried, at the same time, to get out of here? Maybe that's the answer. Maybe we *all* have to be tired of playing it safe, of turning our backs on what's just outside, slaughtering those on the other side of the door. Maybe it takes everyone! Did you ever think of that?"

The room stayed silent for a long moment. Then, the Englishman stepped forward, telling the Captain, "I will admit that such a thought has never crossed our minds, but I will tell you one that has. In the play *Julius Ceasar*, the bard has the Lord of the Romans say; 'Cowards die many times before their deaths, the valiant never taste of death but once."

"A thousand," whispered Gregory. When queried as to what he meant, the Confederate answered, "I heard that one before, 'ceptin' I heard it as 'a coward dies a thousand times.'"

"Yes," answered Ling. "Well, I do not think I can bear nine hundred and ninety nine more demises such as this one." Walking to the far wall, he returned with a sword which he fastened to his sash, saying, "let us see what is now on the other side of that door."

Throwing his weight against the panel along with the Captain and Gregory, the General found he had to move as more bodies joined in the effort. Eight hands pushed against the door. Then ten. Twelve. Finally, after a undeterminable period of struggle, a voice called out behind the half dozen at the door.

"I ran away, because I was afraid."

Turning toward the speaker, the Conquistador addressed he who had been in the shelter the longest, saying, "Abruk, we were all afraid."

"Yes," the man agreed, his head low, "but you were afraid for the moment. I have been afraid always. Always until now."

Stepping forward with purpose, the last of the warriors placed his hand upon the door with the others. Silently, the panel receded into the wall, revealing a shattered vista outside to the cluster of soldiers. Smoke filled the air, the sound of explosions flicking through the filthy haze, mingling with the roar of machines and the screams of the dying. Gregory asked the Captain,

"Is this... where you were? Is this your war?"

The Captain squinted, unable to tell if the burning, ruined landscape was the one he had escaped or not. Pulling his weapon down from his shoulder, he fed it a fresh supply of ammunition.

"We're soldiers," he answered simply. "They're *all* our wars, aren't they?"

Gregory smiled and nodded, unslinging his long rifle. Behind the two, swords were unsheathed, powder was tapped, blades were readied, and one after another, men stepped out of their blissful shelter into the smell of blood, the sight of death and the jaws of freedom.

Jeffrey need to tell someone something very important, the problem is, he need to somehow tell himself. One day looks just like another —exactly like the others— was it boredom, routine or something else? If something else, could he change it?

THE BIG THIRTEEN

JEFFREY REALLY DID NOT NOTICE. NOT AT FIRST. NOT FOR A WHILE. THAT was the point, after all. But—

When it finally did happened, however, it was on a Wednesday.

Well, of course it was.

Again.

It was a Wednesday, early in the day—actually, it seemed maybe even microscopically earlier than the day before. A Wednesday when the creeping suspicion that had been nagging fearfully in the back corners of his brain finally broke through. A horrible nightmare of a notion, finally loose within the conscious dimensions of his mind.

It was triggered, of course, by the oddest thing. A dribble on his bathroom mirror in the shape of a "K." Like a leftover letter from a child's secret message—finger-writing on vapor and glass. How it got there he had no idea, but it frightened him in an odd way, because he realized it meant something.

Had triggered something.

What had been triggered was but the barest of whispers. Jeffrey knew the source of what he had heard was internal, realized it was nothing supernatural, no luring demon or beckoning succubus, or any such rubbish. He could tell. He had seen something—realized *something.*

And now he was telling himself something. Something a part of him felt was important—like a frightened private on sentry duty, breaking radio silence against the strictest of orders because he honestly believed he needed to warn others of an impending disaster.

Jeffrey had begun to notice a pattern to his life. Oh, he knew everyone fell into ruts on occasion. Realized the monotony of daily life could sometimes begin to take on a repetitious quality that gave one to believe they could perform certain tasks with their eyes closed. In their sleep. Yes—

He knew all that.

But, on the other hand, he had begun to notice something more… what would be the word… yes—

Insidious.

Or at least, he thought he had noticed such—hoped he had not.

Jeffrey Sayler had fallen into a stretch where one day just seemed like the next—like the next. One after another. Nothing changing. Eating the same breakfast. Catching the same train—seeing the same faces reading the same newspapers. Every day after day. After day.

After day.

After—

"I don't know what you mean, Jeff. You're bored? Is that it?"

Day

Not the same people at work doing things they were supposed to do in this or that regimented fashion. Not neighbors performing their routine in a comfortable manner, seeing to this chore or that, being predictable in the way all comfortable people are predictable.

No—

Jeffrey was seeing the *exact* same people, doing the *exact* same things—the exact *same* people, doing the exact *same* things.

At the exact moment they were supposed to do so, in exactly the same way they were suppose to, for the exact same reasons, in the same amount of seconds, at the exact same volume, with the exact same enthusiasm—

The *exact* same enthusiasm.

The exact same *everything*.

As Jeffrey paused his mind boggled, actually contracting and expanding as his neural centers overloaded briefly. Trying to digest the notion that he was living the same day. Over and over and over.

And over.

Everything he had seen and done so far that day, getting up, having breakfast, washing, dressing, leaving home, getting to work, sitting at his desk—all of it had been the same as the day before. Exactly the same in every detail. He was sure of it. Exactly the same as the day before, and the day before that. Twelve days of exactly the same.

Twelve.

And now, now he was living it again. All of it. It was the big thirteen and there had been no changes, not a breath out of place. Every crease, every wrinkle, every hope and sigh and reliable disappointment—all of it part of a monstrous repeating loop churning out the pre-determined choices of his life like coffee beans in a grinder, his supposed free will and self-determination reduced to a fine powder. One grain of it looking exactly like ten thousand others.

As he forced his mind to keep racing down the corridors of actual thought, struggling to focus upon ideas that highlighted this new train of inquiry—that were not part of the seemingly iron-clad script he seemed doomed to follow—a part of his memory told him his friend was about to speak.

Actually, Bill had been standing near his cubicle for some five minutes, jabbering on about the files needed for the McKenzie report, just as he had done every morning for twelve days. But now, his mind made a prediction, as if he needed convincing of the horrible notion that had taken over his mind. In just Bill's voice, in a flawless mimicry of his tone and volume, just two seconds before he spoke, the voice within his brain whispered;

"Hey, you even listening to me?"

Not only did it let him hear the words, but it also added the knowledge that Bill would add the action of reaching over with his left hand, with two of his fingers bent at an odd angle so that they would more poke his shoulder than push it, while saying;

"Hey, yoo-hoo, you with us in there?"

It gave Jeff all of it just before Bill could speak his line, make his gesture and then speak again. Correct tempo, right body temperature, sunlight outside the window in the distant wall correctly luminescent. Everything. He could see it all coming, could predict every moment because he was remembering it.

"Hey, you even listening to me?"

Bill said, reaching over with his left hand, two fingers bent at an odd angle so they more poked his shoulder than pushed it. "Hey, yoo-hoo, you with us in there?"

For the thirteenth time.

The big thirteen.

Jeff jumped at the touch. Again.

Again.

Standing, Jeff ran away from his friend. He did not excuse himself, gave no thought to the fact he was doing what he was doing at his place of work. *Why not?* he asked himself. What could it *possibly* matter?

Seized of an urge, Jeffrey Saylor turned and left his place of work. What did it matter? What could it possibly matter what he did? He refused to be caught up in the pattern. Whatever it was. Whyever it was.

He had seen *Star Trek* and *Doctor Who*. He knew there were a thousand possible scientific explanations for what was happening to him. All of them theoretical. All of them either irreversible or dependent on some complicated, one-chance-only way out.

What was he supposed to do?

Reaching the outside of the office, Jeff grabbed at his head, trying to stop the pounding within his skull. Hundreds of questions slammed away at him. What to do? Which way to go? Stay at work. Break the pattern of breaking the pattern by staying at your desk. Run. Get away. Find drugs. Drink in the middle of the day. Go home. Back to work/on a cruise/ go eat/eat anything/the hell with calories/the hell with everything/ the hell with anything/with anything/backtowork/whattodowheretogowhy mewhymewhymewhyme—

Jeff fell against the wall, begging himself not to scream. What good was getting locked away, spending whatever time he had left in a cage, begging the indifferent to listen to him, that his crazy story was different. His crazy story was the one that was real.

The thought sobered Jeff, silencing all the warring sections of his brain for the moment.

Catching hold of himself, Jeff went back inside his place of work. Knowing he needed time to think, he found his friend and made a feeble attempt to explain his behavior as a failed joke. Then he went to his desk and assumed his practiced "I'm busy" pose. For once, however, it was not a pose. For once Jeff Saylor really was busy.

As the hours droned by, Jeff threw all his effort into trying to remember more. What was the pattern? If he could remember just one more coming event, and then cause it to not happen, he reasoned, perhaps he could break the pattern.

Obviously, he told himself, running outside was part of the pattern. I've done it twelve times before today. Today was thirteen. But, the thirteen day of what? How long had the whole thing been going on, anyway?

Suddenly Jeff realized, what he had done thirteen times was realize that he was stuck in the first place. He had not been living the same horrid, boring, ordinary day over and over for only thirteen times. It had merely been thirteen days since he had first realized he was trapped in his loop in the first place.

Tears formed in Jeff's eyes. Sitting at his desk—people walking by, arms filled with files, taking no notice of his pain and terror—he wept silently, staring—dumbstruck. He could not remember any more. He had no other clues. Knew not what came next.

And so, having no better ideas, he returned to his apartment. He stood outside the door to his tiny chambers unthinking, merely standing, for some length of time he could not remember. Finally he went inside, closing the door behind him. Throwing his bag on the living room's only chair, he slid out of his jacket, still wondering what he could do, when suddenly, a new idea struck him.

If he could not remember any more of what came next in his day, his never-ending day, then he would stop reaching for more, and work with what he had.

"The K," he thought.

The K he had seen stenciled on the bathroom mirror. He had been telling himself something. Who else could have done it? It had to have been him.

Hopefully Jeff headed for the bathroom. Turning on the hot faucets in both the shower and the sink, he then shut the door behind him to help maximize the water's effect. In a few minutes a slight steam began to build within the room. Jeff closed his eyes, saying a silent prayer as he took several deep breaths.

Then, opening his eyes, he felt his arm reaching up, watched in detached fascination as his finger touched the steam-slick mirror. And, even as he watched himself sketch out the first straight line, a voice from the back of his mind whispered—

"*Kill...* "

Degreed line descending, ricocheting off the first—

"*Yourself...* "

K completed.

And then, Jeffrey Saylor woke up.

Sitting in his bed, head twisting from side to side—mind wondering what he was looking for.

A bad dream, perhaps? He had no idea.

No. He had one idea.

He had an urge to get up and go to the bathroom.

To look at his mirror.
And so, Jeffrey Saylor arose. Once More.
And went to his bathroom.
His mind screaming in fear.

The Great War was over, and the Empire was rebuilding and searching for its lost colonies. Captain Florg stared in disbelief at ruined cities on Ortise, a once beautify and unspoiled world; once planetside the Captain and crew searched for the answers to this enchant mystery.

TIME TO SMELL THE FLOWERS; TIME TO TALK TO THE STONES

"O, call back yesterday, bid time return!"
William Shakespeare

THE CAPTAIN STARED AT THE MONITOR—AT THE RUINED CITY SPREAD OUT all about his ship. It was a panorama of debris unequaled in his experience, even if one included the war. His report to Fleet was overdue but somehow, the officer simply could not find it within him to tear his eyes from the viewer. His aide waited with practiced patience, micro-recorder hanging at his side.

"Captain Florg, sir," ventured the sergeant, "the Empire's lost worlds before."

Florg turned, staring. The look in his eyes actually forced the non-com to take an involuntary step backward. "Not like this," the officer said in a harsh and ragged whisper. "No. We haven't. Never like *this*."

Sergeant Rater did not speak further, could think of nothing to say, actually. Colony Ortise was a disaster. In truth, only the barest traces of their people remained. "All right—computed. It has been an aching long time since we've been out this way," snarled Florg suddenly. "But still, what? Tell me; give me an idea. What went on out there?"

He received no answer.

Ortise, far from the center of the Empire, stretched to its furthest rim, the ancient stories called it one world in a million. Fresh, uninhabited, inviting—lush with the steam of paradise—colonists of every stripe had flocked to it. Of course, someone should have checked on them long ago. Indeed, they had been on their own so long, the joke was they had been blessed with enough time to both work out the secrets of space travel on their own and then come home.

But, first communications had been cut off. And then, that small matter of the war with the Reis—the never-ending conflict which thrashed the Empire backward, inward, galaxy by galaxy. So terrible had the eons of shattering warfare become the accepted common wisdom in everyone's mind had been that the end was inevitable. And then, joyously, there had come the accidental discovery of Feggel's Law.

Simple, innocuous as it was, still the weapons based on its principles turned the tide, subsequently saving the Empire. Feggel, however, had no answers for rebuilding that which had been lost. That remained as slow a process as always. Thus century after century, millennia on top of millennia, worlds were reclaimed, the Empire was rebuilt. A hundred thousand generations and more stretched their awesome limbs and the vast domain was repossessed.

Once whole, once every single shattered state had been resurrected, the search for the colonies was begun. Some had survived—flourished, even. Ortise had not.

The captain clicked off his monitor as Rater said, "I don't understand it, sir. The buildings out there—most every one of them was built for something a lot smaller than us. Tall homes for runts."

Florg surveyed his aide critically for a moment. Rater was a good soldier, possibly the best in his command, but his biases did have a habit of showing through.

"You have a point," the captain answered. "Aspirations, perhaps. A lonely people reaching for their gods, trying to be nearer the universe."

"Yeah—you think so, sir?"

"Maybe. Or maybe the garbage just got so deep the only way out was up."

The captain walked toward the entrance of their occupation headquarters, a huge structure like all the rest, but one with a cavernous interior compared to most of the city's cramped buildings. The team's historian suggested it to be a place of religious significance, citing the altar-shaped construct toward the back, as well as other indicative artifacts he had uncovered. The only thing Florg cared was that its roof kept the planet's rain off his back.

A crewman entered through the building's narrow front entrance. Releasing the tab-lock on his helmet, he removed the bubble, gulping down refreshing lungsful of fresh air. His tongue reflexively curled around his snout as he enjoyed the chamber's cool, clean oxygen. Purifiers had been mounted in the command post when it was determined that the atmosphere was tainted with numerous viruses. The ship's medics were fairly certain they were most likely responsible for the fall of Ortise's civilization, but it was thought they would also prove to be within acceptable limits. Not one to compromise his crew's safety, Florg had ordered the planet-fall suits to be issued for all outside work until the green light was given. He knew the discomfort caused by folded spine plates and cramped tails, not to mention the gag of constantly rebreathing the same, stale air, but a few sore muscles and bad breath were small prices to pay to stay alive in an unknown atmosphere.

Florg returned the sweating private's salute as the soldier reported, "Captain, sir. Weather's breaking finally. We'll be able to start work again soon."

The massive commander smiled, showing a number of bright, sharp teeth. "Good. Get the muck out of the tractors and start clearing the paths again. I want to know what happened here. Excused."

As the crewman turned, lumbering back toward the exit, a ray of the freshly revealed sunlight broke through the large portal filled with colored glass overhead. The captain could not translate the alien scene, of course, but he could appreciate the well-ordered juxtaposition of colors.

"Well, they certainly could create beauty," thought Florg. "I wonder, though, how many of them understood it?" Then, turning back to his sergeant, he ordered;

"Rater, turn our lazy ship-dragons out into the sun. I want ever tail-wagger soaked through his suit and smelling of swamp in five minutes."

The sergeant saluted and hurried out the door, growling orders in every direction. Once alone, the captain moved through the echoing hall. "So," he thought, "now we find out just what happened to all those who came here so long ago."

Florg's stare pierced out over the decay of the island once known as Manhattan. Stepping forward over the debris in front of St. Patrick's, he snapped his helmet bubble into place and then joined his men in probing the mystery of what had happened—to the city around them, the world around it, and to Colony Ortise, which apparently had gotten lost somewhere along the way.

It took several weeks to draw the pieces together. All traces of much-hoped-for Ortise were gone. Pitifully small descendants—hopelessly regressed, almost embarrassing reminders of the great peoples of the Empire—were all that remained.

Florg called the mission specialists to order. The geobiological team reported that with but a few exceptions the planet's demise was uniform.

Aerial studies showed that their immediate surroundings were fairly representative of the entire global situation. Small bands of alien mammals hunted and cultivated here and there, but not to any extent worth noting. As further reports were given, Florg commented;

"All right, let's turn to the last page. Give me the egg itself. Rebuild local chronology for me from the landing of the first Ortise ship until the time we curled our descent orbit."

"My department, Captain," answered Chelt, the ship's historian. Groans went up around the table as the rotund reptile rose from his chair. Paying the insolence no heed, the portly lizard, accustomed to being disliked, announced in a tone meant to imply other departments had been lax;

"As best can be compiled from the scant facts gathered by our researchers, the Ortisians were victims of both the planet's bad luck and the War. The Reis cut off supplies. That meant the back-up ships never arrived; no tools, no building stores, smelters, processors, et cetera. All they had were the clothes on their backs, several years rations, and their wits.

"Without tools, however, trapped in a hostile environment, they were sadly, over-civilized folk in a harsh and unchanging world—gentlebeings surrounded by a barbaric wilderness. As best we can tell, they continued on, reverting to tribal ways of life for tens of millions of years. Then, some catastrophe of cosmic proportions befell them."

"'Some' catastrophe?"

"Yes, captain," sneered Chelt. "Our staff is at odds. Some feel it might have been a glacial period which did them in. Others say the impact of some large foreign body from outside the atmosphere is to blame. Still... "

"That's it?" The captain's tone did not imply satisfaction. "Ice and smoke and the Empire loses a world? Paradise? That's all it takes to lose Paradise?"

The historian, who had begun to take his seat, rose once more.

"The Ortise and all their stock," the obese lizard resumed, clearing his throat, "long necks, gliders, swimmers, they covered the world—but lost it. The fur-bearers we've noted, they managed to reach some level of ascendancy, for a brief period, but also lost it through planetary mismanagement, along with a scattering of nasty confrontations, all the usual subculture mistakes."

Florg did not miss the snideness in the historians following request; "May I be seated, sir?"

"Mind your tongue, Chelt."

"Mind your rank, Rater."

"Shut up, the pair of you," snarled the captain. The order brought an unsettling silence not broken for several long moments until one of the other non-coms finally asked, "On your advisement, sir, what should I task my crews to next?"

"Task them to packing up. We're moving out."

As the assembly excused themselves, Florg strode to the back of the cathedral.

"Going out, Captain?"

"Yes, Rater." Florg chewed his lower lip for a moment, then added, "Keep everyone busy. I think before we cramp ourselves in for another ten cycles, I'm going to go for a little run." Looking at his sidearm, the captain considered strapping it on, then ignored it, adding;

"If I'm not back by daylight, send out a few search teams. But don't make them look very hard."

"Captain, sir... "

"Yes, sergeant?"

"You're not, I mean, you wouldn't have anything, ah... in mind? Would you, sir?"

"Not a thing, Rater. If anyone asks, I told you I was going out for a run. And you didn't notice anything different about me." Florg stopped for a moment, then repeated softly;

"Just tell them I went out for a run."

Someone outside bumped into a station beacon and cursed loudly. A commotion ensued, but the sergeant did not seem to notice. Instead he stood motionless as the lamplight outdoors danced across the glass colors above the door, filling his eyes. Then, the light swung back into its regular position, the loud voices disappearing as it did so. Rater blinked the dazzle out of his eyes, looking about himself for the captain.

But his commander was gone. As the sergeant had expected.

Florg had worked at sorting events through his mind as he passed the extensive ruins north of the city. He paused briefly as one of Chelt's great finds. "The Divine" linguist Konrin had interpreted the engraved stone. They had pawed over the structure, similar to their headquarters, with particular skill. Chelt had pompously announced that the site might be sacred to all beings, but the captain found no more peace in it then than he had when it had first been uncovered.

Turning away from the ruins, Florg headed for the open plains. Dinosaurs of his breed loved to release their speed. Clawing open the ground, each great stride placed dozens of yards between the runner and his recent past. In less than half a day the captain reached a place where Ortise was still green.

Before the years of deep space duty, Florg had been a distance runner, not one of the best, but one content with his abilities. At every planetfall the great lizard stretched his legs, getting in as many hours as possible. Those moments of freedom were what he lived for, no matter where he found them. Ortise was no exception. There was a difference this time, though.

This time, he had no intention of returning.

Near daybreak he came across a water path beyond which lay a series of black-scorched cliffs, a sharp, blue-green patchwork lacing the stones.

"Like home," he thought.

He knew no full zenith star would brighten the trees, but at the moment it was enough to bring back memories of earlier, more tender days. He could see his homeworld in his mind, his old school—Margla. If only she could have understood him, what he wanted, why he had denied himself so much, so often... but she had contracted with a loud, low-level construction worker, leaving Florg and his running and his poetry behind.

Sighing quietly, the captain moved on.

In the distance he sighted a discoloration to the grass their biologists had warned could mean higher levels of toxins. Changing course, the captain chose to run along the waterway instead, which was how he found the first of the footprints. It was nothing natural, nothing any of his party had made.

"Aliens."

Curious, Florg followed their trail northward for a short while, following the sporadic prints as best he could. Unfortunately, after a half a day of running along behind it, he could not find the creature responsible for laying down the tracks. Disgusted, he sat beneath a twisted fruit tree, complaining aloud to the wind. Finally, he curled to take a nap. The sun was still hot in the sky. He would bask a while, he told himself, and then move on.

Florg smiled to himself as the wind whispered its way through the tall grass. He watched several butterflies flitting aimlessly by—the small, fragile creatures intriguing him. Somehow their delicate beauty brought to mind a song he had written in his college days. Smiling again, both at the memory of the accomplishment and the childishness of the verses, he sang it to himself—

"Time to smell the flowers,
Time to talk to the stones,
I need more time, before I'm all bones,
Before the duty comes on.

"Time out of suit, Time out of mind,
Time that's not theirs,
Time that is mine,
Before the duty comes on.

"Time to smell the flowers,
Time to—"

Florg broke off sharply, listening for a repeating of the sound he was certain he had heard. He waited in the tall grass, fighting the paranoia of imagining cold, alien eyes upon him. But, his mind whispered, was it paranoia? After all, he had survived too many campaigns to not know when something was near. Coldly, he stripped away the fear response suggesting that the local beasts could cause him any harm.

Concentrating, his patience etched in stone, his clawed hand slid down his side to his holster. Halfway there he remembered, he had not taken his sidearm.

"Smart boy," he murmured, at least a part of his mind disgusted with his actions.

Then, he heard the approaching animal again. His eyes scanned the ground around him, spotting a nicely jagged rock. His paw encircling it, he pulled it to himself. Then, taking a deep breath, Florg sprang to his feet, his arm poised, ready to strike down that which was stalking him. As he roared an oath, his eyes scanned the grass, looking for his target.

He found a small alien closing on him—humanoid, bipedal; female, he thought. She was a tiny thing. Suddenly Florg felt foolish holding his rock, a thing half the size of the alien. He let it fall from his hand. She did not run. As the dinosaur stared, the creature mewled at him. With a sigh, knowing the things proved useless more often than not, he pulled free a device from his belt. Clicking it on, he asked;

"Can you understand me?"

"Yes," the word came out of the machine. "Are you about to ingest me for fuel?"

"Eat you?" Florg shuddered at the distasteful thought. "No, of course not. Why should I want to do that?"

"The male parent has told us the lizard myths. Powerful they were, strong—rulers of all. But hopelessly stupid—with brains the size of tiny, hard-cased nuts."

The captain's grin disappeared. He unconsciously scrunched his brows to show his displeasure with such an assessment, but the girl did not understand the gesture. Instead she tugged at his arm for him to lower the translator so she could speak once more.

"From the Aerial-Command Battle Dreadnought 74 are you? The one leveled outside the ruined metropolis to the west?"

"Yes."

"I believed as much. I was curious. I am not certain I should continue with this conversation, however," the machine translated in its typical, flat formality. "The male parent has dictated we are to avoid contact with the lizard myths. I am not doing as ordered, and could therefore be punished."

"Understandable. You go home. I will not follow."

"Thank you for not consuming my life," answered the machine for the girl. She headed back into the tall grass with a child's casual trust, never thinking to disbelieve the massive reptile. Florg watched until she disappeared, then for long after. Until the sun went down. Until the planet's solitary moon rose and lit the plains below him.

When he finally made the attempt, he did not sleep well.

Five revolutions earlier, the captain had left the ship. Sergeant Rater had allowed for a daily routine set at a casual pace, one filled with many breaks and rec periods. It had still taken the crew only three days to prepare for take off. While many enjoyed the chance to simply be idol, more than a few crew members had begun to grow restless.

"Rater... "

"Historian... "

"Where is the captain?"

"I don't think I really know."

"You don't think you know 'what?'" Chelt stared at the sergeant through the non-coms seemingly nonchalant silence. Uneasily, a nearby lieutenant offered;

"He's waiting for you to say 'sir,' Rater."

"Oh, and here I thought he was waiting on something important."

"Sergeant, just who in all the silver worlds do you think you are?"

"That's easy," spat Rater in disgust. "I'm the slick the captain left in charge; remember? Like he always does. He said ten days rec and lounge, with the ship getting loaded within the first five. The ship's loaded. The men are recing and lounging. The captain went for a run. He'll be back when it's done. How many times do you need this explained to you, tubby?"

"You insolent little frog," snapped Chelt. "He's not coming back, and you know it, you lying bastard. You're covering for him. He's deserted. I know the signs. He's gone space-bugged."

"Someone in this crew sure seems to have done that."

"You don't fool me. You're covering for him; he's deserted, and you're both going to pay for it."

"Oh, Chelt," came a voice from the back of the cathedral. "Must you always be so gloomy?"

"Captain Florg, sir," shouted Rater, smiling as he overly-snapped to attention. "Historian Chelt, sir, has been insinuating, sir, that you would not be coming back, sir."

"Well, I guess he was wrong, sergeant."

"Yes sir, sir. That he was indeed, sir. As usual, sir. Permission to jump on his tail, sir."

"Don't push your luck, Rater," offered the captain.

"No sir, sir," answered the non-com. "That's not my style, sir."

Chelt and those with him left the headquarters area in a sour hurry. A short while later, when everyone but Rater and the captain were out of the cathedral, the little sergeant whispered, "Oh captain, but did you ever have me worried."

The non-com flopped heavily into a nearby chair, curling his tail around one leg. As he scratched his forehead scales in mock exasperation, Florg answered, "I had faith in you, Rater. I knew you wouldn't let my emotions get the best of me."

"What happened, sir? I mean, what went on out there. If you don't mind the asking, sir?"

"If you can't ask... " The captain let the words hang for a moment, then continued on, his voice soft and apologetic.

"I guess I was just tired. I needed some time to get away from it all. I supposed I just didn't care anymore. I wanted some... time. That's all. Just some time."

Florg told his aide about his run, and the girl, and all the hours he had spent simply running and thinking. And running and not thinking. When he finished, the sergeant asked;

"So what in all that convinced you to come back to our smiling faces?"

"Nothing. I was still caught up in the unfairness of Ortise not being here—of fate cheating me. Again. Robbed of the chance to bring the silver worlds paradise. To have some for myself. All those years, locked in our ship—metal walls, metal skies—year after year to get here.

"For what?"

Florg stared at the glass above the cathedral entrance for a long moment. His eyes unmoving, he offered finally, "Let's face it; I'm getting old. I'm old and tired. Tired of the fighting, tired of the never-ending pushing upward and outward. I just don't care anymore."

Florg went silent once more, continuing to stare. How long would it be, he wondered? A century, a week—how long before the Empire pushed itself up against another force like the Reis, starting it all over again? Trillions dead once more, and some new paradise lost. All for what.

Finally stirring, the great lizard said, "anyway, to answer your question, last night I searched until I found a nice grove of trees I seen earlier, curled up underneath them, and went to sleep."

"Why, sir?"

"Because I was looking for something I'd seen there."

"And... "

"And, I found them."

Reaching to his side, Florg unclipped a folding transparent sample box from his belt. One filled with butterflies.

"I woke up this morning and they were all around me... on me, in the trees—everywhere. I yawned, and as they took off into the sky, flying through the early morning light, it passed through their wings, blended with their colors.

"It was beautiful." The captain pointed to the stained glass over the doorway.

"Like that, only out in the forest, away from the ruin." He reflected on what he had said, then added;

"Like what Ortise was supposed to be."

Rater rose and crossed the room, joining the captain beneath the doorway. Pulling a non-regulation flask from his pocket, he took a drink, then handed it to his friend. Florg took a long sip, then handed it back as Rater asked;

"So... why'd you bother to come back?"

"Because," Florg answered, his tone calm, reflective, "when it all is said and done, this is where I belong." A sweep of his hand toward a specific direction showed the sergeant he meant aboard their ship, not on the planet.

"When the Empire meets its next challenge, I want to be at the discovery point, not sitting on my tail somewhere safe where I can read about it thirty years later."

The captain tossed another sample container to the sergeant, telling him, "And we'll take these little ones up with us—sort of a reminder that someday they'll be spreading our ashes out there in the void—where they belong."

"And the duty goes on, right sir?"

Florg shrugged. Striding back to the command table, the great lizard returned to his chair as his aide studied the butterflies further. Looking at them closely, he exclaimed;

"Hey, captain—we really taking these little guys with us?"

"Yes we are," answered Florg. "I'm going to fill my cabin with them, and then the whole damn ship. And if it turns out they make a mess, we'll give a sweepole to Chelt and let him clean up after them... like a good historian."

Sergeant and captain laughed together. As Florg unclipped several more sample bags from his belt, Rater observed, "You know, sir, these things, they're cute and all, but they don't look like they figure on having real long life spans. I don't want to get all sour on you or anything, but I don't think these little guys last very long."

Florg sighed, smiling at the same time. He held back for a beat, then said;

"Tell me what does, Rater. Tell me what does."

John was stressed; some things just didn't make sense. Like why was it always starting daylight saving time?

THANK GOD IT'S FRIDAY

"OH, GOD," COMPLAINED JOHN, MORE EXASPERATED AT HIS WORK PLACE'S bureaucracy than he'd ever been before. "I just can't get anything done around here."

The manager of the Anti-Trust Division sat back in his chair, trying to remain calm. How, he wondered, his blood simmering, mind reeling. How could they possibly allow such a thing? It just didn't make any sense.

"What's the matter, big guy?"

Ed had stuck his head in the door of John's office. He had a way of knowing when his boss was reaching the boiling point. As usual, the sight of his assistant's understanding smile knocked several degrees off John's internal thermometer. With less than his usual restraint, John snarled at Ed, telling him,

"Can you believe it? The front office told Finster he could go home early. Go home early—on a *Friday*? Have they lost their minds?"

"Well, the guy's wife *is* having a baby," offered Ed.

"I don't care if she's having a Volkswagen. The damn kid'll be there when he get's home. In the meantime, how are we suppose to get the Connelly shipment together? That's supposed to fly by five. Five o'clock today. And you know what it means if it doesn't."

"Daylight savings blues," laughed Ed. Seeing that John was not laughing with him, the tall man smiled again, saying, "Look, I'll head down to the warehouse and get the boys organized. We'll get Connelly out on time. You've got my personal 'Big Ed Guarantee.'"

John thanked his assistant as the man headed off to save their jobs. Damn the people in personnel, he thought. Goddamned them. How could they *do* such a thing? He just couldn't understand it—no matter how hard he tried.

In fact, he couldn't understand the whole Daylight Savings Cure business at all. Not from the very beginning.

He remembered how it had started, with all the rumors and then the news reports. Everyone's computer was going to crash when we got to the year 2000. He was no computer expert, didn't understand the mechanics of the problem. He only knew what everyone else knew. Back when computers had first been invented, their systems had been geared to an internal clock. At the time, no one had thought to set the clock to turn over in 2000—Lord, that was decades away—why bother?

But, as the years had slipped by, the newer models that followed had not been upgraded by the same kinds of artists who had breathed life into their predecessors. They had been assembled by technicians who merely concentrated on the parts that interested them, leaving the whole to be wondered over by others—others who did not arrive on the scene until it was too late.

No, thought John, no one noticed the problem until there was nothing anyone could do—not until all the stock markets, all the defense grids and traffic controls, the weather and communications satellites, all the web-sites and bank records and education files and tax statements, the traffic monitors and well... everything, just bloody *everything* was tied into the old system and they couldn't change it.

Like most people, John couldn't understand why no one could come up with a way for everyone to just tell their computers it was a new year. Press a button and "poof." All better. That they hadn't even come close to finding a way just didn't make any sense. But, that they couldn't was the one thing all the experts agreed on, so like everyone else, John believed them, and waited for the end.

It's funny, though, he thought, how the world's changed. Before, when you could actually plan further ahead than a week, everything was so different. So on edge. Now, people, nations, everyone seems to get along so much better. With everyone's tension aimed at the damn machines instead of each other...

John sighed and turned back to the Connelly paperwork. That was what was important. He filled in the columns as he needed to, getting his end of things done and ready to process along with what Ed was handling. Still, though, as he looked at the amazing amount of math he was finishing in mere seconds, his confusion returned. Computers could do so much. So smart, and yet, still so stupid.

And yet...

I just don't get it, John admitted to himself. The only thing the scientists had been able to think up was to keep telling the damn machines that we'd reached daylight savings time again. It was the one thing built into the original systems that allowed for adding and subtracting real time. And so, to stretch out the deadline dropping on Man and all his progress, they—the large, ever-ridiculous "they"—had decided that every weekend would be the beginning of daylight savings time. Weekend after weekend, more and more time dropped into the schedule, tricking the idiot boxes into giving the bright boys who had gotten everyone into this mess in the first place another few hours to work on the problem.

At least, it had started as hours.

John stared at his calendar, his eyes red and tired. He hated the thing. It was one of the new ones—the ones with nothing but Fridays, Saturdays and Sundays printed on them. No year, no dates, no numbers. Just Fridays, Saturdays and Sundays. And then, his door suddenly crashed open. Young Wayne stuck his head in, rolling his eyes and laughing as he blurted,

"Have you heard—Saturday's four months long this week!"

John sighed.

"Oh, God," he complained once more, talking to the walls only. "I just can't get anything done around here."

While outside, in the halls and streets and across the land, the people hunted and gathered, waiting for someone to figure out how to teach their masters to count to two.

The crew of the E.A.S. Roosevelt was on a diplomatic mission to planet Edilson, an alien world where nature itself fills the air with music, and whose inhabitants don't so much talk, but sing to communicate. But there's a problem, the Danierians, the Confederation's longtime adversaries are also there to bargain with the locals for strategic resources. Now's the time to sing like your life depends on it.

EVERYTHING'S BETTER WITH MONKEYS

"What a piece of work is a man! How noble in reason! how infinite in faculties! in form and moving, how express and admirable! in action, how like an angel! in apprehension, how like a god! the beauty of the work! the paragon of animals!"
William Shakespeare

"Were it not for the presence of the unwashed and the half-educated, the formless, queer and incomplete, the unreasonable and absurd, the infinite shapes of the delightful human tadpole, the horizon would not wear so wide a grin."
F.M. Colby

THE ROOSEVELT WAS THE FIRST OF THE LONG-AWAITED DREADNOUGHT CLASS, a single ship stretching for nearly half a mile, inconceivable tons of metal and plastics, crystal and biomechanical feeds, brought together from Earth, the Moon and the asteroids that, when ultimately combined into an end product, became something unheard of—something utterly incomprehensible. And thus... so the thinking went... unbeatable, as well.

She was, in the end, a sum far greater than her parts. The *Roosevelt* was known as "the cowboy ship," for it had been that cocky gang of rocketeers labeled as the Moonpie Cowboys who had built her. They were the wildmen of the mightiest nation in the system's Advanced R&D Team, and it was their spirit that infested her—as well as programmed her still not-quite-understood artificial mind.

The *Roosevelt* was the opening number of a new kind of show, the all or nothing-at-all first born of the Confederation of Planets—big, because she had to be. The first ship with functional energy shields, she needed room for the massive protonic engines essential in powering such revolutionary devices. And for her thousands of attack aircraft, hundreds of them merely hanging off her sides. And for her extensive guns, her big ticket—the whisperers and the pounders—and all her hundreds of thousands of missiles and bombs.

She was the solar system's first spacecraft carrier, a mobile prairie outpost, a relentlessly strong, self-determining fortress in space. Capable of housing as many as 10,000 sailors and marines, the great ship was meant to explore the galaxy, to chart the universe, and to bring prestige and riches to the human race in general.

But, that had been when that particular track meet had thought it controlled the only runner on the field. Reaching the edge of the system's outer planet's orbit, the Roosevelt was hailed, in English, Spanish, Dutch, Jamaican, and eighty-three other standard languages, by a small, obnoxiously shiny craft commanded by a small, and equally obnoxious alien life form that was all too happy to deliver its news.

The quite unexpected messenger announced to the finally-capable-of-interstellar-traveling human race that this accomplishment had gotten them an invitation to join the awe-inspiring Pan-Galactic League of Suns, an organization of worlds begun by the Five Great Races. It was an announcement that, essentially, the party was over before it had begun, that all the planets worth anything were all sewn up, all intelligent species discovered, all franchises in all the marketplaces possible well-established and even better protected.

The news came as a crushing blow to the adventure-craving crew of the *Roosevelt*, and for their first two years, eight months and fifteen days in space they showed their resentment in many a creative and colorful manner. And then, suddenly, all the rules changed. Thanks to that first, bold human crew in space, the entire galaxy discovered the League was a sham, that their claims to have everything under control were simply so much eye-wash, and that there was still plenty of unknown universe out there, teeming with mysteries and excitement—enough even to satisfy the collective curiosity of the crew of the *Roosevelt*.

Within weeks of that revelation, more than a dozen trans-galactic federations had begun to struggle into existence, including the *Roosevelt*'s hometown group. Once made up of only six of the Earth's neighboring planets, because of its pivotal role in pulling the Pan-Galactic wool from the galaxy's eyes, the Confederation of Planets had already expanded to a membership of some seventy-eight worlds, proving, quite nicely, the old adage that everyone does, indeed, "love a winner."

Which is why the crew of the *Roosevelt*, one fine galactic star date, from its stalwart captain down to the lowest chef's assistants and protonic bolt tighteners, was in a rousing, near giddy, mood. They had started their space-bound careers in defeat and through a luck understood by only the most perverse of gods had rolled it over into unbridled victory. So recent had their triumph been that, truthfully, most on board were still at a loss for words when it came to explaining exactly how their good fortune had come about.

"I'm tellin' ya, Noodles," announced Chief Gunnery Officer Rockland Vespucci, more commonly known to bartenders and military police officers across the galaxy as Rocky, "there ain't nuthin' that's gonna trip things up for us again."

"Incautious words," answered the aforementioned Noodles, better known to top notch wire-and-screw jockeys everywhere as Machinist First Mate Li Qui Kon. "As Confucius said, 'he who stops watching for falling fruit will be first to get bonked by an apple.' "

"So, we just reinvent gravity."

Both sailors turned at the sound of a new voice indicating their being joined on the observation deck. As they did so, Technician Second Class Thorner and Quartermaster Harris came into view. As Noodles took exception with the tech's off-handed comment, accusing him of not taking theoretical physics seriously enough, Thorner spread his meaty hands wide, answering;

"Hey, it was just a joke. But com'on, really, look at the way things have been cruising for us. Earth is out in front. We've got the edge. It's our game from now on."

"I've got to agree," chimed in Harris. Taking a deck chair, he leaned back, putting his hands behind his head as he added, "Fate keeps lobbing us softballs, and we keep knocking them out of the park."

"He's right, little buddy," added Rocky. Grinning from ear to ear, staring out into the vast black, Rocky cavalierly added, "Criminey, it's almost enough to make a guy wish for some trouble."

And, it was at that moment that Fate, as she so often does when those bound to her decrees begin to act as if they had somehow negated her sway over their existence, chose to prompt the commander of the good ship *Roosevelt* to broadcast an announcement.

"Attention, this is your captain speaking. We've just received orders to proceed to the Kebb Quadrant to begin negotiations with the inhabitants of the planet Edilson. More information will be zimmed to us shortly, but we're to make best possible speed, which means, ladies and gentlemen, it's time to once more bend the fabric of space and time and be on our merry way."

"Edilson," asked Harris, "where in the wonderful world of color is Edilson?"

"And so it begins." All heads turned to the latest voice to join the conversation. As they did, one of the thinnest individuals to ever muster enough soaking-wet-weight to make it into the Navy added;

"The MI boys are just beginning to appreciate galactic rotation. Which meant that mudball was absolutely destined to hit our radar."

The speaker was Mac Michaels, a balding, bespectacled razormind out of the science division. As the others continued to stare at him, scratching their heads, he spread his hands like a high school math teacher about to share the wondrous joys of algebra as he said;

"Right now Edilson is nowhere, a low rent piece of real estate totally off the charts. But, if you calculate the rotation of the galaxy's set pieces, four hundred years from now, it's going to be in the veritable center of every-thing." Noting the group stare of complete lack of comprehension slamming at him from every angle, Michaels sighed, then added;

"It means that those who are far thinking will want to strike an alliance with Edilson now, so that when the time comes, they'll have an ally situated smack in the center of everything."

Michael's words made sense. Earth was expanding, making friends and teammates everywhere its representatives went. Enemies as well. If the Confederation of Planets was to maintain its presence, to continue advancing in power and prestige, let alone to be able to handle itself in the political and economic arenas of the universe against the likes of the Pan-Galactic League of Suns and others, this was just the kind of advanced cogitation they should be pursuing.

And, as the gobs headed off cheerfully to their various posts, their pride in the planet of their birth swelled. They came, after all, from a forward-thinking world, one clever enough to send them off to negotiate with a solar system that would not really be worth having as a pal for centuries. That, they knew, whistling merrily as they took up their duties, took foresight. It took brains.

If they had possessed the brains to realize just how much desperate luck they were going to need to survive their upcoming expedition, however, they might have thrown in a few prayers in between all the whistling.

"All right then," growled Captain Alexander Benjamin Valance, as he reached for what was to be the first of several large drinks, "tell me someone has discovered something to explain whatever in hell *that* was."

The *Roosevelt* had arrived at the Edilson Well far in advance of the time required for their diplomatic team's meeting with the planetary council. In their best dress uniforms, the captain and his senior staff along with the ship's resident diplomatic officers had disembarked, prepared to put the Confederation's collective best foot forward. "An unmitigated disaster of incalculable proportions" was the phrase one might use to describe their meeting with the Edilsoni who came to greet them—but then, *only* if that one were trying to put the best spin possible on the most unfortunate encounter between dissimilar species since the Log Cabin Republicans first came across the D.A.R.

"Ahhh, if you're willing to consider some non-sanctioned information, sir... "

"Meaning?"

"Meaning," answered Valance's aide in a slightly lowered voice, "data acquired from outside official circles." When the captain only stared, the look in his eyes indicating his aide should just simply speak, the woman cleared her throat, then said;

"I did a records swap with a Chambrin starsweeper a few months back. Running a search through those files, I've managed to pull up some records from a couple of freelance Embrian traders who passed through this sector a few years ago—Iggzy and Cosentino Shipping."

At first, everything had seemed swell. The planet's inhabitants turned out to be an semi-amorphous life-form. Neither male or female, the Edilsoni could, with some difficulty, stretch and remold themselves into any manner of shapes if they desired. Normally, however, they were rubbery, blue-skinned, watermelon-shaped folk who walked on three appendages roughly two to three feet in length. The melon of them—their torso as well as skull—was surrounded by three tentacle-like arms, as well as three eye-stalks, their disturbingly large mouths sprouting from the center of their heads.

"And what did these shippers report?"

The captain and the others, of course, were no strangers to aliens. They had encountered all manner of varied life forms since hitting deep space, and not once had any of them so much as raised an offending eyebrow at anyone or thing they had met. Not when they had watched the Georgths groom each other and subsequently devour their findings, or when they labored to decider the language of the Mauzrieni, the only race in the galaxy to communicate through farting. But the Edilsoni, they... well... they were different.

"Their report tallies pretty much with what we just crashed against." As the aide read through her findings, the captain and his diplomatic squad fell further into the abysmally deep funk they had brought on board with them. For a while they had been able to hold onto the hope they had simply not understood what had been happening. But, sadly, they had.

The planet Edilson possessed a singularly peculiar make-up. Much of it was formed on unstable rock. Not the kind given over to earthquakes—or edilsonquakes, if you would—but the kind that produced the type of environment found in Earthspots such as Japan or Yellowstone National Park. Edilson was, in short, one great big steam-manufacturing ball, and due to its odd rock formations, anywhere the steam leaked out, it filled the air with various streams of continual sound.

Over the millennia, the Edilsoni had cultivated these passageways, giving their planet an unending steam-driven soundtrack. They filled vents with crystals and cymbals, fashioned all manner of horns and harmonicas, even planted bamboo-like reeds where the steam could leak through, making music in every corner of their world. Of course, as one might imagine, this had more of an effect on the population than to simply dress up their days.

"There's no doubt about it, sir," said the aide hopelessly. "The Edilsoni sing and dance to make conversation. It seems they can't even understand races that simply 'talk' at them. In fact, they distrust any species that isn't comfortable doing so."

"Distrust?"

"Yes, sir," said the woman, absently as she continued to read from the stream crossing her handscreen. "Seems they even went to war with one of their in-system neighbors when they stopped up the steam vents on the grounds of their consulate here."

Captain Alexander Benjamin Valance found himself as close to despair as ever he had been since taking command of the *Roosevelt*. "Why," he thought, imploring what gods might be left in his ever-shrinking corner of the galaxy, "do these things keep happening to me?"

This was worse than when his crew had shaved the sacred monkeys of Templeworld. Or when they had conned the guards of the Pen'dwaker Holding Facility into allowing them to transform the prison into a gambling den for their Intergalactic Crap Shoot of the Millennium tournament. Or even when they had sponsored their infamous inter-species mixer where they introduced the debutante daughters of the leading politicians of the Pan-Galactic League of Suns to the various bears, cows, pigs, and chimps they were transporting to the Inter-Galaxy Zoo on Chamre XI.

It was worse than when they had stolen the *Roosevelt* and declared war on a cookie factory, more disastrous than when their pie fight had clogged the ship's protonic engines with strawberry, pineapple, and cheesecake filling, along with graham cracker crumbs, whipped creme, and rhubarb. Of course, such nonsense could not impede the performance of such mighty machines, but it did play havoc with Admiral Morey's white-glove-and-I'm-not-kidding inspection.

It was, in his opinion, worse than anything they had ever done before and most likely would do any time soon. Because, quite simply, for once his insane-as-a-flock-of-dice-addled-cephalopods crew had not done anything. He had no one upon whom he might cast the blame for this one. For once, the captain of the Roosevelt was as stuck as stuck could be, with no options in sight.

"So," he said, weakly, looking for a third highball while turning to the others in the room, those others besides himself responsible for getting the most important treaty in the history of Earth signed, "who's got any really bright ideas?"

The thundering lack of enthusiastic response did not surprise him greatly.

"Tell me again," asked Noodles, not at all certain about the wisdom involved in what he and Rocky were attempting, "why is it we're stealing a shuttle craft and heading for the surface?"

"Look, little buddy," answered the gunnery officer while he gave Quartermaster Harris the high-sign that they were ready to launch. "The captain is tied up in knots about his meetin' with these beachballs down below—right? Now, it seems gettin' these mugs on board with the Confederation is a big deal and so, I was thinkin', if we could crack whatever the big problem is, we could kinda make up for some of the little improprieties we've... well, you know . . ."

"Getting ourselves court-marshalled would probably add some small ray of happiness to the captain's otherwise present dismal outlook."

"You machinist, you're always so gloomy."

"That's only the machinists who run around with Italians."

"Look," replied Rocky, as he eased the shuttle out the side bay doors while Technician Second Class Thorner kept the perimeter radar jumbled so they might avoid detection, "we're a couple of clever guys. We figure out how to smooth things so the Confederation beats the League and all the other bozos to signin' up this bunch, and we'll be spendin' the rest of our days sittin' around swimmin' pools."

"With cleaning equipment," responded a particularly glum Noodles under his breath. He did not bother to argue further, though. Once Rocky had made his mind up on something, it was rare the machinist was ever able to talk him out of it. The reasons why he went along with said schemes were many and varied.

First, he liked Rocky and did not want to see him end up in more trouble than he could handle. Second, he was fairly certain the gunner had saved his life during one of their many drunken escapades, and so he felt a certain amount of obligation on that front as well. He also had to admit Rocky had a point. The *Roosevelt* on the whole would be in for tough times if Edilson decided to take a pass on joining the Confederation of Planets. Lastly, however, he went along with his pal's crazy plans usually because it just always turned out to be more fun doing things his way.

Machinists are a dull lot, he thought, keeping the notion as quiet within his noggin as possible. He would never admit to such a thing, of course. If questioned on the verve and vigor of his profession, he would point to the many fine activities he and the rest of the ship's tool jockeys enjoyed, from their shipwide Call of Cthulhu LARPs and their free-style origami fold-offs, to the week out of every year they lived for, their Sexy-Robot-Building Competition. Privately, he feared Intelligence Officer DiVico's assessment, "I've seen lead foil that was snappier than the average machinist," might sadly be true.

Regardless, it was but a matter of minutes after take-off that the pair of gobs found themselves loose in the capital city of the planet Edilson. After walking about more or less aimlessly for a half an hour, confident from their observation of various street signs and cafe notices that Edilson to Pan-Galactic to Earth Basic 9.8 translation was more or less working fine enough, Rocky approached a passing rubbery watermelon of an Edilsoni and asked;

"So, what's the story around here, chief?"

Bending back and forth so that all the eyes ringing its head could scrutinize the individual addressing it, the random citizen decided it had no idea what this bizarre new species wanted and, doing its best to make a motion with its shoulderless body that would translate to an alien as a confused shrug, it went about its business. The gunner gave his buddy a look meant to convey his mixture of confusion and annoyance, then tried again with the next native to pass by. The results were the same.

After that, both sailors attempted to communicate with the locals, trying this or that different idiom, working to keep their questions as simple as possible in case their problem was merely some translation difficulty. Nothing helped. Eventually, having been working on questioning a large flow of Edilsoni moving toward a stadium of sorts, they found themselves having been moved along with the flow to where they were indoors, awaiting some sort of performance. Frustrated, but hoping whatever was about to be presented on the field before them would give them some sort of clue, they managed to purchase a container of what seemed to be fried, bacon-flavored grass, and two milky fruit drinks which came in a kind of squeeze-bag affair. As they settled in, an announcer came out onto a small side stage and sang an introduction.

Since it seemed that all that he was introducing was the formal presentation from some alien world or the other to the Edilson government, the need for a tune-filled introduction struck the two humans as odd. When it turned out the aliens making the presentation were Danierians, Rocky and Noodles both began to titter with amusement. Bulbous, dour, and as exciting as a panda in fishnet stockings, the boys chuckled over how utterly awful the following would have to be.

"Danierians are gonna try and get these guys' attention," scoffed Rocky. "Now this, I'm glad I'm here ta see."

The chief gunnery officer's joy was short-lived. As he and Noodles finished off the last of their Crunchy Goodness snack pack, a troop of some four hundred Danierian warriors, outfitted in full battle gear, marched onto the field from three triangularly situated entrances. Flags unfurled, horns blaring, drums setting down an impressively unshakable cadence, the troopers met in the center of the parade ground, shouting out in their lumbering cadence as they began to file into formation;

> **"Denieria, it is our home,**
> **That roasting world, so far away,**
> **Denieria, its red sky and foam,**
> **It's the best, on any day."**

Looking first at each other, Rocky and Noodles then began to scan the crowd around them. Unlike their attempts to communicate with the Edilsoni on the streets, the Danierians were getting through to the natives. Indeed, as their simple forward marches began to intertwine, the crowd began tapping their tentacles to the martial rhythm.

> **"We're here to tell you about our world,**
> **How splendid it is, to live in peace,**
> **With Danierian banners, everywhere unfurled,**
> **And all strife and despair made to cease."**

"Noodles," asked Rocky, "is this as bad as I'm thinkin' it is?" When the machinist nodded in agreement, his partner answered, "Yeah, I was afraid of that."

> **"The galaxy is filled with lies,**
> **Other races present intentions, but disguise**
> **Their true meaning,**
> **There's no gleaning,**
> **What, oh what, is an innocent race to do?"**

Rocky shuddered, thinking he had a good idea what was about to be suggested.

> **"Face front! And join**
> **The United Coalition**
> **Of Danierian Worlds.**
> **Be a member of the winning team,**
> **It's a lone and vulnerable planet's**
> **Dream come true!**

As the marching and singing continued, Noodles was struck by how the Edilsoni were responding to the ever-more-intricate step-pattern the warriors below were developing. With every increasingly complicated side turn, with each spin of their weapons and the tossing of banners from one team to another, the native inhabitants gave out with more and louder appreciative whistling noises. And then, the warriors offered up their next-to-final chorus;

> **"Others offer chaos,**
> **We bring rules,**
> **Those who turn down order,**
> **We slaughter as fools!"**

Eliciting cheers from every corner of the arena. As the Danierian Dress Guard broke into an even tighter, and it must be said rather snappy (well, snappy for Danierians), close order drill, chanting "Go Danieria" on every left step, the Edilsoni began singing to one another and performing a variety of three-legged jigs which left the two sailors both astounded and, it had to be admitted, a touch frightened.

> **"Submit to our will,**
> **It's for your own good,**
> **Don't wonder if we kill,**
> **Just do what you should."**

"Little buddy," whispered Rocky, "I'm thinkin' we'd better get back to the *Roosevelt*. The captain's gonna wanta know about this."

"He's not going to want to know it," answered Noodles, reaching for his bag o'juice, "but he needs to."

And with that, the swabbies returned to their borrowed shuttle craft, even as the Edilsoni picked up the admittedly catchy chorus of "Submit, Submit, just do it," sending its singular message wafting out over their capital city in all directions.

"So," asked Rocky quietly, "just how much trouble are we in, captain?"

"Vespucci," sighed Valance, heavily, "you only did what you did for ship and homeworld, and you did good, so let's just say you two have a bit of credit in reserve against your next knuckleheaded shenanigan—all right?"

"Sweet deal, sir."

At that point the *Roosevelt*'s commanding officer moved into as high a gear as his hangover would permit. With confirmation of the true nature of Edilsoni communication in hand, as well as intelligence on how effective had been the Danierians singing and marching negotiation, he dismissed the two gobs while ordering a channel opened to Earth High Command at once. Quickly outlining his overwhelmingly insurmountable problem, his desperate honesty was rewarded with the worst type of military logic.

Since his was the only ship in the area, the mission was still his. And, since he was the ranking officer, he and his diplomatic staff would simply have to dance and sing their way into the hearts of the planetary government and win the day. In the meantime, while Valance and his command staff were reduced to trying to form a not-completely-painful-to-listen-to barbershop quartet, Rocky and Noodles headed for the galley to wash down their planetside snacks with something a little more substantial than milk juice.

"Listen," said Noodles, after finishing his fourth tall and frosty mug of something-more-substantial, "you know, I wonder what the captain's going to do."

"Not our concern," answered his pal. "Hey, we're heroes for once. Little tiny minor heroes, sure. But, considerin' the esteem we're usually held in around here, I'll take it."

The machinist nodded, non-commitally. Rocky was right. The two of them had pushed their luck within the bounds of Navy regs to an extreme not seen since a drunken Admiral Chester William Nimitz had attempted to steer an aircraft carrier up the Venetian canals in search of a combination pizza parlor/chianti distributor/bordello he had been assured by Enrico Curuso was "really primo." Still, it was not in the machinist's internal make-up to simply allow nature to take its course. Running his finger around the inside of his mug to get the last delightful bits of foam, he licked up the delicious residue, then said;

"So, you think the captain can handle things?"

"Well, sure," answered Rocky automatically. Draining his own mug, he added with an equal lack of thought, "the captain's aces. Ain't he got us outta every mess we ever got ourselves into? He don't ever need any help—he's always got the answer."

"Not to be contrary, Rock, but... if the captain didn't ever need any help, then he wouldn't need a crew."

It was not so much Noodles' words, but the tone with which he delivered them that caught the gunnery officer's attention. Squinting hard, as if that might instantly negate the effects of his own eight tall portions of more-substantial, Rocky finally answered;

"You mean, you think the captain maybe can't handle singin' these guys into the Confederation?"

"Do you remember his trying to teach Christmas carols to those kids back on Embri?" The gunner shuddered at the memory, his fingers unconsciously reaching up to his ears to see if they were bleeding.

"So," asked Rocky, fairly certain he knew the answer he would receive, "you're sayin' that ah... you want us to steal a shuttle on the same day we already stole one shuttle, and then use said shuttle to head back down to the planet so we can interfere with the most important mission the *Roosevelt* was ever given?"

"Yeah—you want'a?"

"Hey," answered the gunner, grinning from ear to ear, "does the Buddha drink Mint Juleps?"

"Isn't that usually my line?"

"Ahhhh, tell it to the board of inquiry."

"Oh yeah," laughed Noodles. "Good thinking."

And, with no other pints of more-substantial in sight, the two swabbies got down to planning their course of action.

In all honesty, Captain Valance would never have believed it was possible for four people to sweat so intently. Indeed, the puddle growing around his feet, as well as those of the Roosevelt's intelligence officer, her diplomatic attaché, and the ship's doctor, was spreading with such vigor, it left the Edilsoni to wonder if the human contingent might not actually be melting. To be fair, the makeshift quartet had tried their darnest, calling upon the spirit of a thousand long-sung sea chanteys to aid them in their hour of desperation.

Sadly, though, King Neptune had not seen fit to shower them with any such bounty. In fact, it had to be admitted that their feeble attempts to harmonize had failed so miserably that the Edilsoni's visceral reaction to their singing was the only thing that kept the aliens from noticing how utterly terrible the humans' lyrics were. Finally, when the four paused for a breath at the same moment, although it was obvious they had only covered a third of their points, the Edilsoni prime minister practically fell over his podium as he leaped forward to interrupt, asking if that concluded the Earth Confederation's presentation. Valance was just about to throw in the proverbial towel, considering losing the planet and his commission favorable to provoking interstellar warfare, when suddenly a shout was heard from the back of the amphitheater.

> "If you kind and noble Edilsoni will permit,
> I'd like to step up, while you sit... ,"

As Valance stared in disbelief, he saw Machinist First Mate Li Qui Kon actually doing a handy little two-step, making his way in between the central two rows of spectators down toward the staging area where he and his fellow officers had been dying by inches.

> **"And discuss with you the ramifications,**
> **Of inter-galactic political integrations."**

Reaching the captain and his officers, Rocky urged them to vacate the stage, telling them in an exaggerated stage whisper;

"Don't worry, sir. I think he knows what he's doin'."

"But Vespucci," answered Valance, "singing and dancing... a machinist?"

"With all due respect, a *Chinese* machinist, sir."

> **"There are species descended from fish and bugs,**
> **Others that crawled up from oozing slugs,**
> **Some came from birds and some from rats,**
> **Insects, clams, giraffes and bats,"**

"Chinese moms, sir," added Rocky. "How'd he say it? They expect their kids to... well, they have to be a credit to their family."

> **"And they're all fine, in their own way,**
> **But they're kind of singular, I must say,**
> **Bred for a certain uni... form... ity,**
> **They lack that one human odd... i... ty."**

"Mrs. Kon, you see . . ."

> **"The thing that makes us the ones to choose,**
> **That quality that guarantees you never lose,**
> **It's our single greatest facility...**
> **Our hard-won, irritating...**
> **"Un... pre... dic... ta... bility!"**

"She wanted an entertainer in the family."

And then, at a hand signal from Noodles, waiting in a lurkercraft hidden in the clouds, Technician Second Class Thorner began their free-air music broadcast, as well as sending down a blinding purple spotlight, illuminating the machinist in an iridescent glow as he warbled—

"Oh, everything's better with monkeys,
We're the best bet in the show,
I'm certain you're getting a lot of offers,
But trust me, simian's the way to go."

While Noodles spun around, setting himself up for the next stanza, Rocky caught the captain's ear once more, telling him;

"Five years of tap and jazz dance, six of voice training, and apparently eight years of piano which, from what he says, were a really serious mistake."

"Yes everything's better with monkeys,
They're curious, funny, and true,
They'll stand by your side, go along for a ride,
And they'll make sure you get what you're due."

As Noodles went into a complicated dance routine, one that seemed to Rocky he had seen in a revival of "My Fair Lady," the two of them had been lured into by promises of a different type of entertainment, the gunnery officer and his captain began to notice that the crowd was responding favorably to the performance. Indeed, those who had been previously fleeing from the caterwauling of Valance and his officers actually seemed to be returning to their seats. While the captain dangerously tempted Fate by allowing his hopes to rise from actual imprisonment to a simple court-martial, Rocky sent the signal to Mac Michaels up above with Thorner to both turn up the music and begin the fountain of lights display. As the crowd began to "aaaaahhhhhhhhh" in synchronized harmony, Noodles went into his big finish.

"Yes, we earthlings, we make mistakes,
We've got our bad eggs, who will always disgrace,
We spill our own blood, and we're not always smart,
But the one thing I can assure you is...
The human race has... got... heart!"

And then, in that instant, even as the entire ship's company of the *Roosevelt* Machinist's Saturday Evening LARP Society surrounded the stage, decked in full costume from their upcoming Bambi versus Godzilla extravaganza, accompanied by all the final entries in the Sexiest Robot of All Time competition, all around the stadium Edilsoni began to jump up from their seats. Unable to restrain themselves, the rotund aliens began humming and dancing, slapping tentacles, spinning on their mouths, and in short throwing themselves with total abandon into the fierce joy of Noodle's song.

"We're not perfect,
We don't claim to be,
Hell what do you expect?
Twenty thousand years ago,
We were all still monkeys!

"But you can trust me, you can trust that fact,
'Cause even after all this time,
You throw crap at us,
And I guarantee...
We'll throw it right back!"

The captain, of course, could only be overjoyed by the obvious shift in the average Edilsonian attitude toward humanity. But Rocky was set to wondering. He had seen the response the natives had shown the Danierians. They had gotten into the rhythm of things, had seemed ready to sign on to the program, so to speak. But, the reaction to Noodle's presentation was overwhelming. The aliens were actually dropping down onto the stadium grounds and rushing the stage, eager to join the machinists' newly forming macarana formation.

"But we'll stand at your side,
We'll be there at the end,
We make lousy dictators,
But we make really good friends.

"Yes, everything's better with monkeys,
The bad ones mixed in with the good,
So, show a little trust, but keep your eye on us,
And everything—
I'm saying just everything—
Will work out, as it... sshhhoooouuuulllidddddd!"

And in that moment, as Noodles dropped to one knee and delivered the greatest display of jazz hands since Bob Fosse starred in "The Al Jolson Story," the long unfathomed secret of the Edilsoni came to light. Although the race *could* communicate through speech, they were *actually* a telepathic species, one bound by a hive mentality. As the native population cheered, not just there in the capital city's stadium, but across every continent, in every corner of the planet, their human guests' minds were suddenly filled with billions of voices, all of them sharing in the wonder that was the unquestionable uniqueness of the human race.

"Do you get it, Vespucci," shouted the captain, straining to be heard over the multitudinous ringing within his mind, "the Edilsoni have rejected every offer that's come their way because no one else has ever opened up completely to them!"

"Jiminy," answered Rocky, still a little befuddled over exactly what had happened, being distracted as he was by coordinating the start of the *Roosevelt* fireworks display, "I didn't think his song was that good."

"It's not the song," cried Valance, tears streaming down his face as an utterly alien race's reflected understanding of the true nobility of the human spirit washed through his mind, "it's not the song."

What happened over the next few days became somewhat of a blur in the intergalactic news items out of the Kebb Quadrant, the official reports sent from the *Roosevelt* back to the Confederation, and to be honest, in the minds of most of the ship's crew. That last, however, had more to do with the planet-wide party spontaneously thrown by every individual on Edilson than with any deficiency in the human ability to comprehend the situation.

Distrustful of aliens who masked their true intent, the Edilsoni had turned down every offer of alliance over the two hundred years since first contact. Understanding better than any others the upcoming importance of their world, they had kept communications open with all, dangling the hope of eventual alliance with one world, or league, or whatever, to keep any one of them from invading.

"Four hundred of your years," their prime minister eventually sang to Valance, "is not a great deal of time, galactically speaking, but it did give us some room in which to maneuver."

They had responded as well as they had to the Danierians because, vicious and cruel as that race might be, at least they were honest about it. Their warriors had held nothing back emotionally on the field, and for once someone had shown the Edilsoni true intent. Luckily, as the prime minister was happy to admit, someone else had come along and done the same who had something better to show.

The surprise hit of the negotiations, or whatever one would call the drunken insanity that had transpired on Edilson, had been the trio of

Thorner, Harris, and Michaels, who had taken to the stage in their dress kilts to not only sing the Scottish ballad, the Blue Ribbon song, but to show off the fact that the Edilsoni were not the only sentient beings around who walked on three legs. Valance had been mortified at first, but the riotous response of the natives to the spontaneous gesture had been so positive the captain had been given no choice other than to return to attempting to drink the prime minister under the table.

In the end, the Confederation of Planets got the wished-for deal with Edilson. Valance was showered with praise from Earth Central, which he translated into as much shore leave and good favor as he possibly could for his crew. The next issue of the Monthly Newsletter of the Grand Gaggle of Confederation Machinists tripled in size and, once the ship's doctor had been able to synthesize enough Hangover-B-Gone, the crew of the *Roosevelt* had been able to finally remember how to break orbit and set a course that did not skew to a basanova beat.

Heroes all, loved and admired by an entire world, showered with gifts, the men and women of the *Roosevelt* set off for whatever the universe had in store for them next. The Edilsoni could tell the earthlings were reluctant to leave, and yet somehow eager to be on to whatever came next, and loved them all the more for it. But, beyond that display of all-too-human confusion of purpose, beyond everything they had heard and felt and learned of the gorilla-spawn who had won their hearts, there was one single moment that gave them greater insight than any other.

Being a collective species, having no actual experience with the idea of male or female, sons and daughters, or any of the other mammalian building blocks of individuality, nothing revealed more to the Edilsoni about their human visitors than when the prime minister met privately with Noodles. Asking the machinist what boon he might ask for his part in that which a united Edilson believed was the cementing of their security for the next four centuries, offering him anything the wealth and might of an entire planetary treasury might secure, the sailor asked if he might send a real-time message.

Yes, Noodles explained, he could send notes to Earth via the *Roosevelt*, but because of the distance they could take months, sometimes *years* to reach their intended destination. He did not want to send anything exceedingly long, he told them, just a few words. Understanding his request, touched to the core of what he had thought until meeting human beings was an emotionless heart beating within his breast, the prime minister not only agreed, but without the machinist's knowledge, he sent his own note as well.

Which is why, while the U.S.S. *Roosevelt* broke orbit and headed back out to their next destination in the stars, on the planet Earth, at 12/17 Seloon Street in one of the quieter corners of Canton, China, Mrs. Xiu Yue Kon received two messages. One that read;

"Thanks, Mom."

And a second that read;

"Yes, good Earthwoman, thank you, indeed."

It was so obvious that no one could see it against the mundane backdrop of life, and even at that, one had to be dragged to the point of understanding, and forced to accept the truth. But now that you know the truth, can you convince anyone else of it? After all, it's just a highway...right?

EXIT 14

> "Where ignorance is bliss,
> 'Tis folly to be wise."
> Thomas Gray

YOU HAVE TO BELIEVE ME, HAVE TO UNDERSTAND... I, I MEAN, I DIDN'T WANT to know this. Not any of this. I didn't expect, I was just trying... wanted to figure it all out, explain how it could happen again and again, over and over, with nobody ever noticing. I mean nobody... questioning or complaining or commenting, even. Ever. Day after day, every *single* day, work days or weekends or holidays—and at any time... four o'clock in the morning, it just didn't matter—

It didn't make sense. At least...

Not at first.

I mean, all right, yeah, sure... it's not like nobody ever said anything. I guess, really, people were complaining. But they did it in the way they complained about anything. About taxes. About the homeless. Their boss, their favorite sports team... they would talk about it, make the angry, inpatient sounds of the modern era, but then they would just lump whatever they were going off about in with one of the ten score other massive injustices which were tormenting their lives.

Blathering, ignorant morons. Unconscious, unaware. Each and every one of them just another part of the smug sea of humanity, all nothing more than cells in a barely conscious hive mind that laughingly believe there is something special about them.

There isn't, you know. Anything special about anybody, I mean. It's all a sham. Oh, I don't mean the mindless congratulatory culture, fourth grade graduations treated like the bestowing of Ph.Ds... although that is a part of it, of course. The ordinarying of the human race. The pacification, vanilliation, dumb-bruting, downward spiraling of mankind, all proceeding right on schedule. And there's not a thing to be done. That's the problem, it's already too late. It's over. They're everywhere. They—

Wait... I'm sorry. I'm rambling. I can see the words I'm typing, after all, I do realize just how crazy they must make me sound. Of course, considering that they say insanity is simply believing something no one else believes, I suppose I must be insane—perhaps the most insane person on the planet. Because, believe me, there's no convincing anyone to see things my way. There is no way to believe what I've come to believe, what I was forced to believe by all that I've seen.

And, trust me, I had to be forced. There's no way I could have made up something like this. I had to stumble across it. Had to have it shoved in my face. And even then, like Thomas, I had to be grabbed by the hand and have my fingers pulled forward and shattered in the blood of the inevitable before I could comprehend this nightmare upon which I have stumbled.

See, no preposition at the end of that sentence. Could a crazy man do that? Come to think of it, maybe only crazy people do that to begin with. And that's my point. Merely choose to follow an older sense of communication as the one which is proper, and already you're on the road to crazy. People are so quick to judge. To dismiss.

To ignore.

Not that I'm anyone special. I was like that, too. But then I found all the missing pieces in front of me for no more than the slightest of moments, but that was enough, just that one, singular instance was all that was needed to knock my vision sideways. I see things differently now. Like when as a child you finally realize the policeman is not your friend, or that someone has sex with the teacher you simply adored in the third grade. The world views we assemble for ourselves shatter with each new level of reality we encounter. That's what I'm trying to tell you.

I've seen the only one that matters.

And again, I can hear myself, can gauge the level of instability I must be projecting. So, allow me to pause, to collect myself. To try and explain. And yes, I know I already stated that I don't believe that I can convince anyone of my story, and that even if I do manage to find someone who might be willing to accept my story, that I don't believe there is any hope left to us as a race. But still, it's always possible that I might be wrong. That somehow we could...

No. I'm forcing myself to stop. Enough is enough. I'm simply going to tell you what happened to me, and then, I simply don't care what happens after that.

My story starts roughly eleven years ago. My son had managed to earn for himself a full scholarship to Providence's prestigious Brown University.

My wife and I were, as you must suspect, wonderfully pleased—both for him and ourselves. He had always been headed to the medical profession, and we had determined to find the means to make this happen for him, no matter what the hardships might be which accompanied such a task. To learn that he had not only been able to attend the school of his choice, but to do so for free, it was the greatest of weights lifted from our shoulders. We would not have to mortgage our futures, work endlessly past the retirement age.

My wife and I had married later than most, had our son later still. One loves their children and wants to do everything possible for them, but the practical considerations of life can weigh quite heavily at times. To have that burden removed had left us giddy, and we had celebrated his good fortune as if it were our own, because partially, it was.

Living in New York State, we fell into a comfortable pattern concerning our son's visits. He would come home via the bus or train, or crowding into a car with some of his friends, for a weekend or holiday visit. When it was time to return, I would drive him back. My wife suffered from a frailness which made long drives most uncomfortable for her. Thus, our son would dote on his mother when home, and then we would enjoy our time together on the way back. I loved those drives, and the fact that I would have an equal amount of hours in the car alone afterwards never concerned me. It was our routine, and I looked forward to it.

My wife's passing came quite unexpectedly. She had always made her yearly visits to the doctor, dutifully submitted herself to whatever tests were recommended. None of them caught the embolism which would take her from me. It was, as they say when there is nothing else left, simply one of those things.

But, it was also the intersection of coincidences which prompted my discovery. Alone, suddenly, I found myself with far more time to think. To reflect and wonder. Things dismissed earlier now stayed within my mind. After all, I had far fewer distractions to displace them. And, the one thing I began to wonder about with increasing frequency was my drive to Providence and back. Or, more specifically, about one specific segment of it... the three miles of Interstate 95 in Connecticut leading to Exit 14.

What had captured my attention was this. When driving toward this particular section of interstate, every time, every single time, when I reached the Connecticut border, one of those large black, electric lightboards would flash the warning that one should expect delays between exits 11 through 14. Every time. They were always there. The delays, I mean. Waiting for me.

Sometimes you would think there might not be any delay. Despite what the sign was flashing, you would think, there couldn't be a delay, I'm traveling too fast. You see, Interstate 95, at least in Connecticut, is intelligently marked. The exits are numbered in proper distances. What I mean is, as you enter the state, if you're getting off at an exit three miles across the border, it will be Exit 3. Go another fifty-five miles, and the exit will be Exit 58. So, if you're roaring along at seventy miles an hour as you whiz by Exit 9, and the sign warns you to "expect delays starting at Exit 11, you'd be justified to think that you were not going to find a major slow down only two miles ahead. You would be wrong. Often times, I would be going more than seventy miles an hour, just like all the other cars around me. At Exit 9, at Exit 10, onward, another quarter mile, and another, another, and then—

Bang. Stop. A wall of cars, not moving, or only crawling forward. Beginning exactly at the off-ramp of Exit 11. Every time. Every time I drove up 95, "expect delays from Exit 11 thru Exit 14." And, at the exact spot where Exit 11 began, not halfway between 11 and 12, not five hundred feet before 11, not anything else at all. Never. Not once. Right at the beginning of Exit 11, traffic would rush to a crawl. Stop in its tracks. And drag its way to Exit 14.

And then, even more strangely, once Exit 14 was finally reached, then traffic would resume its top speed. Never was there something that might explain the delay. No accidents. No construction. Nor was there ever something for the idiot horde to rubberneck over—some poor soul pulled over by a state trooper getting a ticket, or a set of cars that had just been in an accident waiting for the police. Maybe a stalled vehicle waiting for a tow truck. Perhaps someone changing a flat tire. A flock of deer. A fire. Bigfoot.

Something.

But no, not once. Never was their anything to justify the routine slowdown. And, after a while, that wasn't the only spot. Other sections of 95 were beset with the same insanity. Every few months, another three, four mile section would erupt in the same unexplainable nonsense.

Once my wife was no longer with me, no longer there to comfort me, to distract my obsessions, to sympathize and thus lessen my anger at the monstrousness of the world, I began, I must admit, to obsess over these pockets of entropy. Finally, after my son's Christmas visit had come to a close and we were to head back to Providence once more, I determined to study the three miles of 95 when we encountered the usual slow down. I would put forth a true effort to see if there was something to the curve of the road which so frightened drivers that they had to slow to a crawl. Or, something about the design of Exit 14 that it forced people to cut across traffic to reach it.

These were, of course, fairly trite attempts at an explanation, but I found myself boiling over with a need to understand this impossibility and, well... I had to start somewhere. And so, when we reached Exit 11, I watched, I inspected, I studied. And I found nothing.

I created reasons over the next few weekends to visit my son, always careful to make them casual drop-ins, claiming it did me good to just get out of the house. I would take him out to eat, stuff a few twenties in his shirt pocket and wink about every young man's need for beer money, and then head off. I made the visits as short as possible so as not to annoy him since, after all, I really wasn't making the drives to see him, but to have a reason to pass through the Connecticut Triangle as I began to call it. After a while, I didn't bother with the trip the rest of the way to Rhode Island. I would simply pass through Exits 11 through 14, turn around at Exit 15, and then go back through them again. Sometimes I might make the circle more than once. One weekend I made the circle seventeen times in a row.

And every time, the same thing happened. I would reach the edge of Exit 11 and traffic would slow to a crawl, only to rush back up to normal speed the instant Exit 14 had been passed. And that was when I couldn't take it any more.

I was moving forward, approaching Exit 11 for the eighteenth time in a row. Circling from Exit 10, I moved forward as I had every other time that day, and then, as I saw the half mile warning, I began to slow. Moving over to the extreme right lane, I decelerated to fifty miles an hour, then forty-five, forty, thirty, twenty...

Cars honked all around me, swerving, throwing themselves forward, their drivers cursing me, shaking their fists. What did it matter, I wondered, staring forward, watching in horror as the traffic began to slow. Everyone that had damned me, braking, drawing to a halt, surrendering to the inevitable. And suddenly, I could not bear to be a part of it once more.

Pulling off the road, I shut down my motor and simply stared, watching as car after car jammed on its brakes and joined the mindless, unexplainable crawl forward. My mind raced as I watched the creeping traffic, desperately attempting to find some reason, some explanation. Of course, it could not, but as the chatter within my mind continued, I noticed something I had not before. Yes, every time I had driven to that spot, even before trying to find an answer had become an obsession, when it was just a pattern I had observed, I had wondered about it.

As I sat there, watching the traffic flow slowly past my position, I realized that for the first time, I was really thinking about what was going on. I remembered that I had always meant to study the area, to try and explain the phenomenon, but once I had passed the Exit 11 sign, I... I hadn't. Not really. Somehow, it had become... unimportant. In fact, as I sat behind my wheel, staring, I realized that I had never before really thought about what the answer might be.

I know... I know it doesn't sound like I'm making sense. I... I don't know how to explain it. It's just that... when I was actually in between Exits 11 and 14, suddenly... knowing what was going on just didn't matter anymore. Not until I had passed through to the other side.

Then, as I would hit the gas and begin rolling along once more, the standard responses would flow. Anger at the delay. Furious cursing of the idiots who must have caused it. Disgruntled, self-righteous, pissed off—not knowing the reason, not caring, glad it was over, that it had been endured—

And then, my mind filled with horror. Indeed, that had been the pattern. Suddenly, it all became clear. Driving up to Exit 11, first there would be the dread—here it comes again. No escape, doomed to relive the pattern, why can't anything be done... then, driving into the void, the empty waste between 11 and 14, and every thing would change. Focus would crash inward, concentration would be completely on maneuvering my vehicle. Total absorption in the task of driving.

It was insanity, I realized, to be driving one-handed, relying on forty-five years of experience to move along at seventy miles an hour, and then to suddenly be gripping the wheel and watching all the cars around me as if I were in a death race when I was moving no more than five, ten miles an hour at best.

What was happening, I wondered. What in the name of God was wrong with that accursed spot?

Suddenly my Connecticut Triangle label seemed more than slightly appropriate. It rang with a terrifying truth, one that left me sweating, filled with fear as I sat quietly along the side of the road. It took me nearly ten minutes after my revelation to realize I was gripping the steering wheel as if I were hanging off the side of a building. As I unclenched my hands, I found I had dug my nails into my palms so deeply I had drawn blood. My fingers were cramped and sore, white from the tension.

I thought to get out of my car, to walk along the road, to go past the exit sign and move in tandem with the crawling lanes, to see if I might notice something I could not from behind the wheel. What I thought I might notice, I had no idea. Nor did I find out. Tired, frightened, I instead started my car and turned off at Exit 11, cutting back to the on-ramp for 95 West. Drained, defeated, I turned and ran, slinking off to what I imagined was the safety of my home.

But, as the wise man said, we can't go home again.

I made it back to my domicile, but it would never again be my home, a place of safety. There was no security anymore. I had no reason for believing such, but I knew it was true. I did not know how I knew it, could not prove the idea, but from the moment I pointed my car back toward New York and ran away, I knew deep in my soul that my life had changed forever.

Pulling off at the rest stop only a handful of miles down the road, I parked in the shadow of the McDonald's there, closing my eyes and hiding in the darkness. Sliding down onto the seat, I lie there for I don't know how long before I started sobbing. I don't know how long I did so, or when I stopped. By the time I sat up again, it was dark, and I was numb.

Tired of my fear, tired of caring, I started my car and drove home. I have little memory of that journey—how fast I drove, what the traffic or the weather were like—no mundane facts come to mind no matter how hard I try to recall them. All I know is, when I reached my home I felt a terrible shame. How soft had I become, I wondered. Just how useless was I that I could allow something as simple as a traffic slowdown to turn me into a bawling coward?

Yes, it was unusual. Yes, there were things about it that might go beyond coincidence. But still, I asked myself, had anything actually happened to me? Had I been in any danger? Had there been some sort of threat presented to my well-being? The answer, of course, was "no." I had simply collapsed. Folded at the first sign of... of what? Danger? Trouble? What kind of danger?

Other parts of my brain worked to remind me of the staggering impossibility of everything I had seen and done being some sort of colossal coincidence. There had to be some sort of... of *something* happening. Sunspots, mass hypnosis, leprechauns... something.

And, as I dragged myself through my front door, embarrassed at my cowardice in running away from *nothing*, I determined in that moment that I would not rest until I understood what was going on along Interstate 95.

Which means that was the moment that my life, for all intents and purposes, officially ended.

I started, as anyone might, by searching out anecdotal evidence. Meaning simply, I went to the Internet, I talked to my friends, to my co-workers, to relatives—to anyone, actually—searching for those who might have ever experienced the same thing. I found them.

The Internet was actually filled with sites mentioning the same phenomenon. And it was everywhere. Stories came from every continent that had roads, from every country. Even Germany, even on the Autobahn, the world's fastest highway, there were spots that jammed that could not be explained. Not by departments of transportation, not by scientists. Not by anyone.

And, as for the people I spoke to directly, those I was able to interview in person, when I asked them if they could relate to what I was describing... they could. All of them. Oh, some could only recall this or that monstrous traffic jam, a snarl caused by a horrendous accident, or endless constructions, and there was nothing wrong in that being their only conscious memory. But, many of them, most of them, in truth, knew what I meant. Had been there. Had stories of their own to tell.

Many, of course, had travelled Interstate 95, had been as inexplicably slowed for the same three miles as myself. Many had other spots to tell me about. Indeed, so many mentioned a several mile stretch of the Staten Island Expressway I was forced to see it for myself. It was far closer to my home than the area I had been questioning folks about. I told myself, if I was looking for proof that there was something damned odd going on in the world, here was possible evidence only a handful of miles from my home.

It was, of course, a perfectly obvious next move, to drive over to Staten Island and witness this reported spot for myself. My brain practically shouted at me, waiting for me to go, puzzling over why I didn't immediately head for my car. It took me almost a week, but I finally realized that I was not heading over the Verrenzano Bridge for one very important reason—

I was terrified.

It came to me while I was shaving. As I stared into the mirror at my face, watching my hand move, scraping away the foam and whisker bits, I caught a look at my eyes and I saw it—fear. White knuckled terror was squeezing my chest, robbing me of breath and nerve. I stared at myself, at my two-thirds shaved face, into my eyes, and there was suddenly no doubt as to why I had not driven to Staten Island. I did not want to. I did not want proof I was right. I did not want to know that I was not crazy.

And why would I? Why would anyone? Do you understand what that moment meant to me? Can you possibly find a instance in your own life to compare? How can I even explain the fact that I did not want to be right, that I wanted to be insane? Because, if I was not, then what I had been accepting as a truth would *actually* be true.

And, in the moment of that realization, I knew I was correct. I knew. Shaving the rest of my face, I finished dressing and, instead of walking down the street to the subway so I might head to work, instead I walked to my car and drove to Staten Island. Coming off the bridge, I headed directly for the expressway and drove to the other end of the island, and then turned around and headed back toward Brooklyn.

I circled at Exit 5 and joined the flow of vehicles, thinking at first that I had perhaps made a bad choice. Of course, I told myself, traffic was snarled. It was rush hour on a weekday. I was in traffic headed toward Manhattan. Of course things were moving slowly. For a moment, I was almost relieved.

And then, I reached Exit 11—Bradley Avenue. Everyone that mentioned this particular slow down agreed, it was here that the crawl ceased and things began moving forward once more. And, as it had been described by so many, it happened. Granted, the rush hour traffic still moved slowly forward, but as Exit 11 was passed, the barely moving parade began to pick up speed. Tears formed within my eyes as the speedometer moved from barely above zero up to the "10." I pulled off at Exit 13, found a diner, and went inside.

I wanted to eat to make certain I wasn't imagining things due to low blood sugar. I also wanted to be with other people. Even if I wasn't talking to anyone, didn't know any of them… they were people, after all. There was comfort in that. And, while I ate, I formulated a plan.

I would wait an hour, and then repeat the experiment. I would spend the day going through the same spot, at regular intervals, and compare them one to another. I had started in the morning rush hour. I would gauge the difference between that and the mid-morning lull, the noontime rush, the afternoon shopper's spree, the evening rush hour, as well as 8:00 and 9:00 and every hour after until…

Well, of course, I didn't know what would constitute "until," but it didn't matter. You have to understand, I was barely in control then. Even assembling that much of a plan within my mind took all my will power. Indeed, when the waitress brought me my check, I managed to somehow thank her, but when she laid the bill there before me, I froze as my mind fell into despair over its consequences.

You have to understand, turning the check over meant knowing how much it was for. Knowing that implied it was time to get out my wallet so I might pay it. Realizing that meant it was time to stand. Time to walk to the cashier. Time to leave. Time to get out on the road and prove what I already knew.

I couldn't. I couldn't do it. My legs, when I tried to stand, merely trembled. I knew I was strong enough to rise, that there was nothing physical wrong with me. But, I could not stand. Could not bear the thought of proving the existence of another Triangle. Proving it. That was the part I could not bear—the absolute knowledge that there was an actual phenomenon. That something was happening.

But what, I asked myself? What could it be? How could such a thing be possible? Was it sunspots, some sort of inter-dimensional waver, spectral energy from vengeful ghosts...

Somehow, while my brain threw one random insanity after another at me, I managed to pay for my meal, leave the building, and enter my car. Sitting behind the wheel, key in the ignition, hand ready to turn it, seat belt in place, I stared through the windshield, slitting my eyes against the quite bright morning sun, seeing nothing.

Finally, however, I did drive away, heading back to the expressway, driving west so I could turn around and drive east. I did it then, and again at noon. And again between lunchtime and the evening rush hour. And again after that. And again. And again. The staff at the diner began to notice my frequent meals. I can't imagine what they thought I might be up to. How could I, when I really didn't know myself.

When finally I drove past Exit 12, headed for home, I felt numb. Drained of all vitality. Empty and alone. I had made the trip from Exit 5 to Exit 11 some ten times. That had been enough. Whatever was going on in Connecticut, in Dusseldorf and Entfield and Rio, in Toronto and outside of Phoenix and everywhere else I had read about, was also going on in Staten Island. Something was causing drivers to slow to a crawl for a few miles—at any time of the day or night—for no apparent reason.

It was true. I had my proof. The only thing was, proof of what? So it happened. So hundreds and thousands of people were willing to swear it was a common occurrence around the world. So what? What did it prove? What did it mean? Why should anyone care?

After a while on Staten Island, I had begun to feel the same crawling noise within the back of my mind I had felt on Interstate 95. More than once, when I would reach the center of the disturbance, I would begin to hear, or feel, as it were, a kind of chatter in the back of my brain, a garbled static the meaning of which I couldn't really figure out.

After I got home, I thought on that fact for quite some time, finally determining that the next day I would have to simply return to Connecticut, to the spot where the communication or whatever it was had been strongest, and see if I could find a way to enhance it. Make it stronger. Hear it clearly.

At first I thought to head straight there, and might have actually done so if I had not gone to the bathroom first. As I was cleaning my hands, I happened to notice my reflection in the mirror. If I thought the image I had seen when shaving was disturbing, I was horrified at the trembling mask which confronted me then.

I had become a creature completely composed of fear. My eyes were etched with terror, sunken, bagged by dark circles. My cheeks seemed sunken, my lips trembling. My hair, obviously unwashed for days, soaked with sweat, was tangled in stringy bundles—wild and disgusting. For a moment, I wondered how bad had I looked in the diner? How crazy must I have appeared to the staff? To the others around me?

Sitting down on the toilet, I buried my face in my hands and cried. It was not a noisy bawling, but simply a release of sorrow, a giving in to the terror and self-pity it inspired. After a while I finally stood, stripped away my clothing and then stepped into the shower. Making the water increasingly hotter, I showered for some long time, soaping myself from head to toe, using the bar to wash my hair as well as the rest of me. In some way I think I believed for a moment that simply making myself clean might change my outlook, my view of what I had come to realize.

It didn't.

When I left the shower I didn't bother to dry myself. I simply walked to my living room, stretched out on my couch and went to sleep. When I awoke, I knew it was time to leave for Connecticut. I didn't listen to my messages. Didn't have breakfast. Didn't fix myself a travel mug of coffee. Nothing mattered. Nothing but heading for the mid-way point between Exits 11 and 14 on Interstate 95 and trying to figure out what was behind the impossibility I seemed to have discovered.

Dragging on the first clean clothes I discovered, I returned to my car and numbly situated myself behind the wheel. An hour and three quarters later, I had reached my destination. Of course, traffic had slowed to a crawl at Exit 11. It had to, didn't it. As I pulled off the road onto the shoulder, I placed my car in park, turned off my engine, and then sat. Quietly. Preparing myself.

The first thing I did to prepare myself for what I felt had to come next was to take hold of the one thing that I had brought with me—a bottle of Jack Daniels. I looked around for a moment, feeling somewhat stupid, then finally tilted my seat back a bit. Reclining, I closed my eyes and settled in to try and relax. The small part of my brain still capable of trying to relate to the real world thought this was a good idea—making myself appear to simply be a weary traveler might keep the helpful or the law from disturbing me.

And then, once I had assumed the position, I tilted back the bottle and drank as much as I could in one swallow. I am not what you would call much of a drinker which I was hoping would work in my favor. I had been so tense, so wound up for so long, I was hoping that a goodly amount of alcohol, coupled with the fact I had not eaten since the night before, might allow me to clear my mind for the task ahead. After two more good belts, I recapped the bottle, dropped it into the back seat, then settled in to see what might happen next.

At first I was afraid I might simply pass out. From the fear and stress and exhaustion, but I didn't. I didn't fall asleep—instead, I listened. Not to the noise of the passing motorists or the occasional sound of the breeze. No, I listened to the sounds beyond, past the walls of normal hearing. I listened for anything that might guide me to whatever it was that held the answer to the insanity around me. I closed my eyes… allowed my mind to drift… and listened. And eventually, I heard something.

Far in the distance, beyond the limits of my conscious mind, I began to get a sense of what was happening. Had been happening. Would continue to happen. I can not explain how I know the following other than to say that I had traveled the segment of 95 that I had so often, not merely passing through it, but studying it, listening to it, observing, hoping to understand, attempting to pierce the veil, that finally, my mind made contact with another mind—or, I believe more correctly, a race of minds—which views us as nothing more than a food source.

Somehow, pockets of entropy have been set up throughout our world. I can not explain how they work, or to where they transport whatever it is they steal from us. I did not see everything I needed to answer my questions during my vision, but I saw enough.

Somewhere, out beyond that which we know, there is a race that visited our planet in the past. The "ancient astronauts" of which so much has been made. When I brushed against their group mind, apparently it amused them that I had done so, and in the way you or I might use a slice of celery to reward a gerbil that made its way through a maze, the consciousness I reached shared our past with me, chuckling as it did so.

Every wild and stupid thing you've ever heard about our evolution being controlled by aliens... it's true. I'm not certain if life started here without their intervention, but we were given most everything that followed by them. They would come in from time to time and give us whatever we were ready for next—agriculture, irrigation, religion, city states, fermentation, whatever. Our history has moved in bumps and starts because we have been allowed to develop as we would while they were gone, but when they returned they would simply impose their latest set of dictates and get us moving in the direction they needed us to move in once more.

Most of the ancient past was a blur to me. I was allowed to see just enough to give me the idea. But, their last period of time spent here came through most clearly. They returned in the very early seventies, and were not happy with our progress. They had not expected us to advance to the skies, let alone outside of our atmosphere. That was a direct challenge to their authority. They didn't like that.

Flooding our minds with the fright and self-interest they had used so often before, they crushed our dreams of leaving the planet, of expanding outward—of ever being more than what they wished us to be. Exerting their influence, they turned us back to the crippling notions of brotherhood once more, diverting our concentration toward the insanity of caring for every crippled starveling rather than attempting to push ourselves forward. And they did it one blurring, hideous traffic snarl at a time.

Suddenly I understood why the Chicago Loop was such a nightmare, why the Washington D.C. Beltway was always so horribly snarled. Their fields were set in spots where human consciousness was distracted. Driving is a complicated endeavor, really. It takes real concentration. And thus, along every roadway possible, their collectors reach out and snag our minds, draining us of ideas and ideals, of spirit and vitality, or curiosity and intellect and drive and determination.

We are, in effect, cattle. They like us contented and docile. Organized sports was their idea. Just like theaters and churches, hordes of people, gathering together, distracted, their attention on something other than the important...

They collect our souls in tiny shreds, in a hundred different ways. The collecting never stops. They don't need to be present for that. They simply return on occasion to make certain we haven't gone off track. They may not be back for a while.

Last time they left, a few years ago, they felt confident we could be left alone for a good stretch. They have us past the point where we might destroy ourselves or the planet. They have stopped us from thinking of the galaxy as a place to explore and conquer. Instead, as NASA and other space agencies close their doors, alter their missions, corporations are taking up the mantle—not looking to bend the great darkness to our will, but to use it to turn a buck. Like all of life, our greatest possibility has become nothing more than another tourist attraction.

I don't know what else I can tell you. I didn't see that much during my vision. It took me hours of sitting here alongside the road to piece together even as little as I typed above. And again, I don't know what else to tell you— whoever you are.

I've sat here typing ever since I came out of the stupor or trance or whatever it was that I experienced. I don't know who to send this message to, who will see it, what will happen.

I don't have any answers. I... I don't have anything, really. I know what I've said here is true, but I also know that I have no way to prove anything I've said, either.

Maybe people are just stupid. Maybe on the New Jersey Turnpike, at that spot between Exits 8 and 8A, where three lanes blossom outward into five, and the traffic always backs up and slows to a crawl, it's not because of what I know is happening, maybe—hopefully—it's just because people are so goddamned dumb that they can't simply drive forward in straight lines.

Oh God, I hope so. I so truly, dearly, hope so.

Because tired, tiny hope is all I have left.

Whoever you are, however this message reached you, I don't know what else I can tell you. What I might advise. I don't see how they can be stopped. We don't know who they are, what they are, how to reach them... anything.

There is no machinery here to dismantle, no way to cut off their leeching grasp. I don't know what to tell you.

All I can say is, if you still pray, then pray I'm insane.

Pray. For all the good it will do you.

About the Author

CJ Henderson is the creator of both the *Piers Knight* supernatural investigator series and the *Teddy London* occult detective series among many others. He has written over 70 books and/or novels, hundreds and hundreds of short stories and comics and thousands of non-fiction pieces. He is a master of hardboiled suspense as well as raucous comedy, and is not shy about saying so even when sober. For more on this truly fascinating teller of tales, he encourages all to stop in at www.cjhenderson.com. He promises free short stories and more humility.

About the Editor

Mike McPhail's love of the science fiction genre sparked a life-long interest in science, technology, and developing an understanding of the human condition—all of which played an important role in his writing, art, and game design. These, in turn, are built upon his background in Applied Science and training as an Aeronautical Engineer, all of which were aimed at becoming a NASA mission specialist.

As a professional author, he has been involved in numerous projects, but he is best known as the creator and series editor of the award-winning Defending the Future military science fiction anthologies—now in their second decade of publication. His body of work has been formally recognized with his acceptance into SFWA, the Science Fiction and Fantasy Writers of America.

As a graphic designer, he is the owner of McP Digital Graphics (founded in 2006), a company established to provide cover art, design, layout, and prepress services. This built upon not only his experience as a game designer, but primarily from his time as the Proofing Supervisor for Phoenix Color Corp doing cover work for the great publishing houses.

As a publisher, he is the co-owner of eSpec Books LLC (since 2014), where his graphics company has become the inhouse design arm of production.

As Airman McPhail, he is a member of the Military Writers Society of America and is dedicated to helping his fellow service members (and those deserving civilians) in their efforts to become authors, editors, or artist, as well as supporting related organization in their efforts to help those "who have given their all for us."

www.ingramcontent.com/pod-product-compliance
Lightning Source LLC
Chambersburg PA
CBHW030856200726
48289CB00003B/770